THE

True Prince

J. B. CHEANEY

Alfred A. Knopf · New York

THIS IS A BORZOI BOOK PUBLISHED BY ALFRED A. KNOPF

www.randomhouse.com/kids

Library of Congress Cataloging-in-Publication Data
Cheaney, J. B.
The true prince / J. B. Cheaney.
p. cm.

Summary: Newly apprenticed to Shakespeare's theater company,
Richard and Kit are drawn into a series of crimes involving members of
Queen Elizabeth's court.

ISBN 0-375-81433-7 (trade) — ISBN 0-375-91433-1 (lib. bdg.)
1. Shakespeare, William, 1564–1616—Juvenile fiction. [1. Shakespeare,
William, 1564–1616—Fiction. 2. Great Britain—History—Elizabeth,
1558–1603—Fiction. 3. Theater—Fiction. 4. Mystery and detective stories.]
I. Title.
PZ7.C3985 Tr   2002
[Fic]—d21   2002072972

Printed in the United States of America
October 2002
10 9 8 7 6 5 4 3 2 1

First Edition

To Nancy,
an extraordinary editor
and a gift of God

Contents

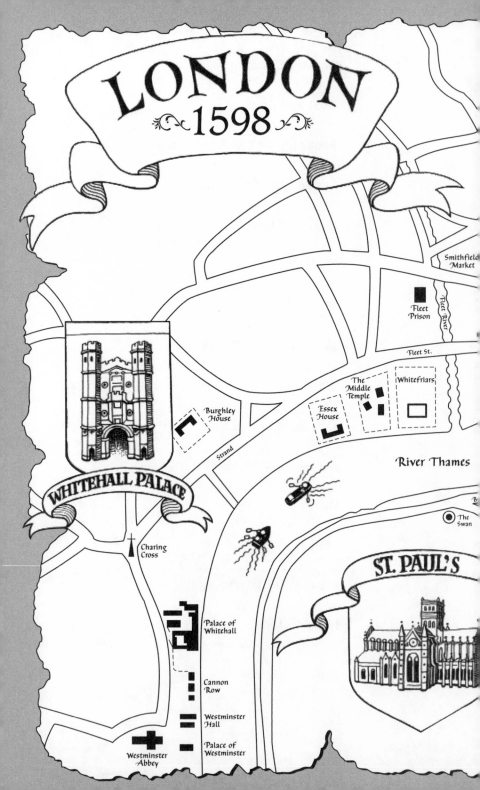

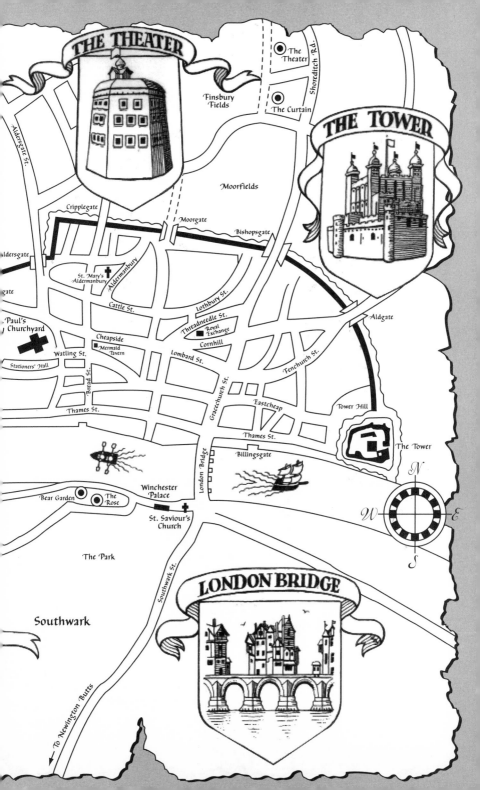

CAST OF CHARACTERS

The Lord Hunsdon's Men:

Principal Players:

William Shakespeare

Richard Burbage

Cuthbert Burbage

Henry Condell

John Heminges

Richard Cowley

William Kempe

Augustine Phillips

Thomas Pope

Edmund Shakespeare (Ned)

William Sly

Apprentices:

Christopher Glover (Kit)

Richard Malory

Robin Bowle

Gregory Lake

David Morgan (the Welsh Boy)

Queen Elizabeth's Court:

Robert Devereux, Earl of Essex

Robert Cecil, Lord Burghley: *Secretary of State, the Queen's chief minister*

William Brooke, Lord Cobham: *the Queen's Lord Chamberlain*

Henry Brooke, *Lord Cobham's son*

George Carey, Lord Hunsdon: *patron to Shakespeare's Company*

Sir Walter Raleigh

Philip Tewkesbury, Baron of Wellstone

In and About London:

Starling Shaw, *penny gatherer at the Theater*

Giles Allen, *a landowner*

Peregrine Penny, *a corrupter of youth*

Tom Watts, *a compatriot of Penny's*

John Clement, *investigator for the Lord Chamberlain*

Bartholomew Finch (Bartlemy), *assistant to John Clement*

Susanna Malory, *Richard's sister*

"Stop! Halt! You'll kill each other!"

Our fencing master said this with a laugh, but for an instant, while my opponent's pale wolf-gray eyes drilled holes in me, I believed him. This was how it went with Kit Glover: practice one moment, dead earnest the next. We had begun with an ordinary rapier match, trading thrusts and parries under Master Cowley's watchful eye as he shouted, "Ward left, Kit! Watch his point, Richard—left foot back. Look to your side—point! Point!"

Then I put too much weight on my right ankle and stumbled a bit. In recovering I made a straight lunge forward that jabbed Kit on the hip. The blunt tip could not have hurt much, but Kit wore his pride like his clothes: just as readily pricked or cut. He went at me with such vigor that I could easily forget this was only a practice round. "Lay back!" shouted Master Cowley. "The foot must follow the weapon, never precede—Kit, do you hear me? Kit!" Heedless, the boy pressed his attack, forcing me to put all my defenses to hard use. Dodging right and left, my eye on his weapon and my hand following his lead, I barely heard our master's cry to halt. Halting didn't seem prudent anyway, with the tip of that foil so relentlessly seeking me out. Faster and faster it came, beating me back until it slipped past a hole in my guard. The cold steel blade slid along my neck, with just enough pressure to hurt. "You're dead," said my opponent as he stepped back, suddenly as cool as the April breeze that gusted over our heads. Once again he had proved he could beat me any time he set his mind to it.

"If you have made your point, Master Glover," our instructor remarked dryly, "pray consent to go a match with Robin."

Kit nodded, taking a long drink from the stone jug of cider left on the stage. The exercise had scarcely raised a sweat on him—just a silvery gleam that complimented his ivory skin and set off his raven-black hair. As for me, I was blowing like a horse and dripping buckets. I picked up my cloak from the rough boards and wrapped it around me to ward off chills.

Robin Bowle stepped up for his match, pausing to slap me on the back with a smile both friendly and anxious, as though to say, "Don't mind him—'tis just his humor." Any tension between Kit and me unsettled Robin, as though he feared that when we finally got around to killing each other, he would find himself in the middle. But I knew all about Kit's "humor." That quick heat and abiding coolness were part of his construction, which helped to make him the finest boy player in London. He and Robin squared off in the approved stance, left feet forward, shoulders parallel. At Master Cowley's command— "Present!"—Kit raised his foil so swiftly that it sang, while Robin crossed his arms over his head and knocked his knees in mock terror. Gregory Lake, sitting out the practice because of a lame foot, laughed at his expression. But at our master's exasperated sigh Robin dropped his fooling and assumed a more serious pose. "To ward!" cried Richard Cowley, and the steel rang. Robin, who was shorter than Kit and three years younger, had put on weight since turning thirteen in the fall. I narrowed my eyes at the two combatants trading their workmanlike thrusts, imagining how their duel would look as part of a play. After barely a year on the stage I was thinking like a player, judging the match not by swordsmanship but by how well it might convince an audience that it was a fight to the death. Robin was now fully on defense, biting his lip as he warded off the thrusts coming at him. Kit's face at the moment showed only concentration, but in it lurked any passion a play might call for: hatred, exhilaration, fear, lust for vengeance. I stared at him, as though to draw some of his assurance and control into me. Then I caught myself at it and abruptly turned away to fix my attention on the Theater surrounding us.

It was a round building open to the sky, with three galleries circling the inside wall. The stage I stood upon was only a platform of rough-planed boards held up by trestles. Here, for six days of every week as weather permitted, the players of our company enchanted Londoners with tragedy, comedy, and romance—to greater or less success.

I had spent an uncertain year learning this trade, but the reason I was still here was due to Kit as much as to me. I had gained some skill as a player, but he had spoken a word for me at a time when all the skill in the world would have done me no good. Why he had done so was a mystery. I could only conclude that facing down officers of the law on my behalf was an act of daring, not friendship—as he did not appear to like me at all. Nor did I like him, exactly; it's hard to like someone who could make you feel, at day's end, that you have been punctured like a colander with your own flaws.

Still, my place in the Company suited me well enough. Though there were times, such as now, when my mind strayed to visions of a warm room in some warehouse where I could add up accounts all day long and see them come out as expected.

Instead, before dawn I had dragged myself out of the bed I shared with Robin, swallowed a cup of cider and a slab of cold porridge, trudged a mile up the Shoreditch Road to the Theater, spent an hour practicing dance and swordplay, stubbed my toe in the Morris dance, taken a snub and a defeat from Kit—and it was not yet eight o'clock. In a few moments the Company would assemble to rehearse a play I had never heard of before yesterday, and that would be the last chance I would get to practice my part, which I must then perform to a boisterous, disrespectful audience at two hours past noon. It was not a large part—one long speech and two short ones, plus single lines in three scenes—but I was expected to get it down pat, plus all my entrances and cues. None of the other actors could be counted on to prompt me, for they had their own parts to occupy them. After the performance we would immediately begin putting together another play for the morrow and would not depart for home until after dark. At times a clerk's position looked very good, or at least very peaceful.

"A match!" sang out Master Cowley. Kit had worked his blade under Robin's hilt and disarmed him. The foil clattered on the stage, and Robin wrung his offended hand, whistling in pain. "'Ware to your right," our instructor told him. "That's where he slips past your defense every time."

"Only because I let him," panted Robin. "I could see he was winded, so I ended the misery for both of us." Kit, passing behind, gave him a jab in the ribs that made him yelp. "I shall take that as your humble thanks."

"—As the dung beetle said to the mare." Kit thrust his foil, then Robin's, into the portable rack, only moments before a stage boy came to wheel it away. His voice made crude remarks sound like high oratory, and all his movements were graceful and well timed and slightly exaggerated—he lived his life in gestures broad enough to be seen from the third gallery.

"Apprentices, attend!" Henry Condell, a senior member of the Company, marched to the foot of the stage and called our names in order of rank: "Kit! Robin, Richard, Gregory!"—a small consolation, that I was not quite at the bottom of the list. We gathered around as Master Condell consulted the scroll in his hand. "You will all be needed for the battle scene outside the city gates. Kit—you must change out of the countess's robes presently after the castle scene, to be ready in time. Use a helmet that covers your face, so you can leave the paint on for your next entrance as the countess." Kit nodded impatiently; he did not need to be told. "We haven't enough helmets to spare one for you, Robin, but if you die as soon as the fighting begins, you can hide your lady's face, eh? Richard—you must fight the whole battle. Take on Kit and don't let him beat you back so soon this time. And Gregory—are you lame today?"

"I twisted my ankle this morning, sir—"

"So eagerly did he leap out of his warm bed," Robin offered.

"You may fall early, then. And get the tiring master to wrap your ankle." Master Condell loosely rolled up the paper that contained our cues and entrances. Soon it would be hanging from a center post behind the stage, where the players would be all but knocking each other down to get a look at it. "By the bye, we have taken on another boy. He should be here by noon, and I bid you make him welcome. He is an orphan, not yet eleven."

6

We glanced at each other. Every season saw apprentices come and go. This new boy was evidently a replacement for Dick Worthing, who had left us barely a month before, when his voice cracked and plunged into the "abyss from which no boy returns" (as Master Condell put it). Dick had joined a touring company bound for France, and I missed his easy good humor. The arrival of this new boy would force us to regroup ourselves as we made a place for him—all except Kit, who would remain on top and pretend to notice nothing that went on below. What made our eyebrows go up as we looked at each other was not the boy's arrival, but his age. I was considered old when I began at fourteen, but ten seemed right young, unless the boy was gifted beyond common. Robin spoke up.

"Does he come from St. Paul's Chapel, sir?"

"No. He comes from Wales." Master Condell was already halfway across the stage. "But he has a certain quality. . . ."

"Quality," Robin repeated, once our master was out of sight. "What can he mean by that?"

"Probably long golden locks," said Gregory as he rolled the paper that contained his lines. "And fluttering eyelashes—"

"—and he doesn't scratch himself on the stage," finished Kit. "What is it? Do you fear he may take your place as Juliet?"

"Impossible," Robin informed him loftily. Snatching Gregory's scroll, he addressed it with the dying words of a lady no one had played but himself. "Oh, happy dagger; here is thy sheath—"

7

Gregory snatched it back. ". . . there rust, and let me die!" As the two of them tried to outdo each other in agonized faces, Kit turned away and sauntered up the stage to where the men of the Company were gathering for rehearsal. Now nearly seventeen, he had long since outgrown such boys' play.

To Robin I said, "Gregory has almost become your equal at dying. He may have an eye on Juliet for himself."

Robin assumed a straight face. "Not until I grow a beard. Then I shall conquer Romeo's part—though not before *he* does, of course." This he said with a worshipful glance at Kit's back.

"What is it makes you think *he* will be trusted with Romeo anytime soon?" Gregory muttered. "The Company may keep him in skirts forever, since no one queens it like himself."

Robin opened his mouth with a quick defense of his hero, but was interrupted by Master Cuthbert Burbage, who burst through the side door yelling, "Richard!" My head jerked around, but he was not calling for me. He stopped a passing stage boy and demanded, "Where's my brother?"

"Gone to hell, sir," the boy answered respectfully. This was an old joke: the area below the stage was known as "hell," partly to distinguish it from the star-painted "heaven" above the stage, and partly because that was where ghosts and devils made their exits.

"Fetch him, then. And be quick!"

The boy darted behind the curtains that shielded the stage supports from view, and Master Cuthbert climbed to the boards. The look on his doughy face indicated dire news. His dramatic entrance had alerted the company members, who gathered around as Richard Burbage released the trap door in the stage and reared his imposing head and chest through it. "What's ado, Cuthbert?" he asked his brother. "Have you just sighted the Spanish fleet off Dover?"

"No jesting. This is serious." Master Cuthbert, usually so calm and milk-mannered, was pacing the floor in great agitation. "Giles Allen has refused to renew our lease!"

His words left an echo. In the sudden, tomblike quiet, Richard Burbage repeated, "Refused."

"Aye. Refused."

"And could you not put him off—"

"No more putting off. No more talk. We have talked for months, and Allen has been a riddle through it all. First he shows a kindly face, then a flinty one, and then he gives us reason to hope that a raise in rent will incline him to see it our way. But this is the first time he's refused us flat. He says he wants to sell the land—even hints that he may have a buyer already."

A tempest from the Bermudas could not have flattened the Company as soundly as those words did. "Then . . . ," a voice quavered from the back of the stage, "what's to be done?"

I knew what was at stake as well as any of them. Richard and Cuthbert Burbage owned the building. When their father, James, had built it, it was the only permanent stage in all of

England, and he was justified in naming it, simply, the Theater. But the land it sat on was the property of one Giles Allen. When the lease expired some time back, Master Allen began to quibble about whether it would be renewed, but never came out with an absolute refusal. Until now. So here we stood: one of the most highly regarded stage companies in London, soon to be without a stage.

"What's to be done?" Richard Burbage climbed out of hell and onto the stage. "What we must do *now* is rehearse for a play to go on at two o'clock. Master Allen will not keep us from that."

Good counsel, but the impending loss of our Theater hit me hard—almost as if it were my own home. Suddenly I was not the same boy who, scarcely an hour earlier, had dreamed of more comfortable work in a counting house.

Even Robin, a veteran of the stage and usually a merry soul, seemed to be undone. His part in this day's play was a tragic heroine—the daughter of an earl who is falsely accused of treason (the earl, not the daughter) and dragged off the stage to be sold into slavery (the daughter, not the earl). At that point in the play, Robin seized the cloak of Thomas Pope and cried, "Alas! What part have I in my father's treachery, that I should be taken in vile servitude and surrender my sweet person to thy lustful minions!"

"None, maid," replied Thomas Pope, "but you are pinching my neck and mashing my toes—kindly loose your grip." Robin blushed and stepped back as Master Pope gingerly tested his foot. The Company laughed, too heartily perhaps, but it relieved some of their strain.

The fourth act was the last for Robin and Gregory and me. Our time might have been better spent studying cues and lines, but we lacked the will. We sat in the first gallery, in the seats reserved for wealthy patrons—a place so near the stage that they could become a part of the play. And they often did, advising the players and making witty remarks as they puffed on their pipes. Robin liked to imitate them when he sat in their place during rehearsals, but today his wit was beaten down. Instead of jesting he fretted, like an orphan soon to be turned out on the street. In truth he was no orphan, but might as well have been: his mother and stepfather lived in Kent, but seldom made the journey to visit him. The Theater was the only home he knew. "Suppose the Company has to disband?" he asked as Richard Burbage made a noble dying speech on the stage. "Would the Admiral's Men take me, do you think?"

"The Admiral's Men are glutted just now with red-headed boys," said Gregory, who then softened his words with a smile. His tongue was as sharp as a dagger, which he sometimes sheathed before it could wound, and sometimes not.

"My hair is not red. It's auburn."

"So it is." Gregory leaned closer, peering at Robin's face. "In fact, those little hairs growing from your chin are the most lovely—"

"What!" Robin clapped a hand to his jaw and felt around it anxiously.

"Put it up, Gregory," I said.

He blinked at me, startled. "'Twas only a jest."

"It's no subject for jesting."

"Our Robin could find a place in any company he chose—you know that. We're the ones in peril, you and I."

I shrugged, but admitted to myself that Robin's harping on the bad news had begun to wear on me. He harped on: "But if the Company disbands—"

"They won't disband," I said. "The Queen herself favors us."

"She doesn't favor our new patron."

With a loud moan, Gregory flopped his head down on the railing that separated our gallery from the stage. For myself, I could have stuffed Robin's mouth with cotton for bringing up another sore point. Lord Hunsdon, the Queen's Lord Chamberlain and the patron of our Company, had recently passed away at a ripe old age. His son George took over the Company, and everyone expected him to take his father's office as Lord Chamberlain as well. But the Queen had settled that position on William Brooke, the seventh Lord Cobham. According to rumor, the appointment caused an uproar at court, where certain gentlemen were still going about with their noses out of joint. But our Company suffered more than bent noses, since we could no longer wear the proud title of

Lord Chamberlain's Men. We were now Lord Hunsdon's Men, which hardly rang with the same dignity and importance. And Lord Hunsdon's Men might soon become Men of the Street. The year was not beginning well.

"All will come right in the end," I said, feigning confidence.

"How?" Robin demanded.

"I am not in God's counsel, so I can't tell you that. But you may be assured that the Company will not take this lying down." I might have put this better, for at that moment a goodly portion of the Company was lying down on the stage, having expired from dagger wounds. Today's play was a tale of bloody revenge and did not improve our mood. "They'll think of something," I added lamely.

"What if they decide to disband?" he persisted. "Other companies have broken apart for less—"

"Hold a moment." Gregory had lifted his head. "Look yonder," he said, nodding toward the front of the theater. "They just came in."

The hired help had arrived: penny gatherers who collected admission to the galleries and serving maids who swept the floors and sold sweets during the performance. But we knew at once which "they" Gregory meant: a man and boy standing just before the first gallery. The man was of middling height with a black beard streaked with gray, but that was all we noticed of him.

The boy was beautiful—his face a little too wide in the

mouth and brow, but cherubic and rosy. A cap of dark, curly hair set off eyes of so intense a blue that the color, even at a distance, made me think of calm summer skies.

Looks matter on the stage—none of the apprentices were ugly and each had some particular appeal that suited him for certain roles. Robin was winsome and lively; Gregory's intelligent face bespoke keenness and subtlety; Kit's noble features and striking coloring set forth dignity and command. And I, with my wide dark eyes and small chin that could so easily be made to tremble, was the picture of pitiable suffering. Or that was my guess; if there was a lady in the play who went mad or killed herself, that part was likely to go to me. But the "quality" shining from this curly-headed boy was pure innocence, as if an angel in child's form stood in our midst.

Playing the Man

*A*fter rehearsal, the boy was brought up on stage and introduced to us as David Morgan—as sweet-faced close up as he was far away, except for his teeth. They were small and brown, evenly spaced in his mouth like a row of worn posts. They looked something other than human, but caused no comment; bad teeth are a mark of Londoners in general.

However, there was no London in his voice. When asked to recite for those Company members who had not yet heard him, his words chimed with a peculiar lilt. Then he sang, and words disappeared altogether in a soft, furry-sounding language I had never heard the like of. That, and his clear sweet voice, cast such a spell that for a moment after he was done, no one moved or spoke.

"Do you speak Welsh, also?" inquired Master Shakespeare, eyebrows raised in a bright, absorbed expression. He wrote plays for the Company and stayed ever alert for any raw material he could use.

"Aye, sir," answered David Morgan with a little bow. "Monmouth was home to me, ere my mother went to heaven and I was sent here to live upon my uncle." The uncle, whom I presumed to be the fellow with the streaky beard, had barely waited long enough to hand off the boy before disappearing. Davy stood before us all alone, a wide-eyed, trembling mouse making a brave show. As I had stood in almost that same place a year before—motherless and uprooted—my heart galloped out to him. The men of the Company showed only thoughtful calculation. No matter his secret sorrows; would he do for the stage?

"He's worth a trial," Master Shakespeare said then. "We've not had a Welsh boy for years." That settled it: both Davy's future and his title. From that time forward most of us referred to him, though not to his face, as the Welsh Boy.

"We thought you might be fetched with that part of him," Henry Condell laughed. "I look for a Welsh lady in your next play. Now to your places, men—and you, boy, let me find you a guardian." He harbored a softness for children: a good thing, as he was father to six of them and a foster father to Robin and me, who boarded in his house. He took the Welsh Boy's hand and swept his eyes around the galleries, where play-goers were already milling to and fro, seeking the best seats. "Starling!" he called to the second tier. A girl's round, pleasant face appeared, framed with wispy curls escaping from her cap. "Take charge of this lad for today, would you? Give him a sense of what he's in for." I took one more look at the boy, who gazed up at the Theater galleries with clear, unsuspecting eyes. No doubt those eyes would be glazed over with perfect confusion by the day's end.

"He's a strange one," Starling Shaw remarked that evening as she bit off a length of black thread. According to our custom on chilly spring nights, we sat at one end of the great room of our master's house. At the other end, Robin, along with Harry, Alice, and Mary Condell, sang madrigals to the strumming of Alice's lute. Near the fireplace at the center, the mistress read aloud to the little ones. Supper was over, the table cleared, and soon enough I would have to climb the stairs to my cold attic room and learn my part in tomorrow's play. But in these few minutes of free time I often chose to rake through the events of the day with Starling. Talking to her came almost as easy as thinking to myself, and this day had given me much to think about. "Strange how?" I asked.

"You know how new boys are, especially if they've not been upon the stage—think of yourself, a year ago: jumpy as a cat."

"Scared as a rabbit, more like."

"Very true. But this boy . . ." She paused over the costume she was mending and twitched her nose as though smelling

17

young David from two leagues away. "He took in everything I told him, without a ripple to cross his face. And he never asked a question."

"That must be because you did such good work of explaining." I made a flapping mouth with my hand. Star was a fair talker, once primed.

"Do curb your wit. He watched the play with the same attention he gave me—no more, no less—and you know how new apprentices watch plays. As though they were either thrilled or—"

"Terrified," I finished for her. "I know. So what ails him? Is he sick?"

"No; bewitched." With an expert twist, she tied off the thread and flipped the garment right-side out: a child's cape of dark blue velvet, embroidered with stars in gold thread and seed pearls. She spread it out upon her lap, like a deep, dark night sparkling with mystery. "Wales reeks with magic, you know. Merlyn was born there, and there he learned his craft, and there he lies imprisoned in the cave under a stone, enchanted by the treachery of Vivien the witch. But the stones and trees remember him and mourn for him, and a lad who ventures too near the seams of that earth—those deep places where the memory of Merlyn has taken root—may find himself caught when the branches shake down their sorrow. The magic sets upon him like dew, so light and fine he may not notice, but it enchants him with a great and deadly calm that cannot be broken, unless . . ."

She raised the needle, and her lively green eyes—the eyes that could fool an observer into thinking she was beautiful— waited for me to prompt her with a breathless, "Unless what?" Instead I took the needle from her and made a little jab with it, along with a popping sound meant to prick her illusion. "He's just a boy. From Wales."

"Did I say otherwise?" She retrieved her needle and attacked a loose seed pearl with it, her expression as pert and businesslike as any housemaid's. "Don't you have a part to learn?"

"Directly. There's another piece of news today—we were told it after you left the Theater." She looked up, alert again. "It's been a day for news," I went on, placidly, "first our land-lord's treachery, then the Welsh Boy, now this. It makes me wonder if we have already used up our allotment for the year, what with—"

"Stow it!" she hissed. "Tell me at once, or I'll ply this nee-dle where it will do some good."

"The Company handed out parts for a new play, to be per-formed two weeks hence. It's called *The House of Maximus,* and Kit is to play the role of Adrian, the hero's brother."

Her eyes went wide, and for a moment she looked more like a little girl than a maid almost sixteen. "At *last.* He finally gets to play the man. How did he take it?"

"Cool as spring water. At least, on the outside. But when

we were ready to start for home, he forgot he hadn't washed all the stage paint off his face until Master Heminges remarked on it."

She giggled and I grinned—Kit shaken from his self-possession was a rare event. "But what is the play?" she asked. "Do you know anything of it?"

"Richard Burbage lined it out. It's a most lamentable tragedy of the usual sort. Adrian's is not the biggest part, but he has the showiest death. He is burned by a poisoned cloak, or poisoned tunic, or something." She nodded; lethal garments were a common means of dispatch in lamentable tragedies. "I sense that the Company thinks little of it. When they like a new play, their eagerness shows, but for this one, all they seem eager for is getting it done. They've allowed themselves only two weeks to learn it, instead of the usual three."

She tilted her head to one side while thinking this over. "Perhaps they are doing it by request—to please somebody of importance."

"Not important enough to give it their best. Richard Burbage has taken a small role and left the hero's part to young Ned Shakespeare. They've given the lover's part to Kit, who has not played anything like it since joining the Company. And . . ." I paused, for this was the moment I had been building to: the major event of the day, for me.

"Yes?" Starling prompted.

"They have cast me as the lady he falls in love with."

Her response did not disappoint; she whistled in astonishment, then glanced down the room at Robin, who was making a great show of good cheer. "So that's why he hasn't spoken to you all evening."

"No doubt." Leave it to her to notice. The "Juliet" parts, as we called them, usually went to Robin, who had the looks for them. But anyone who looked closely at him of late noticed that he had grown taller and bulkier and less pretty. He seemed to believe I had stolen this part. If so, I would have gladly given it back; the thought of playing Kit's beloved made my stomach feel like it was protesting a dinner of old eel. We were usually cast as rivals because the company liked the bite that worked its way into our stage quarrels. "It's not what I would call inspired casting. All in all, a day for unsettling news. What could be next?"

A smile flickered across her face; then she swept the velvet cape from her lap and over her shoulders, clutching it to her chest as one clawed hand shot out to me. "The poisoned cloak!" she gasped, her face contorted in agony. "Beware!"

"Starling." The voice of Mistress Condell floated toward us from the opposite side of the room. "Costumes are too expensive to serve as toys."

"Aye, lady." She pulled off the cape, but whispered to me: "Beware."

21

After only ten days our new apprentice played his first role. Though it was rare to lay a speaking part so soon on a boy with no experience, the players were eager to try him. The play was a bubble of a story called *A Midsummer Night's Dream*, written by Master Will. London audiences love its woodland fairies and enchantments and four bewildered lovers wandering in the forest—and especially the clown, Bottom, who grows a donkey's head. None of it made sense to me in rehearsal, but Robin said I should not insist on making sense: "It's just a story!"

David Morgan played a woodland sprite, whose long speech in the second act should have been shortened. Not that he dropped many lines; he just rattled them off like a catechism. But his voice was strong and round, and at the end of the speech he turned two handsprings and a backflip, flinging himself in the air like a street tumbler as though his weight were nothing at all. This drew a cheer from the audience who had been yawning, and a light shower of applause followed his exit. In the next act Davy sang the Fairy Queen to sleep, and the men of the Company, from the way they glanced and nodded to each other behind the stage, seemed to agree that the boy was worth training.

So he had a place in the Company. But would the Company still have a place? As soon as he could, Master Cuthbert arranged another meeting with Giles Allen, which accomplished nothing. Richard Burbage and John Heminges excused themselves from the next day's performance—a thing most rare—and the rumor was that they had gone to scout for property. That was how matters lay as we approached our performance of *The House of Maximus.*

"You were right," I told Starling on Thursday, the night before. "The Company is performing this play to please somebody—though certainly not our audience."

"Is it so bad?" She never looked up from the pan of dried apples she was picking over for worms. As a housemaid and costume mender at home, and penny gatherer at the Theater, her hands were seldom idle.

"It is," I said. "I could not have told you how bad, until we put on *A Midsummer Night's Dream.* You know the story of Pyramus and Thisbe, that the tradesmen perform for the duke's wedding?" She nodded, her green eyes dancing. "Pyramus and Thisbe" is an overblown, bleeding heart of a "tragedy," a play within the play that always makes audiences weep—with laughter. "Well, *The House of Maximus* is near cousin to that, only it's not supposed to be funny. Sylvester and Adrian are a pair of noble brothers whose family has been brought low: falsely accused of treason; their father murdered; their property stolen. A villainous relative is at the bottom of all this. The brothers vow revenge for the honor of their house, but they've barely started when Adrian—that's Kit's part, the younger brother—falls hard in love with a woodcutter's daughter named Silvia." Here I pointed to myself, and Starling blew me a kiss. "The brothers fall out because Adrian loses interest in seeking revenge. Unfortunately for him, Silvia is really the daughter of the treacherous uncle, who has placed her in the care of the wood-cutter, who is really an evil magician. Adrian suffers various enchantments and does not learn until the end that Silvia was part of the plot against him, and so he wraps himself in the enchanted lethal cloak because it's the only way to redeem his honor. But there's no hope for redeeming the play."

"What's wrong with it? It could be a good story, if written with a fine pen."

"But there's the rub—it's written with a meat ax. When the action slows, somebody gets stabbed or disemboweled. Dull stretches of poetry are laid between the bloody parts. Adrian makes a long speech while dying; it ends with, 'Happy garb, that ends my vile disgrace! Ye Fates: bear me up to a happier place!'"

She held her nose. "Alas! Poor Kit, to speak such with a straight face! Is no one letting slip who wrote this?"

"I'm sure the chief players know—Burbage and Shakespeare and a few others. But they're keeping it close. The rumors all agree that some nobleman at court thinks he's the poet of the age and longs to have his plays per-formed by a distinguished company."

"Who could it be?" Starling loved a mystery—I could almost hear the hum of her busy mind as she harried a worm out of an apple core with the point of her knife. "Sir Walter Raleigh, do you think?"

"Raleigh's poetry is better. And his influence at court is not so great just now. Our author is a bold, impetuous sort, with enough sway to get his way. Someone like Essex."

"Essex is a warrior, not a poet. Perhaps it is Burghley."

"Burghley!" I scoffed. "The Queen's Secretary? He's too busy with state business to write plays."

"How do you know? Do you visit him once a week and share his burdens? 'Alas, Richard, the Queen has ordered me to write a new treaty with the King of Spain. I think I may write a play instead.'"

I slipped a piece of apple out of her bowl. "Resist the temptation, my lord. It's harder than it looks."

She grinned. "You would be surprised how many seem to think it's easy. Today I overheard a lady in the third gallery instructing her servant on the elements of a well-wrought play. She seemed to think our Shakespeare was a mere upstart. But how is it with you and Kit? Have you managed to fall in love yet?"

"Hardly." I thought back over that day's rehearsal, when Kit had "wooed" me under the watchful eye of John Heminges. It had not gone well—he took my hand as though it were a piece of liver and spoke of my "moon-bright orbs" and "swanlike neck" in a voice that would have better called out a challenge to combat. Master Heminges kept reminding

25

him that I was his beloved, not his enemy, finally bursting out with, "Why so cold, boy? Love melts a man!" Kit blushed to a shade I could not recall seeing on his face and muttered that he could hardly play the scene as a puddle, which only provoked his master further and cut our rehearsal short.

"They should have cast Robin as Silvia," I told Starling. "Kit could probably muster a bit of affection for him. He speaks to me as if I was a fortress and he a warrior laying siege. He comes to conquer."

"He always comes to conquer. But what's the state of his fingernails?"

I knew what she meant. In spite of his seemingly perfect confidence, Kit's fingernails were often bitten down to the quick before an especially demanding performance. "They're bleeding already."

"Ah. Becoming a man may not be so easy as he— Ow! A pox on thee!" This was said not to me, but to Ned Condell, age seven, who had thrown a tennis ball to land precisely in the bowl of worms.

Clearing the bowl and ball of worm guts brought an end to that conversation, after which Starling drilled me on my lines for Silvia and agreed with me on their quality. "Whoever wrote this play must be *very* important, else the Company would have used it to start fires. But perhaps there will be enough stabbing and disemboweling to please the audience."

Next day, Kit dressed downstairs with the other men and soon was pacing the length of the tiring room. He often paced before a performance, but without a full skirt or train to sweep around at the turns, he seemed strangely off balance. He jerked where he was wont to flow, and watching him, I felt an apprehension that did not bode well for the afternoon.

As Starling had suggested, sometimes an audience will think better of a work than the Company does. But on this occasion our opinions matched perfectly. The first scene consisted of tedious complaint by Sylvester, which almost put our audience to sleep before Kit swaggered on as Adrian. A fight with the wicked uncle's men roused them briefly, but once Adrian met Silvia nothing would please. During the courtship scene, as Kit professed his undying love, the groundlings became more and more restless until someone called out, "Enough, lad—you'll talk her to death!" In the brutal laugh that followed, an orange peel landed on the stage. Kit threw his shoulders back and set his feet wide apart and spoke louder—but faster, to speed the scene.

This is a practice of raw amateurs, and startled me so much I almost forgot my lines. I had worked long and hard over the past year to slow my speech, and yet here was Kit bumping along like a cart rolling downhill. Presently he caught himself and began cutting lines and feeding me new cues. This sort of invention, called "thribbling," came easier to him than to me. By the end of the scene he was all but pointing at me when it was my turn to speak, and the murmurs of the crowd began to sound like the growl of an angry beast.

We left the stage arm in arm, simpering at each other, and broke apart the minute we passed through the door. "Why couldn't you follow me?" he burst out angrily. "I gave you your cues, and all you could do was flop around like a fish out of water!"

"Me?" I sputtered. "*Me?* That was—that was the most— You cut that scene up like a butcher!"

Richard Burbage intervened and sent us our separate ways before we could attract the attention of our audience—who would have gladly trooped back to the tiring room to watch us instead of the play, which continued to sink in their estimation. Silvia's death scene, where she stabs herself in remorse for her part in Adrian's downfall, came none too soon for me. By then I fully sympathized with her despair and pulled the knife from its scabbard with such passion the audience fell silent. When the blade plunged and sheep's blood spurted from a concealed bladder in my gown, ladies in the surrounding galleries made a collective gasp. Robin and Gregory, as a pair of twittering maids, followed as my body was carried off the stage. Something else followed as well— a spatter of applause.

"There," Gregory announced, as the litter bearers dropped

me without ceremony in the tiring room. "What do you think of that?"

"Think of what?" I said, grasping his offered hands as he pulled me up.

"That sound. You're the only one—" He broke off because Kit was passing on the way to his next entrance, his face so hard we felt it like a slap. "You're the only one to win applause this dismal day," Gregory continued, when Kit had passed. "You can be sure *he* noticed."

I pulled off the heavy wig and ran my fingers through my hair, as though to air out my head. "He has enough worries of his own." I could watch him now that my part was done and saw him carry himself more and more like a girl putting on mannish ways. It appeared he had lost his footing—in the duel with Thomas Pope he lost it literally and fell smack on his behind. The groundlings laughed.

By then Gregory and I were standing in the back of the musicians' gallery waiting for the play to be over. Gregory had spent a pleasant afternoon observing Kit's downfall, but I was exhausted, and the laughter of the groundlings gave me no satisfaction. This was the same crowd Kit had so often swayed to tears and outrage now mocking him, and all I felt was pity. Envy, rage, even irritation are enlivening emotions, but pity just makes one tired.

"Oh good, here's the cloak," Gregory remarked. "Go to it, Kit. Die like a man—silently."

Instead Kit spoke his lines to the last gasp, as though forcing the audience to take him at his word:

"O cloak most black, consume me into dust;

The pale smoke of honor to the gods I trust."

That last line was done rather well, I thought, but my opinion was not shared. "Here's a smack from sweet Silvia, to hurry it up!" sang a voice from the floor, and a rotten apple bounced off Kit's shoulder, followed by a hail of nutshells.

Most of our performances, whether comical or tragical, end with selected players capering out on stage to perform a jig or Morris dance. But the author of *The House of Maximus* had requested that the work not be trivialized in this manner. So it was allowed to stand on its own—meaning that it fell with a thud. After throwing the remains of their noonday meals, the audience left in a foul humor.

Gregory and I descended into a scene as dramatic as anything on the stage. Kit was literally throwing off his clothes, starting with the jewel-hilted sword and gold-studded belt. One or two of the actors made consoling noises, but he was having none of it—he tore at his costly doublet so savagely that a button flew off, and the tiring master cried out in protest.

"Calm yourself, boy!" Richard Burbage commanded sharply. "You bear your own share of blame for this play." I heard the warning tone in his voice as I bent to pick up the belt, but had little time to wonder about it before something caught my eye—a folded square of paper falling from Kit's silk shirt as he pulled it off. Robin approached, as pale as an egg, offering a warm towel for Kit to wipe the paint off his face. "They're fools," said he, with a jerk of his head toward the house. "Knaves. Tomorrow they'll be eating out of your—"

Kit silenced him with a truly vile suggestion and stalked into the far reaches of the tiring room to retrieve his clothes. Some of the men sighed and shook their heads.

"It's just his humor," Robin whispered. "He's never been laughed at."

Overcome by curiosity, I drew aside and opened the paper Kit had kept tucked away in his costume. In an elegant slanted hand—the new Italian script that had taken hold amongst the gentry at court—the writer wished Kit well on this most auspicious occasion: "As I trust all my effort on your behalf will be rewarded, so you too may expect your reward by serving my words this day. Your true friend—" The note was signed with a curious flourish that might have been a C, E, or T.

Well! thought I, putting the message together with Burbage's remark about bearing some blame for the play. If nothing else, Kit knew the author—

Hearing footsteps, I guiltily threw down the note and started up the stairs to the upper room, stealing a glance behind me. Kit reappeared, still buttoning his doublet, his face like a thundercloud as he scanned the floor, then scooped up the note and stuffed it out of sight. He passed on through the tiring room and out the door. No one bothered to remind him that he would bear a heavy fine for missing a rehearsal. At that moment he clearly cared not if the Theater collapsed about our ears and buried us all.

VILLAINOUS COMPANY

*T*he next morning Robin and I were barely up and dressed when a great pounding broke out on the front door below. We glanced at each other, then gathered up our shoes and hurried down the two flights of stairs to see what was afoot. John Heminges had arrived, which in itself was not unusual, for he lived in the same neighborhood and walked to the Theater with us almost every morning. Today he appeared early—but Kit, who boarded with him, was nowhere to be seen.

John Heminges was a firm, broad-shouldered man with yellow hair turning sandy and a disposition to match his sunny coloring. He had a good head for business and could always be counted on to sound the voice of reason in any dispute. But at the moment he looked the opposite of reasonable, as he paced the width of the great room with one fist striking his palm over and over.

By the time we arrived, he had worn a track in the floor rushes. ". . . no reward for all these years of training and oversight. You know I've tried to be fair—more than fair—as loving as to my own child. For the last year his behavior has grown more and more brazen, until this—" He could not, apparently, find words for *this,* so he threw up his hands. "It is not to be borne."

"Of course not," Henry Condell said, in the soothing tone used to pacify lunatics. "We will set a fitting penalty in time."

"Penalty?" John Heminges stopped short. "What penalty but expulsion from the Company?"

"John." Master Condell reminded him, with a jerk of his head in our direction, that open ears were drinking in every word said. "That can be settled later. For now we have more pressing business."

"Then let us be off." Master Heminges picked up his hat from the table and started toward the door with no pause, as though he had merely changed the angle of his pacing.

Henry Condell turned to us. "You boys must walk to the Theater alone. Tell Master Burbage we'll be along in time for rehearsal—"

"Nay." John Heminges turned at the door, one hand on the latch. "Let them come. They should see this—Robin especially." Then he was out the door, leaving us mystified. Our master looked from us to the empty doorway and back again, frowned, shrugged, shook his head. "Come along, then. We'll add something to your education beyond stage deportment, eh?"

So we followed them down Aldermanbury Street and on toward Cheapside, in an opposite direction from the one we usually took. Cheapside, the street that forms the spine of London, was filling already with water peddlers and tinsmiths, carters and housemaids on their way to market. And beggars of every description—sightless, legless, armless, hopeless—all wrapped up as well as they could afford against the morning chill. The gray dawn was made gloomier by the cries of the unfortunate: "A penny, sir. A penny for a poor soldier whose strength was spent in the Netherlands. . . ." "A farthing, young master, to feed my gaunt-ribbed child!" "Pity a blind man, good people; pity the blind!" Add to these the singsong chants of peddlers hawking their wares and the church bells beginning to toll out seven o'clock, and it made a rackety way to greet the morning. Londoners are so accustomed to noise that they don't hear half of it, but I grew up in a country village, where dawn is gently roused by crowing cocks, rather than violently shaken with a thousand voices.

The huge gray block of St. Paul's Cathedral loomed to our left as we veered off Cheapside toward Ludgate. All this time the hats and cloaks of our masters kept well ahead of us— sometimes we had to trot to keep them in view—and Robin the chatterer had kept strangely silent. We both knew that our expedition had somewhat to do with Kit, but beyond that,

Robin was probably as ignorant as I. He and Kit had been close—as close as a lord with a faithful servant, or boy with his adoring hound. On warm nights they used to slip out after curfew to roam the streets of London, skirting danger while keeping out of real trouble. But those excursions had not resumed with the coming of spring this year, and though Robin never talked about it, I knew he was hurt. Kit often showed up at the Theater with the haggard face and dark-circled eyes that indicated he wasn't getting much sleep. Somehow we knew that he had not turned to a life of contemplation and study. "Some lady is keeping him up," Gregory once suggested, with a dig to my ribs. But Kit seemed too much in love with himself to have any left over for a lady. Perhaps his play-writing acquaintance had been claiming his nights—though I could not imagine for what.

Robin seemed lost in his own thoughts and never glanced at me, even when we passed through Ludgate and continued on toward the court district. Here, just beyond the narrow river tributary known as the Fleet, the men turned abruptly toward a gray stone building, climbed the front steps, and disappeared under an arched doorway. "I knew it," Robin murmured, increasing his pace until we took the steps at a run. The building was Fleet Prison.

In a small antechamber just inside the main door we nearly ran headlong into our masters, who were conferring with Will Shakespeare. Master Will's face made a striking contrast with the others: while their expressions were solemn, his appeared bright with interest, as though engrossed in a play. "No, they've set no bail," he was saying. "The magistrate has heard the complaint, but not the defense. That should be next."

"If the Company refuses to pay bail, it shall come out of my own purse." Master Heminges spoke in a tight, strained voice. "The youth is my charge. . . ."

Just beyond them, the broad doorway opened to a courtroom of sorts—a magistrate's chamber for the preliminary hearing of petty cases. I could see the Queen's coat of arms mounted over the bench, where a gray-bearded official in a black cap impatiently shuffled a stack of papers. Two clerks flanked him in lower seats and a bailiff with pike and helmet stood to one side. The witness stand and the offenders' bench were out of my view, but I knew that Kit must be occupying one of them.

"He is *our* charge," Master Will replied. "Calm yourself, John. It may be the very lesson he needs, and so work for the best."

"Soft," Master Condell warned. "It begins."

The voice that was coming through the doorway could not belong to anyone but a player. It seemed to lean forward and take hold of its hearers, placing every syllable like part of an irrefutable argument for the existence of angels or mermaids. Kit had launched his defense like a spring coiled on his tongue.

He could attribute his misdeed to three factors, he said: youth, high spirits, and Spanish sack. Of those three, the wine was the greatest cause. He never had much of a head for it, Your Honor; it takes experience and practice to learn how much a man could hold without losing control of himself, and as far as that particular knowledge went, he was still at school. He threw himself upon the court, confident that a man so wise as our honorable judge would take his youth and inexperience into account and temper justice with mercy.

Master Heminges tightened his lips. "Come," he said abruptly, and led the way into the courtroom, right down the center aisle. Heads turned as we entered: anxious wives and mothers, restless children, bored law students, attentive clergymen. A wooden railing separated the petty offenders from the rest of the courtroom. Masters Heminges and Shakespeare took a bench directly behind the rail, while the remaining three of us filed into the next row.

The minute he saw us, Kit's expression changed. The earnest, eager tone I had heard in his voice flattened—only a little, but enough to notice. By the time we settled ourselves, his expression had become guarded and tight on a face already the worse for wear. A prominent welt marked his cheekbone, and his eyes were puffy from a night in jail. His clothes had not stood the ordeal any better: one sleeve ripped, hose sagging as though someone had tried to tear it off.

"You may save your defense until the charge is read," the

judge told him wearily. "You stand accused of breaking the peace, offering insult to honest citizens, and damaging property. All this court needs to know is, how plead you?"

"Guilty, Your Honor." Beside me I heard Robin draw a sharp breath.

"Very well. Have you anything to add to your defense?"

Kit opened his mouth, then apparently thought better of it. "No, sir."

"You may step down, then." One of the yawning clerks wrote the plea into the court record as Kit stepped down and returned to his place, taking care to look at no one.

Henry Condell leaned forward as the bailiff called another name. "Will, what is this about? What did he do?"

I was eager to learn this myself and inched closer as Master Will turned his head. "I know scarcely more than you, but—"

He was interrupted by an emphatic "*Not* guilty, Your Honor!" from the dock. Immediately after came a screech like a hog being killed.

The noise came from somewhere behind us, and heads jerked up all over the courtroom. A stout woman in working-class garb rose from her bench, pointing a finger that quivered with rage, directly at the man in the dock. "He *lies,* Your Honor! There never was such a bold-faced blistering liar as—"

"Sit you down, madam!" the judge rapped out.

Instead the woman strode forward, her outstretched arm

like the prow of a ship, in perfect disregard of the judge's calls to order: "He promised to marry me, Your Honor!" ("We have heard your testimony, madam—") "So when he shows up at my tavern with two knaves who claim to be churchmen, what was I to think but he was making good on his pledge?" ("Sit *down!*") "And so he says, only we must have a proper wedding dinner before we proceed to the church, where this knave" (she knocked Kit on the back of the head) "—will serve as witness, while the other knave" (waving her arm in a vague circle) "will marry us."

"Bailiff! Remove this woman!"

"And then, after they've eaten and drunk enough to stuff a regiment of Dutchmen, all at my expense, he denies he promised anything." The bailiff did his best, but even after he wrapped his arm around her ample waist and began dragging her toward the door, she would not be silenced. "So what could I do but set my two grown sons on them? The brawl was not my fault, Your Honor—he's the one who brought it on. He's guilty as Lucifer! Guilty, guilty—" The door slammed on a last, high-pitched *"Guilty!"*

In the abrupt silence, I heard a snicker from Robin and saw Master Will's face twitching. Most everyone else looked as sober as our judge, but the courtroom gravity had been stretched very thin. I stared at the defendant, who had brought about this change by denying his guilt.

He almost filled the dock: as tall as Richard Burbage and

at least as thick, with the bearing and presence of a military man and the complexion of a drunkard. His face might have been handsome in a rough-hewn way, but for the swollen nose, fiery as a live coal.

The judge sighed, rubbing his eyes. "As you see, Captain, we have witnesses to the matter and your companion has admitted his guilt. What hinders you?"

"Simple justice, my lord," the defendant replied forthrightly. "'Twas evil companionship that started me on last night's ill-favored venture. I meant to visit the sick, or attend to my prayers, but in spite of good intentions I was prevailed on to leave my humble lodging and take to the streets instead. Company, villainous company, hath been my downfall, honored sir—"

"Go to!" snapped the judge impatiently. "You are the worst corrupter of youth in all of London."

"My lord!" cried the man, holding up a hand that showed a gap where the two middle fingers should be. "I am as virtuous as any man needs to be and as valorous. Was I not maimed in the Spanish Wars?"

"Put down your hand. I have seen it before, and for all I know, you lost those fingers when they got stuck in the bunghole of an ale barrel."

Titters broke out all over the courtroom, as the so-called captain cast down his eyes. "If you please, Your Honor. You wound my good name."

"As if I could do more hurt to that name than yourself. To the point: Did you promise to marry Mistress Oxenbridge, as she claims?"

"If I did, 'twas only in words. Spoken words, things of shaped and polished air that flash but once, then flicker away—"

"Do you intend to marry her, now or ever?"

The defendant looked up, eyes wide. "*Marry* that harpy? By the Mass, no! Would you?"

The courtroom came undone then, as its occupants could hold back their laughter no more. One of the clerks went so far as to crack a smile, as the other bent his head, writing very diligently, shielding his eyes with one hand while his shoulders quivered. Master Will had taken out his table book and was making notes, his eyebrows raised with the eagerness of a huntsman on the track of quarry. Only two people seemed unmoved: John Heminges and the judge.

The latter waved the defendant back to his place. "The destruction of property and breaking of the peace are no matters for mirth. You both stand guilty as charged. Captain Peregrine Penny, stand forth." The large man with the mottled cheeks did so. "You will repay one half the damage assessed and serve thirty days in Fleet Prison."

Captain Penny raised his mutilated hand again. "Your Honor, I protest. 'Tis a poor return for faithful service to my country—"

"Enough! Bailiff, bear him away." I saw Penny's good hand fall on Kit's shoulder and give an affectionate squeeze before he was led away.

"Christopher Glover, stand forth." Kit rose from the bench, as the judge fixed him with a baleful eye. "Your conduct makes all too plain the weaknesses and pitfalls of your profession. Playacting has worked many ills upon this city, but one of the greatest is shiftless fellows who have not enough honest work to fill their days. . . ."

He went on a little longer about the scourge of plays and players, as I felt Master Condell grow rigid beside me. The senior members of the Company were sensitive to the common charges hurled against their profession and made every effort to conduct themselves as law-abiding, church-supporting, respectable family men. Even Master Will's pleasant face had turned to stone by the time the judge was done. For that matter, I might have lodged a protest against the notion that players had too little to do.

". . . As it is your first offense, I shall release you on bail." Raising his voice, the judge addressed the courtroom. "Is there any present to stand bail for Christopher Glover?"

John Heminges stood, clearing his throat. But before he could speak, a voice sounded from the back of the room. "So please you, Your Honor. His bail is secured."

Heads turned again as an elderly fellow came forward. His blue coat marked him as a servant, but without any distinguishing signs to indicate his house. He stopped at the railing and handed the bailiff a sealed letter, which the bailiff in turn passed to the judge. That gentleman broke the seal and read slowly, while John Heminges sank back on the bench, as mystified as the rest of us. Kit glanced back at us, his expression undeniably smug.

"I see." The judge looked up with an impassive face. "Very well." As the servant bowed and left the courtroom, the judge looked our way. "Do I understand the youth's guardian to be present?" John Heminges stood again, red-faced, as the judge continued. "Christopher Glover, you are free on bond, but I pray you take this experience to heart. . . ." With a few more words of exhortation he waved us out of the courtroom and shuffled the next case from his stack of papers.

Once outside, Master Heminges turned on Kit as though ready to settle the issue then and there. But he decided against it, shook his head angrily, and led the way to Fleet Street. Master Will excused himself, claiming some errand. Master Condell caught up with John Heminges, and we boys fell in behind, as always. Robin's curiosity had long since overcome his apprehension. "You must have some well-placed friends," he whispered.

"So it seems," Kit murmured, refusing this invitation to tell us more. For my part, I wished to know who was the "other knave" who had posed as a clergyman to trick Mistress Oxenbridge—he must have been quite a performer himself.

"Who is this Captain Penny?" Robin persisted.

"A corrupter of youth."

"And that barge of a woman—did she really set her two sons on you?"

"How do you suppose I got this knot on my head?" Kit pushed back his hair to reveal an ugly bluish lump on his brow. "Or this cut on my neck, or this stitch in my side, where the ribs are probably cracked?" He put a hand to the affected place and winced. "It took two of us to bring one of them down—I lost count of the things we broke over his head."

"Was he big?"

"Something less than the size of St. Paul's tower. But with about the same measure of wit."

Robin sniggered, as Kit favored him with a condescending smirk. I could have laughed, too, but the chilly silence wafting back from the two men ahead of us kept me from it. Suddenly John Heminges turned, quivering with fury. As soon as Kit was within range, Master Heminges slapped him so hard his head flew back.

Kit's face drained of color, except for the angry red mark on his right cheek. His pale eyes blazed, first with surprise, then rage. Robin and I, and even Master Condell, stood shocked, as though we were the ones slapped. John Heminges was not one to offer violence, nor was Kit one to take it.

Master Heminges raised his hand again, pointing two fingers in a way that, with him, always signaled a stern lecture.

"Today," he said, in a voice as thin as a string, "you are no longer welcome in my house. One more scrape like this and you will not be welcome in the Company; I swear it. Make some other arrangement for your lodging. I've done the best I could by you, Kit. I've been a father to you, as well as I might. But by heaven, there comes a time. If you would throw away your gifts on rakehells and scoundrels, so be it. But I care for my reputation, and you will *not* disgrace me again. Do you understand?"

Kit swallowed once, but did not speak. His eyes spoke for him, burning with a fire that would not be quenched for a long, long time.

No one spoke as we retraced our steps into the city and out again through Bishopsgate, heading up the Shoreditch Road. This was a journey that took most of an hour, not lagging—a long while for five people to hold silent, but Master Heminges's reprimand had left nothing much to say.

As it happened, though, Kit's trouble was soon cast into the shade. On our approach to the Theater a curious sight met our eyes: the men who should have been inside at rehearsal were clustered around the main entrance, many of them shouting and waving their arms. Our masters looked at each other, then quickened their pace until all of us were practically running. The sterling voice of Richard Burbage rang out at our approach. "John Heminges! What a day to be late. See if you can make Master Allen see reason!"

The view before us more than justified the urgency in his

voice. Giles Allen, a stocky little pigeon with a face as round and red as an apple, stood in the midst of the Company, flanked by two marshals of the London watch. Their matched height and shining brass helmets lent authority to the landlord, not to mention the pikes held ready to fend off maddened players. What made the players mad was plain to see: dangling from the landlord's arm were a chain and a padlock.

LOCKED OUT

heard Master Condell groan aloud as he stopped on the edges of a hurly-burly that included all the players, hired help, and stage boys. Robin and I pushed toward the center, where Master Allen stood. He seemed wonderfully composed, though his confidence may have owed somewhat to the presence of the marshals. From every side voices were shouting, "You might have warned us!" and, "This is an outrage!" John Heminges's approach prompted a general shushing.

"What is it?" he asked, reasonably enough.

Half a dozen voices all started at once, but Richard Burbage's quickly overpowered the rest. "We had just begun rehearsal when this strutting turkey cock arrives and turns us out. He claims to have an eviction order from the Lord Mayor—"

"Indeed I do. In this hand." Master Allen displayed a weighty-looking parchment.

John Heminges took it from him and read it with no change in his weary expression. Then he sighed. "I can see no way around this."

"No way *around* it?" sputtered Richard Burbage. "The Theater was built by my father. It belongs to *my* brother and me. He has no right to brazen his way in with chains and parchments and lock up MY BUILDING!"

"*Your* building is on *my* land," Master Allen piped up, in a voice oddly thin for one so round. "Moreover, your lease has expired. I am well within my rights."

"I fear he is." John Heminges looked up from the document. "He cites all the proper statutes—the law is on his side."

"The letter of the law may be," growled Burbage, "but the spirit is not. Look how he gulled us all these months—plain nasty, I'd call it."

"There's no law against nastiness," Master Heminges remarked. He turned to the landlord and asked, "Surely you will allow us access to our costumes and properties?"

"In a day or two," said the little man, with insufferable self-importance, "you will receive permission from my attorney—"

"Shove it down your throat, you beef-witted hedge pig!" Master Burbage snatched the eviction order and shoved it at the landlord's chest, then stalked out into the field and began kicking up clumps of sod. I was glad he had not attended Kit's hearing at Fleet court, or his temper would have given the magistrate more meat for his prejudice against players.

"Why now?" Thomas Pope demanded of the landlord. "Why hold the door open to us all this time, only to slam it now?"

"I am under no obligation to explain," the landlord retorted. "Wait for word from my attorney. Until then, pray you, stay off my land."

After a little more shouting, the scene ended, with Master Allen chaining the main entrance to the Theater and nailing his parchment to the door. The stage boys were the first to leave, followed by Adam Stewart, master of the wardrobe, wringing his hands over the silks and velvets he was forced to leave behind. The Company scattered next, agreeing to meet in two hours' time at the Mermaid Tavern to discuss their prospects. While drifting away, they voiced all sorts of speculation: "The vile bug must have sold his precious land—else why wait until now to lock us out?" "That putrid play we performed yesterday might have been enough to close any theater. . . ."

With so much unexpected time on his hands, Gregory decided to indulge in a truly memorable breakfast. He invited me to join him, but when Kit struck out across the field on a narrow path with Robin close behind, I followed—without quite knowing why. Soon after I turned on the path, the Welsh Boy appeared at my elbow. Thomas Pope, his guardian, either had given him permission to join me or else had failed to notice his absence.

"What do it all mean, Richard?" asked he in his sweet, lilting voice. It was the first time he had sought me out, or anyone else.

"I know not." The Theater hulked silently behind us. The white silk flag that indicated a performance would not be flown today, to the bewilderment of Londoners watching for it. I tried to reassure the boy. "The Company will meet today to find another place. They'll think of something."

"Aye?" The boy did not sound convinced.

We followed Kit all the way to the Thames—another long walk with few words, ending at the stone dike just east of the Tower. Kit turned at the wall and stared at us: Robin and me and Davy, strung out behind him like a kite's tail. If he had wanted, he could have lost us long ago with a rude "Shug off!" Instead he sneered, "You may sit, faithful subjects."

He boosted himself to the stone ledge and turned to face the river, sitting with ankles crossed and elbows on his knees. We scrambled up after him and formed a straggling row: Robin and Kit, me and Davy. The Tower rose forbiddingly to our right, a gray mossy heap brightened at this moment by full sunlight. Ships crowded the near bank, spiky masts swaying as their hulls bobbed in the water. A double-masted French galleass, sails furled, glided smoothly down the tide, headed toward the Channel. To me it felt surpassing strange to be idle on a warm, sunny day: strange, and not pleasant. After a long silence Robin ventured to Kit, "Will you be going to the Mermaid anon?"

"Why? To hear a flock of old hens snap their beaks?" Contemptuously, Kit heaved a gob of spit toward the river.

"It's our future they're deciding—"

"Not mine. You may go, if you're of a mind to be guided by carpenters and grocers."

This was a slap at the Burbages' father, James, and at John Heminges. Both began their adult lives as tradesmen before turning to the stage. But Kit had no room to mock. "Some are only descended from carpenters," I pointed out, "just as some are from grocers."

He rounded on me, as I might have expected, and told me what to do with myself. His own parents were grocers on Bucklersbury Street, though he barely admitted to knowing them. They came to plays now and then, but seemed overawed by their shining son. His mother approached with great meekness, while his father stood afar off and waved, as if Kit were as nobly born as the great ladies he played. It made me sick.

"Honest tradesmen are nothing to be ashamed of," I said. "Better than prison-bait companions."

"I notice you never speak of *your* honest relations at all."

That stung; my mother was dead and my father was not the sort of parent a lad could point to with pride. Kit knew nothing of substance about them, but his insinuation struck close. "You're the only one of us with a mother and father still living," I snapped at him. "You value too little what you have."

"Come off that," Robin complained. "The Theater is locked

52

and barred, and here you sit matching bloodlines. Our future is at stake."

Kit snorted. "Yours may be. But I begin to think that the Theater may go to hell."

"You can't mean that!" Robin straddled the wall and leaned toward him urgently. "That is—I mean—Master Heminges shouldn't have . . . done what he did, but give him his due: he's been a good teacher and guardian. And the Theater is where you won your greatest fame. Everybody knows you're the best boy player in London. The Company—"

"The Company may go to hell, too!" Kit's famous reserve crumbled, as he turned on Robin like a boar at bay, almost snarling. "They care nothing for me—they pretend not to notice I'm no longer a *boy*. They'd stuff me in skirts until I was thirty, if they could get away with it."

Mildly I remarked, "I thought that was a man's role you played yesterday." I almost added, "Even though you ended up playing it like a girl," but tact intervened.

So much for tact; his wrath only increased. "Aye, and you'd expect them to give me good support the first time. Burbage or Phillips should have played Sylvester, but who do they pick but Ned Shakespeare, who has a voice like a pipe and barely shaves and earned his place by virtue of being the playmaker's brother. As for Silvia, well . . . they might have given me some-one I could play off of."

The sheer unfairness of this remark pushed me beyond

prudence. "You play off me well enough when there's a quarrel toward. And Silvia was the only player to win applause, or do I remember wrongly?"

"Stop it!" Robin pleaded. Once again we were making life uncomfortable for him, torn as he was between liking for me and loyalty to Kit. "It was a bad play, I think we can agree on that. The Company should have tried you out on a better one."

Kit uncrossed his ankles and swung his heels against the stone wall—rather like a thwarted child, instead of the near-grown man he claimed to be. Davy, on my other side, was doing the same thing, aimlessly rather than petulantly. "It's a good play," Kit said. "Or would have been a good play, if they had given it the attention they should have."

Robin and I gazed at him with identical stunned expressions. Surely Kit knew a good play from a bad one as well as we did; had he parted company with his senses? In the silence, which neither of us could think how to break, the Welsh Boy's sweet voice bubbled up, softly singing a popular street ballad: "Jolly William, tell me how thy lady doth—"

Swiftly, Kit swung both legs over the wall, dropped down behind me, and grabbed the back of the boy's doublet, jerking hard. Davy landed on his back, his stunned blue eyes filling with sky just before they filled with tears.

As Kit marched away, I shouted at his back, "What is *wrong* with you?" He continued across the field toward Aldgate, seething with the same caged-tiger helplessness I had observed in Richard Burbage. Muttering, I scrambled down to make sure Davy had not broken anything.

Robin dropped down also, then stood indecisively before heaving a deep sigh. "I'm for the Mermaid."

As for me, I had had enough of ranting players for one day. Or so I thought. But after I arrived home, with Davy still in tow, what did Starling and I decide to do with the afternoon but take in a play at the Rose. I helped with her house chores so we could leave early; our Theater's closing was apt to swell the crowds at the Rose and the Swan and the Curtain. At midday the three of us crossed London Bridge into Southwark, that rowdy district where theaters, brothels, gambling dens, and bear pits flourished.

The Rose is home to our chief rivals, the Admiral's Men. Robin liked to compare their players to farm animals, but in truth they were almost as good as our Company. This was only the third play I had ever had the leisure just to watch, a new work entitled *The Downfall of Robert, Earl of Huntington, After Called Robin Hood.* Robin Hood plays always drew a crowd; no Englishman ever tired of the clever outlaw. The Admiral's Men were performing this version for the second time, and to judge by the roar of the audience, they might wring a dozen more showings out of it before the season ended. No tedious speeches or love scenes here: just as a talkative character threatened to outstay his welcome, a sword battle broke out, or the Sheriff of Nottingham showed his nasty mug, or Friar Tuck waddled on with an ale keg. "My lady critic would despise this," Starling giggled. "She was in the gallery of the Theater yesterday, praising the classical beauties of *The House of Maximus*—can you imagine?" We laughed one minute and cheered the next, young Davy jumping up and down with such abandon I had to wonder what he'd swallowed.

When the play ended and the groundlings began jostling their way toward the exits, the boy got away from us altogether. Starling, who had assumed responsibility for him, grew fretful as the minutes passed and we made very little progress through the crowd. "Suppose he's been kidnapped?"

"Who would want him?" I replied lightly, even while admitting to myself that lawless men lurked everywhere and were not above stealing pretty boys for nefarious purposes. Thus I was almost as relieved as she when Davy met us outside, still bubbling over with excitement. I wondered why he never showed such animation on our stage.

"Let's take a boat across the river," he chirped.

"Can't," I replied. "I spent my last penny on the play."

"I'll put the fare."

Starling looked sideways at him. "How could you do that? You had to borrow a penny from me to get into the Rose."

"Aye." The boy's face went as smooth as the summer sky. "And I'll pay it. But I keep a bit of coin put aside, for somewhat that may take my particular fancy." Starling and I raised eyebrows at each other, silently vowing we'd not let him sponge off us so easily next time. But we did not refuse the boat ride. It made a fitting end to an afternoon that turned out pleasant and carefree, and the last of that kind that I was to know for some time.

Master Allen sent word by his agents that he would allow access to the Company's tiring rooms for one day only, and Richard Burbage fired back a notice that he was bringing suit against the landlord for possession of his building. Setting the lawyers on it was all he could do; in the meantime we had a schedule to perform.

After some hasty negotiation, the chief players worked out an arrangement with the owner of the Curtain Theater nearby. The entertainment offered by the Curtain tended toward bear and bull fights, wrestling matches and bloody spectacle. For a price, the owner canceled most of these and gave our Company the run of his stage for three weeks out of every month (the fourth week being reserved for bear fights). It was the best that could be made of a bad situation. Master Cuthbert sent out a division of boys to tack up notices all over London, and performances at the Curtain began the following Monday.

The Curtain was built on a similar plan to the Theater, but different in dozens of ways one would not notice until forced to perform familiar actions in an unfamiliar space. The stage was deeper, but not as wide, so a player pacing off a speech might find himself teetering on the brink before a line was out.

The trap was in a different place, the tiring room walls were closer together, the musicians' gallery was backed by a wall instead of curtains, and on and on. For the first week we continually got in each other's way. Tempers grew short and minor eruptions broke out and every man and boy said things he afterward regretted. Except Kit, who said very little.

In spite of his defiant speech at the dike, he bottled himself up in a sullen attitude and continued playing imperious, passionate, or clever women as brilliantly as ever. As ordered, he had moved out of the Heminges household and now boarded with Richard Cowley in Southwark. This eased the strain between himself and John Heminges, although no one could mistake Kit's posture as one of resignation. He was a walking battle, and I could guess the conflict: one side of him defended his position as the finest boy player in London, while the other rebelled against that very position. No doubt he hated all of us, but for some reason he took it out only on the Welsh Boy.

This antipathy began to show itself in crafty ways. One afternoon I was standing behind the stage with Davy, awaiting our entrance together as a mother and son. Kit was on the stage, as a scheming queen plotting mayhem in snaky tones that writhed and fascinated. Only gradually did I become aware of the boy fidgeting beside me. My own neck itched from the starchy ruff that choked it, but that was an inconvenience that players were expected to endure. After all, the Queen's courtiers spent entire days encased in jeweled prisons, and they managed to keep from scratching themselves in her presence. "Stop that," I told him. "We must go on after Kit is done."

"I can't help it," he whispered. "The shirt is crawling."

I pulled back the stiff high collar of his doublet and squinted down his neck, looking for lice. His skin was far from clean, but neither did it crawl. "I don't see anything."

"You wouldn't. 'Tis cursed."

I looked at him sharply, but before I could ask what he meant, we heard the words of our cue. During the scene I kept a hand on his shoulder and gave him a subtle scratch from time to time, which seemed to help. But he forgot all his cues unless I pinched him, and I noticed that every time Kit looked directly at him, the boy twitched worse than ever. Kit's usual manner with new apprentices was not to torment but to ignore them. But the looks he gave the Welsh Boy were pointed and cruel, as though by looks alone he might drive him out of the Company. After the scene I examined Davy's collar again and picked up a fine grayish powder on my fingers that made them itch unmercifully until I was able to wash it off. How strange—would Kit stoop to such meanness? And if so, why?

Whatever Kit's wishes, the Company had determined to keep Davy, at least until the end of the season. He showed well as a page or young maid, and his tumbling and singing skills pleased our audience. His speeches had to be pared to the barest meaning, because his lifeless delivery of them did not improve, and whenever he had to speak at length, the audience became restless. This was too bad, because his memory was uncommon—just how uncommon no one knew until the day when he was asked to change his lines in rehearsal. "How, sir?" he asked, his wide blue eyes growing wider.

"You are saying the part about the lilies, but we struck that," Master Heminges explained. "Skip down to 'The fairest rose doth bear a thorn,' and speak only the next four lines."

He might have said this in a foreign tongue for all the comprehension the boy showed. In an unlikely show of helpfulness, Kit crossed to him, took his scroll, and skimmed the lines. "Here," he said, pointing. "This place here. Read that."

The boy seemed frozen, his mouth barely moving as he replied.

"What's that?" Kit purred. "What did you say?"

"I cannot read," said Davy.

This brought rehearsal to an abrupt halt, as Master Heminges exclaimed, "Can't *read*?" and other players clamored to know how any boy could get into a theater company without this vital mystery. Davy broke down and wept, pitifully enough to wring any heart, and revealed under questioning that Thomas Pope's housekeeper, who had taken a fancy to him, was drilling him on his lines in the evening until he could say them after her perfectly.

"Well," growled Master Burbage, "ask the lady to start teaching you your letters. And if you've not mastered the art by autumn, you will seek another place. Understood?"

"Aye, sir." The boy nodded and wiped his eyes, and rehearsal continued. I saw Kit's face darken, making me wonder if he had known the Welsh Boy's secret somehow and seized the opportunity to expose it.

Other incidents occurred: if the two had a scene together, Kit was apt to do some small thing—like changing a cue—that would confuse the boy. He did not do it often enough to attract suspicion from the other players, only enough to reduce Davy to a bundle of nerves every time they went on together. One afternoon the boy cried out in pain during a scene when he was supposed to dance and laugh. After the scene I unlaced his gown and found a needle embedded in the corset, at an angle to pierce him when he bent left or right. I could guess who laced him up that day.

These little nips and nudges had begun to stoke a low fire in me. Whatever Kit might have against the boy, no one deserved this. I myself, after a year, was only now settling into some consistency as a player—if Kit had treated me the way he was treating Davy, I would have been shattered early on. With righteous outrage, I climbed to the upper tiring room after the play and held up the offending object. "What's this?"

Kit looked, making his eyes cross. "A needle."

"Do you know where I found it?"

"No. A haystack?"

Robin and Gregory were watching us curiously, so I made

my reply obscure. "Let us say that it was in a place where needles ought not to be, and from now on I'll make it my business to keep watch."

"Please yourself. Standing sentry for needles seems a . . . pointless occupation."

"Be that as it may, I've made it my own."

Words are curious things: "shaped and polished air," according to Kit's reprobate friend Captain Penny. Yet they have an uncommon power. In the heat of the moment I had said more than I meant. Kit's unexplained cruelty angered me, but his arrogance on top of that pushed me to the brink. And with two witnesses I could not honorably take my words back. With no particular liking for him, I had made myself Davy's defender.

MASTER BURBAGE DRAWS A CIRCLE

*O*nce I spread my wing, the Welsh Boy slipped under it; almost every time we were in sight of each other, I would soon find him at my side. His constant presence felt like a splinter—just enough irritation to notice, yet not enough to act upon. Part of the irritation was that he had never learned to keep himself clean. Master Pope's housekeeper gave him one good washing that killed the lice, but his neck was always dirty, and he had to be reminded to clean his fingernails. No amount of scrubbing could purge his smell—not a bad smell, but an old one, like moss under a rock, that worked its way up through the tang of his sweat when he stood still long enough.

That very stillness unnerved me: the unblinking watchfulness, as though he was committing all my words and actions to memory. Sometimes, he was. His reading lessons with Dame Willingson seemed to be progressing slowly, and he used me as a line tutor in the meantime. At least by day's end I could leave him behind and sleep at night—unless Robin was in a mood to unburden his worries on me. Between Kit and Giles Allen he found much to worry about. My own worries increased when the Company scheduled a performance of *Richard III*.

This is one of Shakespeare's most beloved plays: the story of the hunchbacked Richard of York, who schemed his way to the throne, leaving a trail of corpses behind him. The corpses included his wife and brother and two young nephews—mere boys, whom he imprisoned in the Tower and then murdered. The crown rested very uneasily on his head; none too soon he lost it, and his life, in the battle of Bosworth.

King Richard III was one of Master Burbage's great roles. On any given day, it was not uncommon to hear an apprentice cry out in the street, "A horse! My kingdom for a horse!" Burbage had made this line from the final scene almost a password in the city. Londoners shivered in delight every time he clumped on the stage with his dragging hunchback walk.

All the other members of the Company were brushing up their accustomed parts, but one week before the performance Master Heminges announced a change among the apprentices: I was to play Queen Elizabeth, Richard's sister-in-law. Elizabeth, upon my reading of her lines, struck me as a woman who talked too much, but it was one of the most important parts ever handed to me. To be entrusted with her marked a step forward in my progress.

Then Robin, looking as if he had swallowed a lemon, informed me that Kit had played Elizabeth's part since it was created. I considered declining the honor. I had taken one of Kit's parts before and he was not gracious about it; in his present state I feared an assassination attempt. But the Company assigned another role to him: Margaret, the former queen (together with Elizabeth and Richard's wife, Anne, there were more queens in this story than on a chessboard). Margaret had been exiled to France but unexpectedly returns, spewing bitterness and curses. Having no choice, Kit accepted this part—with a vengeance.

Even though Saturday afternoon was drizzly and gray, play-goers packed the Curtain, eager to see the hunchbacked villain meet his well-earned doom. Since I was given only a week to learn them, my lines had been pared back, but even so, by performance time they felt only a little firmer in my head than a custard.

My first scene began well, however. Most of the Company was on the stage as England's royal family, and I was holding my own—until Margaret glided onto the stage in a black gown and hood. I felt a chill run through the building. The heavy gray sky overhead required torches to be set, and a moody light trembled over the scene. Kit knew how to place himself to make the light his ally—when he threw back the hood, his white face leapt out so fiercely that our audience gasped.

Margaret's office is to pronounce doom on all the supporters of Richard who heed not her warning: "Have not to do with him, beware of him; sin, death, and hell have set their marks on him. . . ." Kit's glittering eyes burned through the lines, and it seemed to me he was not speaking of the hunchback. Davy stood close by me as Elizabeth's son, the young Duke of York. While Margaret berated the assembly for past wrongs, Kit glared upon the Welsh Boy:

"God, I pray Him—

That none of you may live his natural age

But by some unlooked accident cut off!"

The boy trembled and shrank next to me, obviously not acting. I put an arm around his shoulder, and I was not acting either.

Kit knew better than to break out of character, but twice during Margaret's tirade he fixed Davy with such dagger-sharp glances that I could feel their edge myself. Shortly before leaving the stage, he turned his venom on the company in general:

"Uncharitably with me have you dealt

And shamefully my hopes by you are *butchered*."

The audience murmured when he left the stage, as though released from his grip, and a voice from among the groundlings called out, "Well done, Kit!" It was a most effective performance; Will Sly could have spoken for all when he said, in character, "My hair doth stand on end to hear her curses." But soon I had cause to wonder if Kit, in his general anathema, had slapped a particular curse on me.

From that time on I dropped lines and missed cues like a rank beginner, enough for some of the players to look at me curiously and Master Condell to murmur, "Are you well, lad?" As my performance declined, my anger grew. Of course Kit could not be blamed for all my failures, but when he tripped the Welsh Boy behind the stage, I felt myself coming to a boil. Davy was running to be on time for his entrance, and directly after passing Kit, he slammed the floor so hard it could be heard from the stage. Since no one saw the crime, Davy took the blame for clumsiness. When he could find me alone, he revealed what had really happened, sniffling, "What hurt did I ever do to him?"

That I could not answer. But soon I was having my own troubles with Kit, in a conversation between Elizabeth, Margaret, and King Richard's mother, played by Gregory. The three ladies are supposed to vent their wrath upon Richard, the "vile bunch-backed toad," but I found myself stumbling over lines worse than ever. My awkwardness threw Gregory off his stride as well. Kit's long speeches were perfect and spoken with such conviction that the crowd hung on every word. As Margaret he saved the scene, but it was Kit, the tortured boy player, who leaned forward suddenly and hissed at me, *"Thou didst usurp my place,* and dost thou not usurp the just proportion of my sorrow?"

What do you mean, *usurp your place*? If he had not been leaving the stage, I might have so forgotten myself as to ask it out loud. With a stab of panic I realized he had dropped several lines. I was supposed to stop him but could not recall the words. In desperation I simply called, "Stop!"

"'Stay awhile,'" Gregory whispered, prodding my foot with his own.

"Stay awhile," I repeated weakly. "And . . ." ("'Teach me how to curse—'" Gregory prompted.)

Fortunately, there was not much to the scene after that— or to my part. Davy went on once more as the ghost of the young prince, but appeared to be so haunted himself, he could barely speak. The boy's miserable face, ashen under the ghostly powder applied to it, pushed me at last to confront his tormenter in the upstairs tiring room.

At least, I tried to confront him. The attempt was not successful at first, for I could hardly get the words out. In moments of deep stress or high feeling my voice fails—a strange impediment for a player, I've been told, but there it is. "What—" I began, and felt my throat closing up. "What—"

Kit stared at me, feigning interest. "What's this? It has two legs, two arms, and a mouth—it looks like some sort of human but gulps like a bunch-backed toad."

I clenched both fists. "Wh-what's this game you're p-playing?"

"Game? What game?"

"This t-t-tormenting of . . ." I found myself struggling for breath. "Gregory—my points—would you?"

Gregory stepped behind me and began unlacing the back of my gown. Robin, biting his lip, was already performing the same service for Kit, so we looked like two over-decorated barges unlimbering for combat. Gregory handed me a damp towel to wipe the paint and powder off my face, all the while with dark glances at the opposition as though to signal whose side he was on. Robin inclined more to peacemaking. "What are you talking about, Richard? Nobody is being tormented."

I took hold of myself, slowing my speech to a crawl. "I . . . know . . . it was you . . . who p-planted that needle last week. And what did you use . . . to cause the itch? P-p-powdered nettle?"

"What . . . do . . . you . . . mean?" Even though he mocked me, Kit's complexion had flushed to a deep shade that his brisk rubbing with a towel could not account for.

"You m-must tell me that—"

"I *must*?"

"Whatever your reasons . . . you've achieved your goal. The boy is—petrified."

"The boy," he repeated, tossing the towel to one side, "is too small for you to hide behind. If you gave a bad perfor- mance, take it like a man." I opened my mouth, but could say nothing, probably because he was so close to being right. "What I've achieved," he went on, pulling off his shift, "is getting a r-r-rise out of you. This is lofty enough, considering what a milksop you normally—"

I threw my corset at his head: not a trifling weapon, with its metal grommets and whalebone stays. It unleashed the tiger in him. He picked up Elizabeth's crown and hurled it at me like a discus, so the clover points caught me in the neck. Robin pinned his arms, but Gregory would not restrain me. Lacking any other weapon, I hurled myself and knocked both Kit and Robin to the floor. Recovering, Kit pounced on me, rolling us so near the loft opening that I might have fallen through it if the other boys had not screamed a warning. He punched me, and I punched him. We had each drawn blood before Richard Burbage stuck his head through the opening, bellowing to shame any bull.

I could not make out what he said at first, but it was round enough to make Kit release me and stand up, looking sullen. Burbage's words came clearer.

"—and depend on it, you'll pay for every farthing of damage to these clothes. Kit, come down at once. Richard, shed those ridiculous petticoats and follow presently."

They all went down, leaving me to look around. I could see what touched off Master Burbage: the tiring room resembled an ambush in the Queen's Wardrobe, with velvets and silks splayed out like battle-sprung horses and beads littering the floor like musket balls. Upon my life, I could not remember doing such damage in so short a time. They'll have our heads for this, I thought gloomily, while untying the petticoat strings. Still, it was almost worth it to coax a little blood from Kit's haughty nose. For his part, he'd cut my lip. I ran my tongue around the place already swelling, then hastily tucked in my shirt, picked up my shoes and doublet, and descended the steep stairway, expecting a heavy fine to be laid on me.

The lower room was empty. Tiring master, stage boys, apprentices, players, and hired men had all gathered on a stage that still flickered with dreadful torchlight under the lowering clouds. Richard Burbage was drawing a large circle on the planks with a piece of limestone as John Heminges hovered at his elbow, protesting, "But we must rehearse."

"This will not take long." Master Burbage closed the circle, straightened his back, and tucked the limestone into a pocket on his sleeve.

"But what if they do real damage, and we're out two players?"

"Real damage can be prevented."

"And bruises, and cuts, and black eyes? Won't our gentle ladies look fetching with black eyes?"

"That's what paint is for. Kit, Richard; stand here, please you."

Master Heminges threw up his hands and backed away, shaking his head. As Kit and I approached, I felt goose bumps rise on my arms, having by now gained a notion of where this wind blew. The murmurs around us fell silent as Master Burbage motioned us to stop.

"Now," said he, "the two of you have never managed to get along since you met. Whatever the bone of contention between you, I propose that you have it out this hour, for once and for all. That is how honest men settle things—"

"It's how *barbarians* settle things!" Master Heminges called from the back of the stage.

"Peace, John," Will Sly spoke up. "For my part, I like it well. Straightforward and simple."

"And," continued Burbage, "as it is bound to happen anyway, we might as well see that it happens where the least possible damage may be done."

Except to my own sweet person! thought I, desperately looking about for an advocate. But of the boys, only Robin appeared the least bit alarmed. I noticed Gregory shaking hands with one of the stage keepers and guessed that he had just made a wager. Of the men, Master Heminges had raised the only objection, and though one or two may have been impatient to get on with rehearsal, few would dare to take issue with Richard Burbage. The only two who might—Masters Kempe and Shakespeare— stood in grave discussion, with occasional glances to Kit and me. They seemed to be comparing our advantages, perhaps in view of a wager of their own. Even the serving girls and penny takers, who had just finished sweeping up, crowded among the men for choice places. I sent a look of distress to Starling, who merely raised her shoulders in a tiny shrug, then smacked her fist against her palm.

"Box, or wrestle?" inquired Master Burbage.

Kit deferred the choice to me. "Box," I said helplessly. My fighting experience was of the untutored kind that consisted of aiming for the soft parts of the opponent while protecting my own soft parts. It might be called boxing.

"Well enough," Master Burbage said. "Remember you must be on your feet by Monday. We'll stop you before you cripple each other—"

"And the faces—the faces!" called John Heminges.

"Very well; try not to go for the other's face. A swollen jaw might pass, but—"

"Richard!"

Our mediator sighed. "Avoid the face, if you can. And below the belt—that leaves a wide expanse between neck and waist to work on, eh?" He rubbed his hands together, and I suddenly guessed that he needed this fight as much as he claimed we did. Better battling youths in plain sight than battling lawyers in court, perhaps. "Stay within the circle; any step outside and we'll push you back in. Ready?"

Kit's flinty eyes told me he was more than ready. And indeed, the whole crowd of spectators appeared ready; I could almost feel their breath, and thought of bulls pawing the ground. I might vie with John Heminges for most reluctant player, but no honorable alternative occurred to me. I prayed a swift petition for speed, endurance, and fists like a hammer as I slowly pulled off my shirt and tossed it behind me. A voice—

I could not tell whose—shouted out, "God speed you, Richard." Another answered back, "Slam him, Kit!" and the battle of the voices was joined.

As we closed in, the shouting made a hedge around us. I heard his name and mine, but saw only him, approaching at a crouch, fists raised. He made a jab at my chin, which told me that he did not intend to go by the rules, and while ducking, I replied with a blow to his side. Then we circled for a while, coming to know each other dreadfully as the world narrowed: just him, just me, each seeking out the other's weakness in the same way, I suppose, that lovers tease out each other's charms.

His first hit, a straight punch to the chest, drove the wind out of my lungs and filled my vision with red. Coughing, I dodged right and left until he emerged from the haze, then swung wildly at his stomach and was amazed to see him double up. Only the shock to my wrist convinced me that the blow was mine, but making firm connection at last seemed to add weight to me. I swung again, expecting my knuckles to jar against his ribs—but missed, leaving myself open. Pain slammed into my own ribs instead. I felt the hurt I'd meant for him, which doubled my resolution to give it back. It was not anger that possessed me now, but a kind of hunger, a craving for the crack of bones. My left swung and missed again, but the right—beautifully—caught him on the point of the chin and flipped him back like a leaf. He caught himself in the midst of his fall, bounced upright again, and came directly at me, his pale eyes as sharp as sudden knives. I remember nothing clearly after that.

They were shouting our names, though at that moment we were not Kit and Richard, but two unleashed winds. We bore into each other until our knuckles were bloody and our eyes glazed. I was down, I was up; we were locked chest to chest, twinned hearts furiously pounding. He was down, he was up; he knocked me out of the ring. The shouting—such a vital animal, it had grown hands and feet—pushed me back in.

I do not know how long it was until a hard thump on the jaw spun me around. Next I knew, my right shoulder was mashed against the floor. Splinters from the rough boards speared up in my vision. From overhead Kit's voice pressed down on me like an unsteady hand: "Don't. Don't get up." But all around me the noise contradicted him, chanting: get up, get up, get up. Slowly I rolled onto my chest, put my palms to the boards and pushed, flinging blood and sweat out of my eyes. The shouts rose with me, thick and fierce.

"That's enough." One voice stood out distinctly, and no wonder: it was Richard Burbage's, the most celebrated voice in London. "Enough," he said again. I gained an unsteady foothold on the stage. Someone thrust a cold towel in my hands. I buried my face in it and heard my name again, but this time in one clear tone that gradually emerged as Starling's.

"Who won?" I asked her as she was patching me up in the Condell kitchen. My voice came out at a rasp, owing to a bruised throat.

"The orthodox view is that he did, but there's no canon to judge by." She was wrapping my chest with linen to shore it up against possible cracks. "Master Burbage failed to make it clear how long you were to stay down. You started up again in far less than ten counts, so it should have gone on, but the Company feared for the damage, I think. No one denies you gave a very good account of yourself. He looks no better than you." She finished the wrapping and pulled the end of the linen so tightly that I gasped. "Does that feel like knives gouging your vitals?"

"No." I took a careful breath. "More like . . . like babies gumming from inside my chest."

She knew not what to make of this comparison. "Well . . . I hope that means nothing is broken." She gave a final pull and tucked in the strip securely. "You'll live, and feel better for it, in time."

Nell the cook had larded my cuts and slapped a piece of raw stew meat on my swollen cheek and boiled up a batch of onions to make a poultice for my throat—with a pot to cook in, I might have made a good dinner. "I felt better when he was pounding me than I do now."

"That's because you were pounding him back. You haven't told me yet what it was all about."

I had told her almost nothing. The Company released me from rehearsal early so she could see to my injuries (Kit had to stay). The walk home—stopping once for me to vomit in the gutter—was too painful for speech. Nor did it help to clarify the matter for me. "I don't know myself what it was *all* about. I don't hate him, for all he makes me mad. Sometimes I think we might be friends, except for the small fact that he hates me."

"But he doesn't—"

Nell bustled in and demanded her kitchen back, so Starling bundled me up—meat, onions, and all—and helped me climb the two sets of stairs to the attic. Along the way we had to fend off the eager attention of the youngest Condell boys, stop to let the mistress gently feel my ribs, and respectfully ignore Alice's pointed remark about warring savages. When we finally reached the room I shared with Robin, she eased me down on the low bed and took off my shoes, but I had to tell her I could remove my own breeches, and would do so once she was out of the room. Then she pulled up a three-legged stool and sat by the bed. "He doesn't hate you. There's more to it than that."

"What?" My brain was sinking into the dark waters of oblivion, but the subject held enough interest to keep me awake a little longer.

"He's the only one—besides me—who knows how good a player you are apt to become."

"Oh." She had voiced this notion before, and it seemed in

the same company with her other flights of fancy. "My performance today must have terrified him."

"Your performance today means nothing, in the balance. He's always seen the promise in you, better than most. I think it challenged him before. But now that he's begun to falter, it threatens him."

"Falter? You mean one bad performance, in that putrid play?"

"One bad performance—one truly bad performance—is too many for him." She was speaking with some passion, as though she had thought this out fully and had longed for the moment to share it with me. "Master Burbage spoke of ending it once and for all today. But I believe it's only begun."

"That's a comforting thought to sleep on." A memory of the way Kit had said that line about being "usurped" stirred in my brain, but that brain was rapidly sinking. "You've drawn too long a bow about his opinion of me. What brought this on today was mainly the way he treats the Welsh Boy."

"*Davy?*" her voice pierced my throbbing ears. "You were fighting over him?"

"In a way . . . I've told you how Kit's been nasty to him . . . I know not why. . . ."

"That's strange."

"How so?"

"I noticed him, in the midst of the combat. He always looks so bland, you can never guess what he thinks, but as he watched you and Kit pound each other, I saw him smile. A strange, inward smile, perhaps even a little smug. . . ."

Her voice faded. Shortly afterward, I felt the covers settle over me, and a light touch on my forehead.

When I woke again, the room was as black as pitch. Robin lay on his back beside me, snoring; Thomas, Ned, and Cole Condell rustled in their box bed on the floor. Through the open window a watchman cried three o'clock, and in some dark recess of my aching head, a bloodthirsty crowd was still shouting. Starling had told me something about the Welsh Boy. I remembered him now, had caught sight of him as I braced my palms against the rough boards and pushed up: saw him watching. And, yes, smiling.

Fat Jack

unday allowed me one day of rest before returning
to the stage on Monday—which I was expected to do, no
matter how sore in the ribs. Kit had a cut on his chin and
a bruised eye I could not remember giving him. But that,
as Master Burbage had said, was what paint was for, and
Kit took more time with the paint than he normally did.
While waiting for him to finish so that I could occupy the
space before the window, I found myself wondering if he
was dawdling on purpose to make me late. The
performance was to begin in only half an hour. His
manner toward me seemed unchanged—cool and superior
as ever—but I feared he might take some subtle revenge.
Gregory and Robin were treating us gently but preferred
avoiding us altogether; they had dressed and cleared out
as soon as possible, leaving us alone.

"That swelling on your cheek," Kit said abruptly. I

looked up, directly into the small hand mirror he was holding out to me. My face, a white-powdered blob, wove in and out of the mirror, while his held steady behind it. When painting ourselves for the stage, we imitated the ladies at court, who in turn followed the Queen's example of an almost dead-white purity of skin. We looked familiar yet strange, as though something had sucked the blood of our essential selves. "You can make swellings less with a tincture of lead," he went on. "Do you know how to do that?"

I shook my head, and he dug among his effects for a lead spoon. Giving me the glass to hold, he showed me how to draw the back of the spoon down the swollen side of my face, creating the palest of shadows. "Don't do it often, or your skin will rough up like a pig's hide."

"Thank you," I said, mightily confused as to where I stood with him. It occurred to me to ask: Do I threaten you? Did our fight settle anything? Is there any way we could be friends? But a silence stood between us, like a wall of glass I dared not break for fear of getting myself cut.

As for Davy, he hooked onto me as I climbed upon the stage and hung close all morning, but spoke no word about the fight. I thought he might have shown some gratitude; did he know what it was about?

"He knows," Gregory told me as we waited for an entrance together later that afternoon. "Robin let it slip when he was trying to feel out the little weasel. The boy all but laughed in his face. Depend on it; you're the only friend he will have soon."

"Why do you say that? Has the Company turned against him?"

"No, but they haven't warmed to him." Gregory's mouth twisted. "There's something about him that's not right."

"In that case, he's more an object for pity than—"

"Do as you please," he said abruptly. "Only if I were you, I would drop him like a hot iron."

That evening the entire Company adjourned to the Mermaid Tavern for the casting of Master Will's latest play. I had heard some of the chief players discussing the work with happy anticipation, though the meat of it did not sound promising to me: a history of the troubled reign of Henry IV. This king had usurped the throne from his cousin but never sat easily on it; his reign, from what I could remember, was plagued with rebellion and unrest. Master Will could coax life from it if anyone could, but I expected a rather solemn evening when I squeezed onto a bench at one end of the table, with Robin on one side and Davy on the other.

On casting nights the proprietor of the Mermaid reserved the long board in the loft for the Company to discuss their work in private. By the time we broke up to go home, we'd be cured like hams in the close, smoky air, but one advantage was that the tavern servers were always bringing us more ale and meat. They liked to eavesdrop on the new plays and be great men amongst their friends when they shared their knowledge the next day.

"Before I begin," Master Will announced, "you should know that I have found so much matter for this subject that it can't all be packed into one performance. Therefore the reign of King Henry IV must be presented in two parts: the first for the spring and the second, God willing, next fall."

Will Kempe laughed. "By all the saints, what treasures did you mine out of old Holinshed to fill a double dose of theater?" He was referring to Holinshed's *Chronicles,* our author's main source of information for the history plays. I had read some of it in school and felt as doubtful as Master Kempe. But Shakespeare surprised me, once he plunged into his reading of all the parts.

As the play begins, King Henry is sick and sad and longs to ease his troubled conscience with a crusade to Jerusalem. But he must first deal with ill winds in his own country. Two of his strongest supporters, Henry Percy the elder and Henry Percy his son (called "Hotspur"), have become dissatisfied with the king's treatment of them and join forces with other unhappy nobles to plot rebellion.

If these three were not enough Henrys already, there is yet one more: the king's oldest son is Henry too, but better known as Hal. Hal prefers carousing in taverns to sitting in council with his father's advisors, and his companions are the sort that no respectable prince would expose to the light of day—

chief among them a fat and cowardly knight called Sir John Oldcastle.

The Percys, father and son, join forces with Owen Glendower, a Welsh lord who has never submitted to English rule. This Glendower is a sorcerer who claims to command supernatural powers, but the real heart and soul of the rebellion is the gallant Hotspur. He lives for glory and holds complete faith in his own brilliant reputation: "By heaven," he cries, "methinks it were an easy leap to pluck bright honor from the pale-faced moon!"

The rebellion gathers strength and power as allies from Scotland join them, and the king is seriously threatened. He hopes for support from his son, but Prince Hal is playing an elaborate prank on his friend Oldcastle: when the fat knight holds up a band of pilgrims on the way to Canterbury and takes their gold, the prince appears in disguise soon after and robs the robbers. (To his credit, he later returns the money to its rightful owners.)

Such conduct makes the king despair of his own son, but when the rebellious Percys bring on a war, Prince Hal heeds the call to honor. He manages to gain back some of his father's regard, especially after saving the king's life on the battlefield. In the final clash at Shrewsbury, Hal and Hotspur go sword to sword, and the prince slays the valiant but misguided rebel. Thus the rebellion is put down and King Henry reconciled with his son, though not perfectly.

And Part Two was still to come.

The Company fell in love with the play at first reading and immediately after joined in spirited discussion over who would play what. The argument was mostly show, since it was assumed that Shakespeare held certain men in mind as he wrote the parts. The portly Thomas Pope would fill Oldcastle's round doublet to perfection, with Will Kempe and Richard Cowley as his fellow soldiers and reprobates. Will Sly was known for dashing roles such as Hotspur's, Richard Burbage would shine as the mysterious Owen Glendower, and John Heminges could outfit King Henry with the proper careworn gravity. Prince Hal seemed almost an afterthought in the midst of more colorful roles. There is more to him than meets the eye at first: though he appears a shallow ne'er-do-well, he reveals strength and purpose as the story unfolds. The role was assigned to Augustine Phillips, but seemed not to have any particular name on it.

Concerning the boys' parts, there would be little discussion; the chief players had already determined these, and all that remained was to hand out the sides. The closest to a "Juliet" was Lady Percy, Hotspur's spirited wife—"And that falls to Richard," announced Master Will, passing down the scroll with my lines written on it. "Robin, you are for Mistress Quickly."

This was a comic role, not a romantic one, and I felt Robin's arm stiffen as he drew away from me. A glance at his face showed his hurt, mixed with the bitter knowledge that he had grown too stout for Juliet. I felt for him, but did not look forward to the sulky mood that was sure to follow.

David Morgan received the role of Owen Glendower's daughter, an announcement that surprised no one. His side consisted only of cues, for the part was all in Welsh. Playing a grown woman would be a stretch for him, but Master Will could not resist making use of his peculiar gifts.

Gregory was handed a mixed bag of messengers and servants, as usually befalls an apprentice when there are not enough female roles to go around. "As for Kit—" Master Shakespeare paused.

Kit was sitting across from me, carefully maintaining an inch of space between himself and Gregory. Throughout the evening he had sat in stone-faced silence, even while the rest of the Company roared with laughter at the antics of Oldcastle and the prince. Now he raised his head, and I was struck by a thought that probably struck the rest of the boys as well: there were no more female parts. "You shall play Ned Poins, the prince's companion." Master Shakespeare passed down the scroll as if it was no great matter, but the Company fell silent for an instant, understanding what this meant. The part was not large, but it could be lively—Poins, I recalled, was the one who proposed the robbery scheme, and he and the prince have a rare old time in the tavern scene that follows. The clear message to Kit was that the Company was willing to help him master this great leap in his career, so long as he stayed out of trouble. I gazed at his face, rewarded by one of the rare moments when it actually revealed him—though what it revealed was a clash of gratitude and resistance. What he said would be a natural response, from most people, but sounded odd coming from him: "Thank you, sir."

Shakespeare nodded, and across the table from him Thomas Pope burst out in a loud laugh. "This fellow Oldcastle—God's truth, this time you've outdone yourself, Will." He had been scanning his lines and now threw his voice into a pious, canting pitch as he read, "'Do I not bate? Do I not dwindle? Why, my skin hangs about me like an old lady's loose garment. Company, villainous company hath been the spoil of me.'" He gleefully rubbed his hands together, chortling, "Fat Jack is worth a fortune to us!"

"To Fat Jack!" cried Richard Cowley, raising his ale tankard. Everyone downed a toast to Oldcastle, who was just the sort of outrageous rogue our audiences loved—yet with a difference that troubled me, even as I drank to him. Plenty of plays included witty servants or fast-talking thieves, but Oldcastle was a gentleman of sorts, and much more than a mere thief. He reminded me of someone, or some thing, but in the smoke and noise of the tavern, with the oil lamps beginning to gutter out and ale buzzing in my head, I could not think clearly.

The assembly began to shift and sigh. In the middle of a

yawn, I caught a view of Kit's face, with an expression of such naked malevolence on it my jaw locked for a moment. The look was not for me but for Davy, who had turned sideways on the bench with his legs dangling over the end and his spine digging into my side. I glanced down at his dark head, bent over a long loop of string between his hands. It appeared to be a game of cat's cradle, but the design was unfamiliar to me. His fingers shuttled with a skill that could only come from long practice. "What's that?" I asked him.

The fingers froze, like a nest of startled rabbits. Then he twitched his thumbs, and the string pattern disappeared as he pulled his hands apart. "'Tis nothing."

Later that night, I sat up in bed with a cry of revelation: "Aha!"

Robin stirred. "What?"

"Sir John Oldcastle. There was something about him I couldn't remember, but now I do—he's one of the martyrs in Foxe." Only the ale had kept me from remembering this earlier; as a boy I had read Reverend Foxe's *Book of Martyrs* countless times, and the copy given me by Master Condell was among my prized possessions.

"Fat Jack, a Protestant martyr?" Robin groused. I had been right in predicting his mood. "Not likely. Now shut up and let me sleep."

I was sure of it, though. Sir John Oldcastle had suffered under Edward III for denying certain doctrines of the Church of

Rome. He made a most noble end, burned for the true faith. Didn't Master Will know that? Or might he have some reason for resurrecting a pious saint as a wine-guzzling libertine? Oh well, thought I, sinking back into the straw mattress; the real Oldcastle died two hundred years ago. He could not come back to haunt us now.

As with most new plays, the Company allowed about three weeks for the players to learn their parts, but this particular new play set an additional task for them: Master Will wished a better setting for it than the creaky old Curtain. Across the river, in Southwark, a new theater had gone up west of the Rose. It was called the Swan, said to hold upwards of three thousand people. Cuthbert Burbage began negotiations to secure it for the opening performance of *Henry IV,* and when he interrupted a rehearsal one morning to announce that the Swan was ours for the last week in May, all the men of the Company cheered.

But most of them were groaning two weeks later, when we had to load our properties and costumes in carts and haul them from Shoreditch to Southwark. The distance was not so great by measure, but it took us all the way through London: over every pothole, past every cart collision, and through every street quarrel that happened to be going on at the time.

The apprentices were given charge of a large barrow loaded with royal properties: crowns, orbs, some costume pieces, and a very heavy throne, all covered in buckram to conceal the cargo from light fingers. Davy added little muscle, so we kept him on watch for most of the journey, while the rest of us sweated and strained and managed to get our clumsy cart stuck in at least half the holes we tried to avoid. The evening had turned rainy, and we all looked like half-drowned rats by the time we had lumbered through Bishopsgate and entered the city.

As we approached Buckingham Tavern, on Gracechurch Street, the door of the establishment burst open and a score of contentious men boiled out of it. We stopped to watch, glad for the diversion. The quarrel surged back and forth like an angry sea until the sense emerged: it seemed to be about the honor of certain people at the Queen's court. As the smaller group slandered the loyalty and fighting ability of the Earl of Essex, a sizable body of defenders spoke vigorously for him, and soon a young man in their midst stepped forward to engage in single combat for their hero. He had some personal insults to revenge as well.

"Call *me* a prissy dame?" he shouted at someone in the opposing crowd. "Call *me* a prancing duck? I'll show you a duck. Have at thee!"

A hard laugh rang out like steel. "Your blade is no quicker than your tongue, boy. I'll test you on that point as easily as any other." An older man stepped out of the shadows, his hand on the hilt of a rapier. When their blades flashed in the damp twilight, my blood surged, as though I had stumbled on a body.

"Make it two points, then!" The "boy's" words sounded fiercer than he looked, with his slim body and refined, almost girlish features. But his fair complexion was flushed with wine and rage. He pulled a velvet cape off his shoulder with one hand and tossed it to the servant hovering nearby, then pulled his dagger. His foe likewise removed his cloak—a plain, sturdy wool one—and looked around for an honest bystander to hold it for him. To my surprise he ignored many eager outstretched hands and tossed the garment to Kit. Then he pulled his own dagger.

The onlookers cheered, for this would be rare sport. Men slashing at each other with swords, or stabbing with knives, were common enough on the London streets, but only gentlemen and fencing masters preferred the new style of rapier-and-dagger. One of each appeared to be squaring off now in the drizzle and the hissing torchlight; the older fellow was no gentleman, but he clearly knew his business.

Something else soon became clear, too. Even though the fight seemed in earnest, I noticed the older man was pulling his thrusts. Though both showed some skill, he was easily the better swordsman and could have ended the contest in short order. "They don't mean it," Gregory murmured in my ear. "Or at least, one of them doesn't."

Some among the spectators had glommed onto the same suspicion, for a voice called out, "Stop playing with him, Corporal! Finish him!"

The young gentleman made the mistake of turning his

head, leaving a hole in his defense as wide as Newgate. The so-called corporal slipped through it and caught a button at the point of the rapier, then sliced it off with the dagger, all so quick the boy scarcely had time to turn around.

"Do you yield?" asked the corporal. His voice was hard, with a curious accent that sounded familiar, though I couldn't place it.

Up until now, the gentleman had behaved rather like a brat demanding his own way; I half expected him to stamp his well-shod foot and whine that it wasn't fair. Instead he sheathed his rapier, straightened his clothes, and bowed with seemly dignity. "I yield the match. But not the honor of my Lord Essex, whom God grant that I may anon be privileged to defend, with better wit and spirit."

This was a pretty way to concede, and the onlookers murmured their approval as his opponent also bowed, low enough to retrieve the severed button and offer it back. "The privilege was mine, Lord Mustard."

The young man turned a deeper shade of crimson and drew his rapier again. "I told you never to call me that!"

"Of course, my lord. Forgive me." The corporal retrieved his cloak, which Kit had folded into a bundle for him, bowed again toward the gentleman, and backed away toward the Buckingham Tavern, his show of humility as thin as water. Smirking companions followed. At this timely moment the servant arrived, riding one horse and leading another. Flinging his velvet cape over one shoulder, the young gentleman swung into the saddle and jerked on the reins. I knew somewhat of horses, having been a stable boy most of my life, and winced to think how the poor creature's mouth must feel. Heedless of all obstacles, the two turned west, scattering dogs, carts, and people before them.

"Lord Mustard," Robin repeated, once they were out of sight. "He must be a member of the Condiment clan."

"Near cousin to the Earl of Horseradish," Gregory suggested.

Scowling, Kit turned to us as we broke out in giggles. "Will you be helping pull this load? Or would you prefer to ride it instead? One idler on this team is enough." That last remark was aimed at Davy, who perched on the front of the cart. Kit knocked him off with a back-handed swipe and picked up the tongue. Gregory rolled his eyes at me and stepped behind to push.

The Company slated three familiar plays before the first performance of *Henry IV* on Thursday, a wise plan since we needed the time to accustom ourselves to yet another theater. Confusion was certain, but Richard Burbage took it very hard when he couldn't find his favorite black doublet for Tuesday's performance of *The Duke of Navarre*. Costumes had to be carefully watched; the Company laid out more money to dress their players than they did to pay them. "It's worth thirty pounds, if it's worth a farthing!" Master Burbage repeated as he turned over the tiring rooms of the Swan, with all the stage keepers and apprentices pressed into searching for the doublet. Since no one would admit to moving it, he had no one to blame.

"But you won't need it until Thursday, sir," ventured Kit.

Master Burbage backed out of the wardrobe crate he'd been pawing through. "Do you object if I take a notion to wear it *today*, Master Glover?"

Irritation made him sarcastic, and Kit knew better than to reply. An hour's search turned up no black damask doublet with gold braid and piping, and our chief player had to make do with a scarlet one. As far as I could tell, his performance did not suffer, but he was in a foul mood for the rest of the day. The missing costume was only part of it—a fly's weight in the ton of his theater troubles—but his irritation spread to all before the day was done.

When I told her of the missing costume that evening, Starling said, "I'll wager a shilling I can find it."

"If I had a shilling, that would be an easy win. We turned the tiring rooms inside out."

"But without me," she said. "I'll find it."

A good thing I didn't bet, for two days hence she did find it. But under circumstances that provided no answers, only raised new questions.

"And where did you find it?" Master Burbage demanded, with a look that mixed relief, puzzlement, and irritation.

Starling made another little curtsey. Just as we were completing our final preparations for *Henry IV*, she had caught us on one corner of the stage and handed over the missing garment. Her manner was not quite like herself: more hem and haw than common, though Master Burbage's imposing presence could wring hems and haws out of the Lord Mayor of London.

"In truth, sir," said she, "I found it—most unlikely I know, but as I had searched everywhere else, it seemed worthy, yet—I found it in the garderobe, sir."

He almost dropped the black doublet; then he frowned, brought the rich goods up to his expansive nose, and sniffed. The garderobe was a little room attached to the theater on the south side, for the use of players who must relieve themselves during a performance. Since our old Theater had an outdoor privy, we thought this a wonderful convenience, though no amount of lime could keep all the odors at bay. "I do detect a whiff of the necessary about it," Richard Burbage said. "Dare I ask where—"

"It was rolled up and wrapped in sacking," she explained, "then stuffed under the eaves, where the ceiling braces are."

He stared at her long and hard, but decided against asking further questions. Shaking out the garment, he gave it a closer inspection. The doublet, limp and wrinkled, put me in mind of a once-stout king suffering from a wasting sickness. "Seems whole, though worse for wear," Master Burbage concluded. "There's a tale here, but all's well that ends well, eh? Many thanks, maid." He fished about in his purse for a penny, which Starling took with another half curtsey. All of us knew that the doublet was not accidentally stuffed in a privy by careless movers, but Master Burbage chose not to comment.

As soon as he excused himself to dress for the play, I said, "It wasn't there the other day—someone would have found it."

"No doubt."

"So—what are you thinking?"

She was a quick thinker; from the moment she found the doublet, her thoughts could have circled the globe at least once. "First of all, why leave it in such a suspicious place?

There must have been no other choice. Whoever took the garment may have smuggled it in under his own clothes, then slipped into the garderobe to take it off. And then—perhaps he heard footsteps approaching, or feared he could not slip it back to the wardrobe unseen."

"Was it someone in the Company, then?"

"Well, it stands to reason. Any outsiders would be noticed in the tiring rooms. Perhaps a hired man?"

The Company had hired four extra players for the week, all of whom had worked for them before. My first thoughts ran to the question *Who?* But what I asked was, "Why?"

She made a shrug. "Someone may have wanted to do a bit of acting off the stage—impress a lady, or gull a gentleman. Perhaps there's no harm done . . . except for a rip on the left side of the doublet. A clean slice. It's mended, but not well."

"That could have been done on stage. In the course of a battle or murder a knife could slip." Costumes were damaged that way often enough, even with blunt weapons.

"But the thread looks new and the tailor didn't know his business, unlike our excellent Master Stewart—" Abruptly, she noticed that the doors of the theater had opened to admit the public. "I must go, and you must dress. We will talk later." She hurried to the rim of the stage and turned back again. *"Esperance!"*

I smiled, a little anxiously. "Aye—*Esperance.*" This was Hotspur's saying: the motto of the Percy family, meaning

97

"Hope." She used it to wish us well, and that was a wish well taken.

No matter how much the Company likes a new play, performing it for the first time is like meeting in the flesh a person one has known only by hearsay. However carefully planned and wrought, no work acquires the spirit of life until the public breathes into it. Would that motley crowd of canons and clerks, housemaids and horseboys, tradesmen and trollops breathe good or ill?

We need not have feared. *Henry IV* not only came to life, but leapt up and danced, with Sir John Oldcastle in the lead. From the moment a well-padded Thomas Pope waddled onto the boards, the audience began to fall under his spell. Their affection grew and grew, bursting into full-blossomed love when Oldcastle and his fellow rogues accosted the Canterbury pilgrims and then were surprised and routed themselves.

Howls of laughter followed Pope, Kempe, and Cowley off the stage, the three of them chortling like schoolboys as they brushed past Will Sly and me. "They have set us a hard scene to follow," Sly remarked, then squared his shoulders and strode onto the stage with a letter in his hand. I feared that Oldcastle and his crew had claimed all the good will of the audience for themselves, but they soon were cheering Hotspur as well, as he debated with his letter in lively terms. When I entered as his wife, I caught their high spirits.

Lady Percy wants to know why her husband is so preoccupied. Midway into my long speech, I made a snatch at the letter, a move we had not rehearsed. He held it behind him, and over his head, and out to one side, with a teasing affection that Will Sly the player had never shown for me. We were the picture of a playfully loving couple at cross-purposes: I determined to know his business and he just as bent on hiding it, even when I seized his little finger and threatened to break it.

"Do you not love me?" I teased. "Do you not, indeed?"

"Oooooooh!" This came from the ground and galleries both, a response of all the husbands who had heard this ploy from their wives.

Fleetingly, I wondered if my mother had ever said it, a thought that sobered me a little. Sly followed my mood, ending with a promise that I would know all soon enough: "Will this content you?"

Once off the stage, he cuffed my shoulder lightly. "Well played, boy. I'd have sworn I did love you." He strolled off for a chat with Shakespeare and Heminges, leaving me in a glow—through which I caught sight of Kit's stricken face as he went on stage for the Boar's Head Tavern scene.

Whatever happy disease our Company had caught passed him by. He was playing Ned Poins as though the young man felt his mother looking over his shoulder, even while carousing with Prince Hal in the tavern. The audience didn't ridicule Kit; in fact they barely noticed him, especially after Oldcastle appeared. The prince demanded to know what happened to the stolen money, and Sir John obliged him with an outlandish tale of how he was set upon by four, seven, and eleven men in buckram suits—the number grows as he tells it. Finally, when the prince revealed himself and Poins as the "men in buckram," Sir John was dismayed only for a moment. After a pause of exactly the right length, Master Pope exclaimed, "By the Lord—I knew ye as well as he that made ye!" A roar from the crowd greeted this monumental gall, as he went on to explain how he couldn't bring himself to kill the heir to England's throne: "Thou knowest I am as valiant as Hercules, but beware instinct. The lion will not touch the true prince. Instinct is a great matter—I was a coward on instinct." Behind the stage, Masters Heminges and Condell nodded to each other and smiled.

Even Robin gave himself to the role of Mistress Quickly with a relish I had not noticed in rehearsal, and the tavern scene ended in triumph. Several of the players made their exit together, cheerfully commending each other, but without a word to Kit. I was standing nearby, ready to go on, my buoyant spirits a contrast to his drawn and anxious face.

"I'll tell you what," I ventured, "you seem to be trying too hard. If you would let down your guard and feel your way into this part, you might—"

"Let down and feel yourself," he snapped, just before stalking away. On reflection I could understand how galling it might be to a veteran to have a green lad tell him his business—like a schoolboy pointing out to a university man that one plus one always equals two. But strange as it may seem, I may have learned something that he had leapt over to reach his exalted position. Well, thought I, if he's so set on the hard way—let him take it.

For the concluding scenes, all available players were impressed into the army, marching back and forth across the stage as King Henry prepared to fight the rebels at Shrewsbury. After the opening clash, I escaped to the gallery in time to see Prince Hal meet Hotspur, an engagement long awaited by both. "If I mistake not, thou art Harry Monmouth," challenged Hotspur.

"Thou speak'st as if I would deny my name," replied Hal— aware that his rival regarded him as little more than a tavern brawler. They fell to with swords. As they were swinging at each other, Oldcastle appeared. He had been avoiding battle all along, but suddenly it caught up to him in the person of Douglas, the wild Scot, who rushed on to attack him without so much as a challenge. After a brief exchange of blows Sir John fell (to cries of shock and dismay from the audience). The boards had scarcely stopped rattling when Hotspur stumbled and Hal ran him through.

"Oh, Harry!" Hotspur cried in agony. "Thou hast robbed me of my youth!"

It was a gripping moment. Even though I knew that Will Sly had died a thousand deaths upon the stage, and the catch in his throat sounded very nearly the same each time, and that in a matter of minutes he would spring to his feet again—even though I knew all that, I was still seeing brave Hotspur die. He continued: "O, I could prophesy, but that the earthy and cold hand of death lies on my tongue. No, Percy, thou art dust, and food for—"

He choked on the last word and gave up the ghost. From where I stood, at the back of the gallery, I could see white handkerchiefs pulled out of sleeves, and not just ladies' sleeves, either.

"—for worms, brave Percy." Augustine Phillips, as the prince, wearily sheathed his sword. "Fare thee well, great heart. . . ."

After speaking a tribute to Hotspur, he turned and discovered Oldcastle's body, as the audience had been waiting for him to do. He staggered, stepped closer, peered down upon his fallen friend. "What! Old acquaintance, could not all this flesh keep in a little life?" When he left the stage to find his father, a moment of silence followed him, punctuated by loud sniffles throughout the theater.

Then Thomas Pope twitched, sat up, and rubbed the back of his neck. The people gasped. Then they cheered—a roar such as I had seldom heard.

"I don't like the ending," I said late that night.

It had taken me all evening to decide this, after a long celebration at the Mermaid Tavern and distribution of bonuses to everyone. Now I was in bed, and Robin sprawled on top of the covers, too tired to undress. And perhaps too dizzy as well, given the amount of ale he'd drunk.

"I like it well; it earned me another half-shilling. If the public is happy, so am I."

"But what's there to rejoice about?" I persisted. "Here's this cowardly lump of flesh who feigns death in order to escape it. Then the true hero dies, and after he's well and truly dead, Oldcastle stabs his honorable body and claims *he* was the one to kill Hotspur. And the prince, though he knows better, not only fails to challenge him, but *rewards* him instead! What sort of lesson is that?"

Robin yawned, as he began pulling off his netherstocks. "'Tis only a story. I've never known a body to fret over plays the way you do. How would you like it to end?"

A fair question, and of course I had no ready reply. "Well . . . Some way more uplifting."

"But Part Two is yet to come. Perhaps Master Will will send good Sir John to hell, and you may lead all the Puritans in a rousing cheer." I sighed; he was becoming tetchy of late, with the tender skin of a hermit crab changing shells. He sat up to take his breeches off, then said in a more somber tone, "What did you think of Kit today?"

"His performance, you mean? Ah . . . I've seen better."

"Something's happened to him. He's come to a river he can't cross."

"Better whistle for a boat, then."

Robin made no response to my wit, but continued to slump, his back to me. "He's leapt across all obstacles so far. He was singing in St. Paul's Chapel when he was seven, have I told you that?"

"You've told me." Many times, in fact.

"And he was acting in their Company at eight, and playing lead roles by ten, and the Lord Chamberlain's Men started borrowing him when he was eleven. He's mastered everything, everything. But not this."

Robin's voice trembled on the last word, and I guessed why he was so shaken. Through the years he had watched Kit like a disciple, following every footstep as though to say, Where this boy goes, so go I. But now the footsteps had come to an awkward hesitation.

I tried to reassure him. "Perhaps he's queened it so long he can't come off his lofty perch. He'll have to humble himself a bit to play low-lifes."

"Perhaps." With a long sigh, Robin sank down upon the straw mattress (which smelled a little moldy this time of year) and held still for so long I thought he'd gone to sleep. Then he spoke again. "Do you remember Captain Penny, from the prison court? The corrupter of youth?"

"Who could forget him?"

"He was in the theater today. Came up to the stage after the jig, bellowing at Kit—something like, 'Ho, imp of fame!

Playing the man becomes thee!' His nose still blazes like a beacon. They talked for a while, and the talk seemed to cheer him. Kit, I mean."

So the captain was sprung from his cage. I opened my mouth to say that Kit could choose more worthwhile companions, but was struck at that moment with the thing that troubled me about the character of Sir John Oldcastle: it was his resemblance to Peregrine Penny.

When a new play meets with success, the Company could expect to stuff the house with it many times over; thus our second performance of *Henry IV* took place only two days after the first, on Saturday. The Company expected a packed house, but received more than they bargained for. We arrived that morning to find the stage keepers dusting off the gilded chairs in the "gentlemen's rooms" that flanked the stage. With a nervous twitch to one side of his mouth, Gregory informed us that our play was to be honored with the presence of nobility.

Robin scoffed, "What of that? I've almost tumbled into an earl's or baron's lap many a time. They're a nuisance." He spoke as if gentlemen were on a level with dead rats to be swept off a doorstep.

"But that's not all," Gregory said. "Rumors are flying as thick as bats. They say Essex will attend. And that he—or somebody—has a complaint about the play. The men are keeping very close about it."

And so they were; on an occasion when they should have been strutting about congratulating each other, Masters Burbage, Heminges, and Shakespeare wore the faces of clerks whose accounts have failed to add up. Their concern had nothing to do with receipts; long before performance time the penny takers began turning play-goers away at the door. Just before the third trumpet, we heard cheers in the audience, sparked by cries of "Essex! Essex!" Apparently that gentleman, as beloved by the people as by the Queen, had taken his seat with a handful of friends.

His presence in itself was no matter for concern—Essex had been a friend to the Company for years, with a well-known preference for Shakespeare. But from the other side of the theater came opposing noises that sounded like jeers and catcalls—a terrible sound to a player. Behind the stage we looked at each other warily. "Well, God guide the issue," remarked John Heminges as he straightened his crown and marched out with a dignity to match any earl's, followed by the members of his court. A hush fell on the theater as he began: "So shaken as we are, so wan with care . . ."

The performance began quietly, but I could feel, as players sometimes do, a certain anticipation building up in our audience. When Sir John Oldcastle appeared, calling, "Now, Hal, what time of day is it, lad?" the anticipation burst loose like a long-held breath. Clearly the fat knight's reputation preceded him; everyone seemed to hold high expectations that were not disappointed.

To those of us behind the stage it sounded like a triumph, but Augustine Phillips came off at the end of the scene complaining bitterly. Prince Hal is supposed to have the stage to himself as he makes a speech revealing of his character—"But they kept interrupting me. Not speaking to *me,* mind, but to each other. No, I don't know what about. 'Twas all I could do to keep hold on my part."

Thomas Pope returned from the back of the tiring room, where he'd poured what looked like a gallon of water down his stuffed doublet—the day had turned warm, and he was already sweating. "We are caught in a most elegant crossfire." Master Pope moved in higher circles than most of us and knew faces we did not. A bit pompously, he explained that we were playing host to two opposing court factions. Sitting opposite Essex and his party were men who were known to loathe him. And one of the loathers was the son of the Lord Chamberlain: Henry Brooke. "So dodge the fire as you may," Master Pope concluded. He intended to make the best of the situation and was the sort of player who could—a lovely thribbler, he.

But Augustine Phillips saw misery before him. "O for a wad of cotton, to stuff their mouths! Their insults are downright poetical—didn't you think?" He asked this of Kit, who had shared part of the scene with him. But Kit only shook his head. He was sweating, too—from effort. As though to make up for his stiffness of two days before, he threw himself into the part with wild abandon, fluttering his hands and goggling his eyes. His lithe body, which had always seemed under control, now threatened to run away with him.

Fortunately the gentlemen sitting too close to the stage became engrossed in the play and reserved their insults to the pauses between scenes—with one glaring exception that occurred near the end. Sir John Oldcastle was alone on the stage, giving his discourse on the subject of honor: "Can honor set a leg? No. Or an arm? No. Or take away the grief of a wound? No. Honor hath no skill in surgery, then? No. What is honor? A word . . ." And so on, until the cowardly knight convinces himself that the thing is not worth seeking: "Honor is a mere scutcheon! And so ends my catechism." The laughter following his speech was especially rowdy from the Essex side, and a clear voice rang out, "Spoken like a true Oldcastle—water from the family *Brooke*!"

A reply came from the other side—the words garbled but the tone very plain. It put me in mind of a snarling dog. Then a disturbance of some sort: a rustling, a chorus of shouts, a delighted gasp from the audience. Questions began flying behind the stage: "Here now! What's amiss?" Richard Burbage cracked the stage door with one hand while holding back curious players with the other, but Gregory, Robin, and I rushed to the musicians' gallery and crowded amongst the musicians, all craning their necks over the rail.

A young gentleman of the Essex faction had leapt upon the stage, sword drawn. A wide-brimmed hat hid his face, but I could guess his age by the way he stood and bounced on his heels. Through the hubbub I could make out his words only with difficulty, but it seemed to be a challenge, delivered in a voice shrill with passion. "I defy all your highblown terms! Come on the boards yourself and insult me again, Brooke! Say it to my face!"

A voice replied, "Crawl back into your mustard pot, Master Philip!"

The youth bolted toward his enemies while two of his friends jumped the railing onto the stage. A brawl seemed likely, but in situations like this Thomas Pope was worth gold. He had been making his exit when the disturbance occurred, but now he rushed back with his own sword out and made a comical show of searching for the voice. "Who calls? Was't a mouse? I'll play your cat, sir; my steel is out and honor pricks me on!" He bent low, pretending to peer under bushes. The young man took his cue and used his weapon to poke him on the behind. Still in character, Master Pope sprang up, treated the audience to a portrait gallery of outlandish faces, and ran off the stage as they roared. The challenger took off his hat and made a low, courtly bow to the crowd before returning to his seat in the gentlemen's box. "Was that Henry Brooke he called out?" Gregory asked me. "The Lord Chamberlain's son?"

At that moment I was too startled to answer. The young man had turned and replaced his hat, and I recognized the same fellow who had caused the disturbance outside Buckingham Tavern: Lord "Mustard," still leaping, waving his sword, and taking offense. Who was he? Gregory didn't know, nor did any of the musicians. Master Pope merely shrugged when I asked him. "Some new lad out to make his mark, I reckon. They all latch on to Essex—hope his glitter will rub off on them."

Money overflowed the coffers that day and spilled into the pockets of the lowliest apprentice. That should have put the Company in a cheerful mood, but all was not well. More than one player remarked that the Brooke side of our court party did not seem to enjoy the play as much as the Essex side. On the way back across the river Master Condell refused to discuss it, but instead spent our time in the boat giving Robin an example of how to shrill his voice like an Eastcheap tavern hostess (earning some odd looks from nearby passengers and boatmen). As we walked up St. Andrew's Hill, Robin raised a whole new crop of worries, wondering aloud why Henry Brooke, who had never before honored us with his presence, chose this day to attend.

A pair of roving minstrels had set up near Ludgate, accompanied by a wild-looking girl selling ballads. She dressed like an Egyptian, in a striped skirt and bright scarves, with dark coils of hair springing loose from a band about her head. "News!" she sang to passersby, beating a hand drum. "Hear our song of the gentleman bandit, the latter-day Robin Hood!"

One of the minstrels struck up the ballad, with a tune and words I had never heard:

> *Draw closer, good people, and give good ear*
> *To the latter-day tale of a knight beyond peer,*
> *Of lordly mien:*
> *Whose booty he will keep but half*
> *When he tickles the rich, the common folk laugh*
> *For 'tis their gain.*
> *In garments rich, of black and gold*
> *He rides the highway broad and bold*
> *And hails his prey.*
> *Unwary marks raise hands while nearing;*
> *Like innocent sheep they go to their shearing*
> *At dusk of day.*

Our master had paused to buy strawberries from a vendor, allowing us to hear the ballad out. The tune was lively and the tale comical, especially when the gentleman bandit held his victim at the end of a pistol barrel:

> *"Thy money or thy life," demanded he.*
> *"And since thy life's no use to me*
> *I'd liefer the coin."*
> *So then he made off with the money, tra-la,*
> *And spread it about like honey, tra-la;*
> *In highway or city, near river or wood,*
> *No mark stands too high for bold Robin Hood.*

Ballads often tell of true events, but I suspected this one was highly decorated, if not run up out of whole cloth. By the end of the tale I was watching the gypsy girl, now busily selling copies of "The New Robin Hood" for a halfpenny apiece. Though not exactly clean, she was pretty in a foreign way that took time to appreciate. She smiled at me, just as Robin broke into my straying thoughts. "Suppose the Lord Chamberlain has somewhat against us? Suppose his son was on a spying mission today?"

I sighed and put an arm around him as we followed our master. "It may do you good to recognize that the world is bigger than the stage."

He looked at me in surprise, as though this thought had never entered his mind.

Banished Honors

*O*nly a few weeks remained until the plague season of midsummer, when London theaters would be closed for fear of spreading disease. The Company hoped to perform *Henry IV* at least three more times—but on Monday, the arrival of a herald from Whitehall cast that plan in doubt. He carried an official complaint signed by Henry Brooke, the son of the Lord Chamberlain. John Heminges assembled the Company on the stage to hear it read aloud. Though the document was perfumed with rose water and flowery phrases, its meaning stank.

Brooke regretted the occasion of this message, but the honor of his family lay at stake. He would have it known that Sir John Oldcastle was his revered ancestor, a brave and worthy gentleman of famous memory. The character presented in the Company's latest play was such a foul slander that Brooke was forced to protest. He reminded us, as though we needed reminding, that his father, Lord Cobham, was the Queen's Lord Chamberlain and would be deeply saddened to make the acquaintance of the scurrilous blot masquerading as Oldcastle on our stage.

So much for my assumption that Oldcastle could wreak no vengeance on us from the grave. I had forgotten one thing from Reverend Foxe's reference to him: his title was Lord Cobham. As Master Heminges read, the threat in the message darkened until it hung over us like a storm cloud. "Who *is* this Oldcastle fellow, then?" Edmund Shakespeare asked his brother. "I thought you made him up."

"You should read more, Ned," Master Will replied. "I don't make people up, I only . . . enhance them." He went on to explain the character and history of the real Oldcastle, who sounded nothing like the Sir John we had come to know.

"If this is slander," fumed Master Burbage, "it can't be laid to you alone. You submitted the play to the Revels Office, as always, and it was approved. If the Lord Chamberlain had wanted to raise an objection, he could have raised it then. Besides, wasn't there a rogue Oldcastle in that old play *Famous Victories*?"

"I took the character from many sources," replied Shakespeare, "plucked from many gardens to make one odiferous bouquet." I had to smile at that, guessing that the fragrant Captain Penny had made one of those blossoms.

Thomas Pope, who had been unusually thoughtful, spoke up now. "There's bad feeling at court. You know how they war against each other, Essex's crowd and Burghley's. And the Queen plays both sides. Essex is still smarting that she gave the Chamberlain's post to old William Brooke, instead of to our patron. The young Brooke is Burghley's son-in-law, you see, so Essex takes it as a personal slight—the Queen's rewarding his enemy. That's what the skirmish we saw on our stage was all about—an Essex man using our Oldcastle as ammunition against the Brookes."

"And he scored a direct hit," laughed Will Sly, "—against us!"

"What does Brooke expect of us?" one of the younger men burst out. "Write Fat Jack out of the play? Or make him over into this spotless Protestant saint?"

"Let them try. I'll cut their sniveling complaints right out of their throats." Will Kempe, ever the clown, drew his dagger and struck a mock-heroic pose. No one laughed.

"If we were to tamper with Oldcastle," Master Condell said thoughtfully, "all of London would swarm the stage and hang us from the ceiling struts."

I glanced up and pictured the Company thus decorating the rafters. It may seem strange that no one reproached the play's author, who knew all about Oldcastle's famous memory and had slandered him anyhow. Perhaps he was registering his own disapproval of the Queen's choice for Lord Chamberlain. At any rate, once they had accepted a play, the Company regarded it as their common property. That meant it was also their common responsibility, and when Master Will spoke again, his words carried no more weight than Richard Burbage's. "There may be no need for tampering with Oldcastle. I'll send a letter to the esteemed Henry Brooke and tell him we receive his correction and will gravely consider all avenues of recourse."

"Like this one." Will Kempe bent over as if in a humble bow, then put his hands on his hips and made a very rude noise. That finally won him a laugh, and the Company broke up for rehearsal in a slightly better humor.

In the midst of packing our goods between theaters and offending important men at court, ordinary plans went forward, such as putting together the summer tour. Our lease on the Curtain ran to the middle of June, after which our only source of revenue would be a small company touring the provinces. Six or seven players and two apprentices would make up the roster. Masters Heminges and Shakespeare would not be going this year, the former because he hoped to make Giles Allen see reason over the summer, and the latter because he was under great pressure to write the second part of *Henry IV*. Even the dogs in the street were baying for it, he claimed, and this was very nearly true. But he also snatched at the opportunity to escape to his house in Stratford, where his wife and two daughters lived.

Of the apprentices, Kit would make one. The other we expected to be Robin, but he received a welcome surprise when his flighty mother remembered to ask for his company at her country home in Kent. Davy was too young, and as for me, I had received permission to return to my hometown in Lincolnshire. Over a year had passed since I had seen my sister Susanna, and her letters to me had taken a carping tone. I will admit to wanting to see her, carping or no, and longed to fill my lungs again with country air instead of the thick, moldy soup that hung over London throughout July and August. That left Gregory, who could make no good excuses, even though he let me know that the thought of spending eight weeks in Kit's company turned his stomach.

Thus our troubled season limped toward its end. The landlord met all the Company's legal charges with charges of his own, until the case grew so tangled that it was laid aside for the fall term. The Welsh Boy continued to hang on me, an ever-increasing weight as the days passed. If I stood still too long, he would come and brush against me like a cat; if I was sitting, I would sooner or later feel his elbow in my side or his shoulder tucked against my arm. And Kit simmered on in skirts. Some spark was missing, though—the power and conviction that had made his duchesses and queens linger in memory. I asked Gregory if he had noticed and received a snort in reply. "If his edge is a little blunt, it's because he's been wearing it away each night."

117

Kit's haggard face on certain mornings seemed to bear this out. Apparently Richard Cowley was not keeping a close watch over him, but the others soon would, if he began slurring lines or stumbling over his feet. One morning during rehearsal he became tangled in his own skirt and almost fell. "Are you drunk?" John Heminges demanded sharply. Showing up drunk for rehearsal was a serious offense, costing the offender an eightpence fine.

"No, sir," Kit replied, with enough conviction to stave off the fine. But then he added, "Not *yet,* sir," with enough sarcasm to make Master Heminges bristle. By all appearances, he had lost his appetite for success on the stage. But something could still move him, as we discovered on the day of our last performance.

The play chosen to end our summer season in triumph was *Henry IV.* Shakespeare had smoothed the ruffled feathers of the Brooke family by a simple device: Instead of changing the fat knight's character, he changed his name. Henceforth, the rascal would be known as Sir John Falstaff.

The morning of the performance promised fair; we knew our parts and knew our play, and no gentlemen had announced plans to attend. A well-filled house would fatten up the treasury and send the touring players off with money for the road, while the rest of us could look forward to some breathing space. With less than an hour left until performance, Robin and Gregory jested with each other, I found a quiet place to go over Lady Percy's lines, and Kit (suited up in breeches and hose again) paced off the tiring room and picked at his dry lips. He was wound tight, but seemed no tighter than usual—that is, until a messenger appeared.

Visitors in the tiring rooms were discouraged—a score of players changing costumes and searching madly for a misplaced crown or sword do not take kindly to outsiders standing in their way. But the man in blue servants' livery simply crossed the stage and walked through one of the doors before anyone could stop him. Once in, he went directly to Kit and delivered a message—and a gift.

"From one who wishes you well," said he, "and prays that certain high expectations will not be disappointed."

He made a bow, offering a black velvet pouch in his open hand. Tributes from admirers, especially ladies, were fairly common: mostly scarves or flowers or scented notes. Kit received the greatest number of tokens, but this looked like more than a token. The presentation and wrapping suggested a piece of jewelry, or a sum of money. Kit inclined his head in reply and took it with a quick, almost furtive motion. His face turned so pale that his lips, in the dusty light of the tiring room, looked gray.

"Have you any reply?" prompted the servant.

"No. I mean—my thanks, of course. My humble thanks."

The man bowed again, in that flattering yet superior manner of servants who belong to the best households, and took his leave. Kit turned, with the velvet pouch in his hand and a distracted look on his face, and walked into the Welsh Boy, who was lurking nearby. Shoving him aside in a way that seemed more flustered than angry, Kit continued on to the back of the tiring room where he kept his things.

The words "certain expectations" lingered in my mind as I recalled the last time a servant in blue had delivered a gift to Kit—when his bail was secured in Fleet court. Most house servants wore blue, so I could not assume that the bail and the gift had come from the same hand. But if they had, why would the first make him smug and the second turn him pale?

It occurred to me that someone would be watching him very closely today. Perhaps I should do a little watching myself.

Shortly before the third trumpet that signaled the beginning of the play, I begged permission from Master Condell to sit in the musicians' gallery, provided I kept out of sight and came down well before my entrance. Once seated on a step behind the lute player, I had a decent view of the house, or most of it. The third gallery gleamed with silks and velvets, gold earrings and silver brooches. All the gentlemen and ladies seemed in high spirits, calling to each other across the house or waving down the penny takers to buy bottled ale or gingerbread. I smiled at the sight of Starling, curls escaping from her cap as always, in conversation with a thin, fair-haired woman in blue. By the way the lady ticked off arguments on her fingers, I guessed this must be the "Mistress Critic" who thought so little of our Shakespeare. Starling tapped her thumbs against the rim of her ale tray, a sure sign of exasperation. As a serving maid, she had to hold her replies to "Aye, lady" and "Indeed, lady"—even when her thoughts were not so agreeable.

I wished I could get a message to her, to watch for . . . what? I myself didn't know what I was watching for, only someone who seemed to be taking a particular interest in Kit. Most of the faces showed little but anticipation for an already-popular play and delight when the play began. I watched closely during Kit's first scene.

This is the scene in which Poins sets up the Gad's Hill robbery and then, after Sir John departs, persuades the prince to go along. Since I couldn't see Kit, I had to judge his performance by voice alone, and he started out strong: "Good morrow, sweet Hal!" But when he began jesting with Sir John, his lines fell flat. It puzzled me. Kit knew, better than I, the tricks of timing and voice that made an audience laugh; he had played any number of witty women to great acclaim. But in playing a man he had lost the knack. As more clever insults went by the wayside, his voice changed—he spoke faster and higher, even as the other two players tried to slow him down. I scanned faces in the third gallery, but none of them revealed any obvious disappointment.

When the scene changed, I had to leave my post and get

myself into a broad-hooped farthingale and skirt. On my way to the upper tiring room, I glanced down to see Augustine Phillips come from the stage and take Kit by the arm. Though he spoke quietly, his voice carried, as a player's will: "What's this? We went over and over this scene yesterday, and you carried it well. Are you bewitched?"

They drew aside and I heard none of Kit's reply. Only one thing seemed clear to me: this would be a good day to avoid him.

I would have avoided Davy, too, but we had a scene together. While waiting for it, we perched on the edge of the loft with our skirts spread on a canvas sheet to keep them clean. The position gave us a fine view of players rushing to and fro below us, scanning the plot for their cues, adjusting costumes and rehearsing their lines. Roars from the house indicated that the tavern scene was working its charm again. "Well," said I, for the sake of conversation, "We should end the season peacefully, at least."

"Aye," Davy remarked—never much for words. His fate with the Company was not yet resolved, for his abilities in June had not risen much above what they were in April. I supposed his uncle would take charge of him over the summer; if so, he might be well advised to find the boy another place. I still pitied Davy—poor motherless scab—but looked forward to a summer's relief from him. His attention was taken at the moment by one of those intricate string figures he wove between his hands. The present design was rounded like a spider's web.

It occurred to me that perhaps this was no idle pastime. "Who taught you to do that?"

His shoulders twitched, as though the question surprised him. "My granny."

"Back in Wales?"

"Aye."

"Is she still living?"

"Aye."

"How does she get on?"

". . . What means that?"

"What is her occupation? How does she support herself?"

He raked a thumb over the whole pattern. "She is by way of being a conjure-woman. Spells and portents. And midwifery besides."

Casting spells and delivering babies did not seem complementary work, but then I understood what he meant: his grandmother was a witch. Such women tucked themselves into dark pockets of the kingdom and scraped out a living in the black arts. "Wales reeks with magic," Starling had said. Owen Glendower, the Welsh lord in the play, boasts of his power to command the devil, but the only "witches" I had ever heard of lived in wretched huts, unable to command from the devil so much as a good supply of firewood. No wonder the boy seemed strange, if he had been raised in a smoky den of muttering spirits. After a moment I said, "Pray you, put that string away."

To applause and cheers from the house, the stage door below burst open and a clutch of players crowded through it, loudly congratulating each other for the most successful performance of the tavern scene yet. As they scattered to change costume or find the plot, Kit remained behind for a moment. Then, believing himself to be alone, he clutched the nearest post and firmly knocked his head against it.

The gesture revealed such utter, naked despair that I had to wonder, along with Augustine Phillips, if perchance he *was* bewitched. My eyes wandered to Davy's hands, now folded serenely in his lap, and for a brief moment the string in his fingers appeared to writhe.

I did not believe in curses and spells. But the boy did. If his string figures were meant for cursing, he was not so innocent as he appeared. When I looked his way again, Kit was glaring up at us with absolute hatred. In a flash of understanding I recognized the source of it: he thought we were in league against him. Not true! I wanted to shout it out loud, but the words stuck. I scrambled to my feet and moved away from the boy, resolving to try and meet with Kit after the performance, to let him know that Davy's game, whatever it was, had nothing to do with me.

As it happened, though, the only meeting we were to have occurred during the battle of Shrewsbury.

Battles are acted according to pattern; if the stage master calls for "skirmish set" or "retreat set," all the players know what to do, though each must be alert and shape himself to the overall design, or the effect is spoiled. When the trumpet sounded the first melee, all soldiers rushed onto the stage and made for each other with pikes and staves and swords. I found myself opposite Kit.

Soon after, I was fighting in earnest, as his swift, savage blows came at me faster than my staff could ward them off. The butt of his pike clipped me on one side of my head, so hard that tears of pain sprang to my eyes. "Stop it!" I hissed. A blow to the other side of my head was his answer; my vision blurred and my legs buckled. Next moment I was on the floor, too dizzy to stand. The trumpet sounded a retreat, signaling all the players to fall back and leave the stage clear for the duel of Hal and Hotspur. But I could not trust my feet just then. I rolled over on my stomach and impersonated a corpse, fighting alternate bouts of rage and nausea as Augustine Phillips's voice rose and fell over my head. ". . . I am the Prince of Wales . . . think not to share with me in glory. . . . Two stars keep not their motion in one sphere. . . ."

As Hal and Hotspur fell to, my head clanged with their swords: Why? *Why?* What cause had Kit to attack me thus? Soon Thomas Pope as Sir John and Henry Condell as Douglas began their duel, and the ringing questions multiplied until I thought my head might crack. Pressed to the boards, my ear

125

picked up every step and slide—and, unexpectedly, a rush of footfalls from behind the stage.

The moment that Pope fell, with a quake of the stage boards and a gasp from the audience, I heard a shout from the tiring rooms. It was followed by a high-pitched cry, not loud—pathetic in its smallness, like the mew of a tortured kitten. No one in the audience seemed to hear it, but their attention was wholly taken by the duel between Hal and Hotspur. I managed to gain my feet and stagger through the discovery space at the back of the stage.

I stumbled into a snake pit—or so it sounded to my reeling brain, for the players had to keep their voices down to a hiss. A violent scene emerged: Kit had taken the Welsh Boy by the neck and slammed him against the center post. Davy's little feet hovered several inches off the ground, his eyes bulging with terror and his cherub's face turning an impossible shade of red as Kit's hands squeezed his neck.

I recall Will Shakespeare chiding, "Down boy, down!" as though to a dog, but the rest appeared to be frozen until Master Heminges stepped forward and broke Kit's hold. Davy collapsed in a heap.

On the stage, Hotspur had fallen as well, and for a moment silence claimed the entire theater. "This is the final outrage," Master Heminges said, his voice drained of expression. He pointed two trembling fingers at Kit: "Gather your things and draw your quittance from Master Cuthbert. We will see you no more."

I expected a protest—from the players, or Robin, or Kit himself—but heard nothing except a wispy voice saying, "Wait. . . ." One of the hired men standing nearby turned his head my way, and I realized the word had come from me. I wanted to suggest that something was amiss here, that in all fairness we should examine the particulars. I opened my mouth to try it again, but Kit silenced me with a murderous look. He had turned to shoulder his way through the players, and at first it appeared he was coming at me to finish what he had begun on the stage. But his entire face looked gray now, as though the fire in it had burned so hot it was already ash. He went by, pushing past Robin as well, who remained with one hand raised.

"Richard," John Heminges said. I turned to him. "Get ready. Two days hence you will set out on tour."

He looked like a stern stranger, this kindly, patient man, but I saw his lower lip tremble as he straightened his crown. The other players murmured as they lined up behind him to make their final entrance, but none disputed him. I was supposed to take part in this scene but hoped they would excuse me. Robin stayed behind also, though the blow to him was not to his head.

"'We will see you no more,'" he repeated as his eyes welled with tears. "After all the years, it ends like that? Just, 'Gather your things and go'?"

"What happened?" I kept my own voice low because Davy

had rolled up in a wad not far away, sobbing. "What brought this on?"

"I know not. That is—" Robin glanced at the boy. "We were just standing about, waiting to go on. He was singing, that's all."

"Davy? Singing what?"

"Does it matter? He always sings. He raised his voice a little as Kit passed, and next I knew he was being strangled."

"What was he singing?"

Quick steps sounded in the back room and a door slammed; Kit leaving, never to return. I pushed myself away from the wall and reached the window in time to see him striding down the Shoreditch Road, a large bundle under his arm. *Never to return.*

"This can't be," Robin said, at my back. "I'll talk to him. If he would humble himself and ask to be taken back, I'm sure they would . . ." He was moving as he spoke, unbuckling his sword belt and searching for a cap.

"What was Davy singing?" I asked again as Robin tugged a cloak from a costume rack to throw over his soldier's garb.

"Leave off, jakes! I don't recall." In spite of his calling me after a privy, I stuck close as we threaded our way through the clutter of the tiring room toward the side door.

"Think about it," I persisted. "It wasn't that long ago." I could not have said why this seemed so important. Persistence paid, however, for he paused at the door.

"Wait. It was that ballad you hear everywhere now. 'The New Robin Hood.' That was it. Will that satisfy you?"

Next moment he was out the door, pelting down the Shoreditch Road, following in Kit's wake.

Dust and Doubts

"S o that's that," I told Starling as she cut parsley in the garden just before dinner. A soft, summery breeze carried the shouts of the Condell children, who were playing Hoodman Blind over by the gate. My head had finally cleared, though Kit had left a knot on the left side to remember him by.

"I'm wondering just what those 'expectations' were," she mused.

"For his performance, I suppose—what else?"

She did not answer directly. "If I had known about the message to Kit beforehand, I could have kept a close watch on the patrons in the gallery. It would have been a welcome distraction from Mistress Critic, who was talking down Master Shakespeare as always. She puts me in mind of Ben Jonson."

Master Jonson was Shakespeare's closest rival, who

claimed to love him like a brother but criticized him no end.

"What else could the expectations be?" I asked again.

"I think this goes beyond the stage. Here's a lad who's known for meeting every mark set for him. He could hold an audience spellbound from the age of eleven. He's been commended by the Queen more than once. Granted that playing the man may set him back a little, but it shouldn't drive him mad. Mark my words: something else is gnawing at him."

This was not especially helpful. I swatted irritably at a cloud of gnats. "He could have waited until *after* the tour to go mad."

She straightened her back, her apron full of parsley. "The tour will be good for you. It will shape you into a well-rounded player."

"Just now I don't wish to be any kind of player at all."

"But you are, whatever your wishes."

"Stop smirking. And stop managing my life."

"I am doing neither. Do I have to tell you what should be plain?" I didn't answer, but she told me anyway. "You are the next Kit Glover."

At this, some line of restraint gave way. "I am no one but myself!" My voice came out louder and higher than I intended—almost a screech—and we stared at each other, equally startled. Then I ran off to join the others in their game of Hoodman Blind, vigorously dodging Ned Condell as I dashed in among them.

131

What advantage in being the next Kit Glover, if eventually it caused me to snap in the same fearful manner as he had done that day?

"TAG!" Ned Condell yelled in my ear. "I've got Richard."

"You must learn to pay attention," Alice teased as she tied the blindfold around my eyes. "The rest of us won't be so easy to catch."

She meant this as a jest, but I took it to heart. If the events of the last two months had proved anything, it was that I should be paying attention.

For most of the next day I was engaged by the Company, helping to haul costumes and properties from the Curtain to storage apartments in Eastcheap. Gregory let me know how delighted he was by the change in the tour roster, and Robin kept to himself; I gathered that his efforts to reason with Kit the day before had ended badly. The other players all seemed to have their minds on crates, boxes, and carts and how many of them it took to move a theater company.

This constant shuffling of properties was beginning to wear on everyone. Tempers ran high in the heat and dust, with cries of "That was my toe you trampled on!" and "Watch where you set that box!" ringing out frequently. Trying to lighten the mood as we hauled a crate up the stairs, Master Will remarked, "What think you, Richard? If we fail to win our theater back, should we set up as Lord Hunsdon's Movers?"

I made an effort to smile. "Perhaps, sir. We could have moved the Theater itself by this time."

"Hah!" His expression shifted. "That's a notion—"

At that moment the tiring master bounded up the stairs at twice his normal speed, squeezing past us. "Master Burbage, a word with you. I was sorting costumes for the tour, and 'tis my sad duty to report that the black satin doublet with the copper lace is missing."

Richard Burbage shoved a wardrobe crate against the wall ("Ow!" came from behind it, and directly Ned Shakespeare emerged limping). "What's this?" he growled, wiping sweat from his brow. "Have our costumes taken a notion to move themselves?"

"Nothing else seems amiss and we can thank the Lord the item in question is of little value, except for its being black. Black dyes are expensive, you know. I had best search these boxes."

Wearily, Burbage waved a hand. "Have at 'em." To Master Heminges he added, "John, I pray thee—I beg thee—please bring Giles Allen around, else I shall go mad, like—"

He broke off his own comparison, but in the ringing silence everyone heard what he had meant to say: "Mad, like Kit Glover." What else could have explained the headlong fall of the prince of boy players? Kit was a fresh wound in everyone's memory, and his name was banned by unspoken consent until that wound healed.

Once the moving was done, only a few hours remained for me to sort out my things and roll them up in a bag supplied by Mistress Condell, then write a letter to Susanna telling her not to look for me this summer. It would add another black stroke to her opinion of players, but I had never managed to change her opinion on anything; no point in trying now. Starling had made herself scarce all day, and I wondered if her feelings were still hurt over my outburst in the garden. But that was not the reason. When the household gathered very early the following morning to see us off, she caught hold of my hand and drew me aside. Master Condell was bidding farewell to his wife and children, and no one appeared to mark us.

A little breathlessly, she said, "I have a thing here for you."

She had made a shirt. "You need more clothes on a tour, because it's harder to keep everything clean. It's not much," she hurried on, before I could speak. "I had that piece of linen lying about. If you no longer need it on your return, I'll cut it down for myself."

That piece of linen had probably not been "lying about" for long, and while not of finest quality, it was good enough to have cost her something. Not to mention the sewing time, which must have kept her up well past midnight. "Thank you." I was honestly touched.

She nodded, and we stood awkwardly, both afflicted for the moment with wordlessness. "I will miss you," I said, realizing how true it was. She and I had not been apart for as long as a day since we'd met.

"And I you." Suddenly she took hold of my shoulders, kissed my cheek, and darted away, like the bird she was named for. I just stood there, blinking, until Master Condell called, "The day's a-wearing, Richard! We must be off."

For all my dread of it, the tour was not so bad. At the very least, I breathed my fill of country air.

Our daily pattern seldom varied: after rousing early from a dusty straw mattress in a fly-specked inn, one of the players would saddle up and ride to the next town. There he would spread word of our approach by reciting a few speeches in the streets and sometimes getting into a public wrangle with local Puritans—both equally good for our fame. Meanwhile the rest of us loaded our two carts and set out in the same direction: Burbage, Condell, Sly, Cowley, Phillips, Kempe, Ned Shakespeare, Gregory, and me, all acquiring a uniform coat of road dust on the way. Master Burbage's dog loped along beside us, a hound named Crab—who would have his own role to play.

By the time of our arrival, the town would be in high expectation and some public space would be cleared for us. Usually this was the inn yard, an area enclosed on two or three sides, with the upper level of the inn forming a gallery for the town gentry. There among the horse dung and heaps of hay, we set up a rude platform for a stage, washed ourselves at the pump, took a long drink of the local ale, and laced each other into costume. The play began as close to three o'clock as we could manage.

Sometimes a local squire who knew our reputation would welcome us to his estate and put us up in comfort; twice a village refused to have any truck with wicked players, and we were forced to make camp along the highway. If the distance between towns was greater than ten miles, we might spend two days in travel. But generally it was road, inn yard, inn; road, inn yard, inn, as the days boiled down to a common stew.

We were not the only players on the road—many of the beggars and madmen we met were masters of the craft. They produced their own sores and wounds with a mixture of unslaked lime and iron dust, with soap to make it stick—a revelation to me, but the men of the Company were well acquainted with such tricks. All agreed that the number of vagabonds was greater than it used to be, as so many soldiers were left unemployed after the Netherlands war. Few beggars got anything from us, except the fellow who threw himself in our path, twitching horribly and foaming at the mouth until Richard Burbage tossed him a couple of pennies. "A tribute from one player to another," he explained to me later. "A man who labors so at his profession—even to eating soap—deserves his reward."

I thought about that for days afterward, wondering if we

players, in the end, were little more than madmen who performed tricks on a stage for a few pennies. I felt like a candidate for madness myself. When we started our journey, I was familiar with only one of the plays on our schedule—*Romeo and Juliet*—but I had never played the parts assigned to me. The other two plays I had never seen or heard of: a comedy called *The Two Gentlemen of Verona,* and a romance, *The Maid of Troy.* Our first performances felt like rehearsals to me, with the added chaos of costume changes, cramming my lines in between scenes, brushing away curious villagers who wanted a peek into our tiring room, and trying to ignore the occasional chicken who flew up to the stage and pecked our toes.

Gregory let his sarcasm overflow on our audiences: "rustics" and "cud-chewers" who counted themselves lucky to see one play every five years. In part, he meant to reassure me: "What matter that you missed your entrance (or confused two speeches, or fainted too early in the scene)? These bumpkins would never know the difference anyway."

But I had grown up among "these bumpkins" and knew them better than Gregory did. They may not have been keen judges of acting a part, as Londoners were, but they understood living and recognized a bad imitation when they saw it. I learned this very early, the second time I played Juliet's mother. Upon discovering my daughter's body, apparently dead, I wailed, "Accurst, unhappy, wretched, fateful day!" while beating on my breast in the approved style. During the brief silence that followed (while I tried to recall my next line), a sober-faced farmer nearby muttered, "Nay, lad—if tha heart was really broke, ta would not punish it so." Some of his neighbors laughed, but he himself never cracked a smile. He knew how a broken heart felt. For myself, I thought of him long afterward whenever tempted to indulge in empty gestures.

So Starling was right again: the tour was good for me as a player. The demands of performing in new circumstances improved my skill in thribbling, while the luxury of playing the same parts over and over allowed me opportunity to delve into their character. Gregory and I sometimes even sat up late, arguing about Romeo's amazing speed at falling in love or Julia's easy forgiveness of Proteus. To my surprise, Gregory had worried over many of the same questions I had. Our talk concerned the characters themselves, not how to play them, but both of us gained conviction in performing as a result of it.

Within three weeks I had found my feet and was feeling easier. Mistress Condell told me once that players could bring a larger view of the world to people stuck in their own lives. When the inn-yard crowds wept over the fate of the young lovers or cheered with the warriors of Troy, my occupation began to seem less like madness.

Or at least it did, until we got to Lincolnshire.

That was my home parish, and as we approached, my anticipation was touched with dread. Lincoln town, where we meant to perform, lay about twenty miles from my native village. That made it unlikely I would see any familiar face from Alford, but if so, I did not look forward to explaining myself. Some of my old acquaintances might regard me as a fortunate son indeed: a boy who had spent his early years shoveling horse dung in Squire Hawthorne's barn, now gadding about with famous players who performed yearly for the Queen. But many in Alford viewed players as little better than fallen women.

Such were my thoughts approaching Lincoln town, but once we arrived, there was no time to think. We had hit a market day, so the players anticipated a large audience and a full purse. Richard Burbage judged the mood of the town and decided to perform *Two Gentlemen of Verona,* the lightest and most nonsensical of our three plays. It was one of Master Will's early comedies, I was told—a story of young lovers falling in love and mixing themselves up and ending with different partners. I thought that Lincoln, a sober-minded town generally, might better appreciate *The Maid of Troy,* but no one asked me. When a sizable crowd had gathered under a westward-tilting sun, the play began.

Though far from a disaster, it was not one of our better performances. This was the play in which Crab earned his keep, for there is a part in it written for a dog. Crab's only skill as a player was to scratch himself and gaze over the crowd with damp, soulful eyes. He had also been taught to raise his hind leg at a tug of his leash, and then lower it at a shout; if the player managing him knew how to time this, the crowd roared with laughter. In fact, Crab got more laughs than any of us, until the last scene.

This scene includes an escape through the forest, an assault on a lady, a boy revealed as a girl, an accusation, a reconciliation, and a whole band of outlaws. But as if that were not enough, when the fair maid I played was fighting off an attack from her thwarted lover, the loose boards began to leap beneath my feet. A tremendous din, like the baying of twenty hounds, drowned out my cry of "O heaven!"

It was, in fact, the baying of one hound: Crab, who had a voice like a bass horn. When he wasn't performing, he slept under the stage, but something had stirred him from slumber and infuriated him besides. He howled like a wolf and bucked like a stallion, beating his broad strong head against the stage. Master Condell, my thwarted lover, stepped back just as the dog made a ferocious lunge that raised the board I was standing on. I cried out again—something stronger than O heaven!—and pitched forward, landing with such a thud that my wig flew off: a fallen woman, indeed.

The audience loved this. With a few choice words Burbage climbed down to subdue his hound (and would shortly discover that some mischief-making boys had crept under the stage and set loose a jarful of bees). Worse things have happened to me, and I was calmly retrieving my wig when a worse thing did happen: I raised my head to come face to face with a pretty maid who looked familiar, especially her scandalized expression. Then I recognized my sister.

"I am only grateful our mother isn't alive to see this," she said.

"I would never be grateful for that," I fired back.

"You know what I mean. You know how she longed for you to become a minister or lawyer. But if she could have seen you today . . ."

Susanna is my twin, but she was born older. We sat opposite each other at one end of a long table in the local inn where our Company was staying the night. As it happened, Susanna was staying there too, along with old Beverly, the squire's cook, and young Walter Hawthorne, his son. They had come to Lincoln town to buy and sell, and our paths had crossed according to God's mysterious ways. Master Walter was a big lout in his early twenties who used to kick me around the stable yard for sport. I had dreamed of returning to Alford some day and daring him to kick me now, but I could hardly make such an offer after he had seen me flat on the boards in a skirt. He stood around smirking until Susanna asked him to allow us privacy, and I didn't like the possessive manner he took toward her.

In appearance Susanna had improved in a year's time. She looked more like our mother, with her broad brow, large dark eyes, smooth auburn hair, and short chin; a quiet beauty that turned threatening when her temper was up. She had hardly begun on the list of things she didn't like about me: "—a *wig* and a painted *face,* and spouting all manner of *non*sense—"

"I told you all that in my letters. You needn't come on like you've just had the shock of your life."

"Reading about it was bad enough. But a thousand times worse to *see* it . . ." and so on.

The players sat at another table, pretending not to listen as we plowed the same ground several times. Susanna relished argument, doubtless because she was so good at it. My only defense against her logic boiled down to this: I knew where I belonged. Finally she threw up her hands in exasperation. "You're as stubborn as ever. How can you be so sure you've found your place?"

"I seem to be rather good at it."

"Good at it! Don't you reckon King David was 'rather good' at adultery, too? What good is 'being good' at anything, if it costs you your honor and your good name?"

What is honor? was the first reply that popped into my head. Can it set a leg? Or an arm? Hath it no skill in surgery . . . Judging by Susanna's face, though, this was no time to quote a scurvy character like Sir John. "Look—I came into the theater by God's provision. Doubt it if you must, but I know it's true. I've learned a lot and come to understand things better—about people, about life, about myself—"

"You've learned about *yourself* by putting on a dress and

playing *women*? Truly I fear for you, Richard. . . ."

Soon it was time for bed and we had worn each other out. We parted angry and frustrated and confused (or at least *I* was confused), but the morning brought some reconciliation. I went to say farewell after we had packed our cart and found her in the common room. Her eyes were red, and her nose too, and I guessed that she'd slept no better than I. "I'm thankful we met," she began. "You've not convinced me all's well, but I will pray for you daily."

"And I for you." My throat tightened, and my voice sounded as thin as hers.

"Just keep watch, Richard—remember the devil is like a roaring lion, seeking whom he may devour."

"I will." Tears stung my eyes as we embraced. "And you keep your distance from Master Walter. Greedy pigs bear watching, too."

"I can manage him." Her voice turned tart again as she released me. "Do write, or I may come to London to see for myself what you're up to."

She came outside with me and exchanged a few courteous words with Master Condell and the other players. We took our leave in procession, Gregory and I bringing up the rear, Susanna waving until we were out of sight.

"I must confess," Gregory said. "Last night, when all were abed, I was tempted to climb that rose trellis beside her window and have a little chat with her. You barely introduced us."

I refrained from pointing out that when he had had the opportunity to speak to her, his tongue appeared to be tied. "She's no Juliet—she'd have pushed you off the trellis."

"The men remarked how much she resembles you."

"What? She doesn't resemble me at all."

"Tell that to a blind man. Master Condell thought it would make a good play: a twin brother and sister who look alike, and she dresses as a boy, and a lady falls in love with her—"

"I don't want to talk about it." Or anything else, for that matter. Gregory got no good conversation out of me for at least two days, for Susanna had put me into a dump—her arguments crawled into my brain and began picking at my confidence: What *would* my mother think? Is this life worthwhile? Is it honorable? Thoughts of Kit returned, with the dread that such a fate might be in store for me.

I have noticed this, though: once you're well launched in one direction, it takes more than a few doubts to change your course. When, at the end of July, we reached the farthest limit of our wanderings and turned back toward London, I could feel the pull of the city. All the towns began to look alike, and I gave up trying to remember their names. Every night our anticipation grew; every day we moved a little faster, shortening the distance. *Home, home,* the cart wheels chanted; *home,* murmured the brooks and streams.

My eagerness startled me; for every one thing I liked about the city, there were a dozen I despised. But when we finally

144

caught our first view of London, huddled beside the Thames and breathing its dank, dense breath, my heart beat faster. The flat-topped steeple of St. Paul's stuck up from the maze of houses and streets like a lighted beacon, guiding us in. "Home again!" Master Condell sang out. Others took up the refrain: home to the Mermaid Tavern, the wife and little ones gathered on the hearth, the clattering streets, the never-ceasing chimes from a host of church steeples.

"Good old stinking London," Gregory laughed, and I could only nod—not trusting myself, at that moment, to speak.

We approached by way of Charing Cross and followed the Strand up Fleet Street. The closer we came to Ludgate, the more there was to see, until my eyes ached from seeing. "Look!" Gregory cried over and over, at the sideshows and puppet motions that had sprung up since we left. "Look: Indian savages from the New World!" "Look—a man-sized snake from Africa!"

Just inside Ludgate a lively tune caught my ear, and directly I recognized the ballad of "The New Robin Hood"—the same tune, but different words. While the Company paused to clear our carts with the customs agent, Gregory and I wandered over to listen. The song was carried by a singer with a lute, while two tumblers pantomimed the action—not literally, because the story told how Robin Hood surprised a gentleman while the gentleman was passing water in a garden. The victim, one "Lord Stuff," was forced to surrender the golden chain about his neck as well as his purse. "But you may keep your water," said Master Hood, before making off with the money, tra-la.

The smaller of the two tumblers jumped on his partner's back and rode into the audience, waving copies of the ballad to sell. He got some applause, but few buyers.

"The song is already old," Gregory sighed. "I wonder what else we've missed?"

Master Condell sent a boy to alert the household, and by the time we arrived, everyone was on hand to greet us, from the mistress down to Roland the dog. The little boys leapt on me; Alice remarked, "You're browner but no taller"; Jacob the gardener slapped me on the back; Nell slipped a sugared plum into my hand; and Mistress Condell put her arms around me, after putting them first around her husband, of course. All of it made me feel like I had been dragged through a warm bath of affection, coming out drenched but happy.

Starling came last. I had wondered what her greeting would be after so long a separation, but from the way she drew me aside and touched a finger to her lips, I saw my homecoming was not the first matter on her mind. "Are you too spent for an adventure tonight?"

I will admit to a touch of disappointment that her welcome was not warmer. "What sort of adventure?"

"There is someone you must meet, after dark." Over my certain protest, she raced on: "Tonight would be best, before Robin gets back from Kent. After supper I'll play rough games with the children and wear them out so they'll drop off to sleep presently. As soon as they do, creep out your window and come around to the door of the buttery and knock twice. I'll be with you straight."

"But where are we going?"

"To a respectable eating house near the Royal Exchange. I'll tell you no more than that."

"If I'm to be cheated out of sleep after eight weeks on the road and trolled through the streets after curfew, should I not know the reason?"

"It wouldn't do, sweet chick. Trust me. Oh—and I am right glad to see you back." While my guard was down, she bounced up and brushed a feather-light kiss directly on my lips. Then she muttered something about work to do, and I saw no more of her for the rest of the afternoon. Devious female!

She played Thomas, Ned, and Cole so hard that they were too excited to drop off quietly. I had to cool them by degrees with stories from the Bible. She had played me too, winding up my mind so tight that even though my body longed for my own straw mattress, I couldn't have slept on a featherbed. The watchman had just called nine o'clock when I squeezed through the narrow window and crept across the roof to the stone trellis. Roland met me on the ground, his growl stilled when I put out my hand for him to smell. Once he knew me, his tail thumped out an invitation to play, but I shushed him and crept around to the back of the house. The buttery door sprang open upon my second knock, and Starling slipped out, wrapped in a shawl. The buttery was where she slept, on a narrow bed amongst the hams and cheeses, and in the summertime she picked up a trace of its sour smell. Yet there always seemed to be a fresh, apple-sweet breeze about her. I felt it as she brushed by me, whispering, "We must hurry. There's no time to lose."

Unescorted females and unoccupied youths are not allowed on the street after dark, unless they can claim pressing business. With a little care taken, though, one can usually avoid the watchmen, and Starling and I covered a quarter of a mile unchallenged. We emerged from dimly lit side streets onto Cheapside, where Londoners bustled about on foot or horse almost as thick as in broad day. Turning east, we proceeded to the three forks. Across from the Royal Exchange, Starling halted under a sign etched with a crowing cock. Warm light stippled her face as she peered through a latticed window. Then she made a nod to herself, threw the shawl back from her head, and beckoned me forward.

The eating house we entered seemed respectable, as she promised: busy but not rowdy, babbling but not loud, full of merchants from the Royal Exchange who carried on their business over platters of roasted meat or fowl. Starling attracted little notice as she led the way to a table in the back corner. A thick post partly hid the table from view, but as we came nearer, I could make out a hand with spidery fingers lifting a pewter mug and long legs stretched out with one ankle crossed over the other. The hand stopped, as if its owner had heard us. Then it set down the mug with calm deliberation. The legs folded under the table and a joint stool scraped against the rough floor as the fellow stood up. Rounding the post, I saw his hand held out to me. Then my eyes rose to his face.

Next I knew, I was heading in the opposite direction with the force of a charging bull as Starling clung to my arm: "Richard! Richard—believe me, it's all well. He means you no harm. Think—would I have brought you here otherwise? Richard!"

I came to myself in the middle of the room, feeling the pressure on my arm and the curious glances sent our way from nearby tables. "Be reasonable," Starling pleaded. "You have nothing to fear."

I could not trust myself to speak, but waited until the leaping tiger in my chest had settled to a discontented purr. Then I squared my shoulders, removed her hand, and marched back to the corner.

The young man who so rumpled my disposition had seated himself and did not bother to rise again. Instead, he peered up with keen hazel eyes from under a rough thatch of copper-bright hair. "Am I so ill-favored that virtuous boys run away in fear?"

Sure he was no beauty, with his thin face and long pimply chin, but I was in no frame for banter. I kicked out the joint stool opposite him and dropped into it, though meeting his eyes took some effort. "Wh—What do you want?"

"You can lower your guard," drawled Bartholomew Finch, in his low, coarse voice. "I only want some questions answered—and they are not about you."

This did not reassure me. Master Finch was no older than eighteen, yet he worked for the Queen—indirectly, as the hired man to one John Clement. Their work was the shady kind, conducted in dark corners and whispering dens as they rooted out criminals and traitors. Young Finch had made my acquaintance barely a year before, when he suspected me to be just such a traitor. He had pursued me with the relentlessness of a hound after a hare. And though I was not as guilty as he believed, he had me well near trapped when Kit had unexpectedly provided my alibi and forced the hound to pursue other prey. Seeing this young man again, I could not help but feel cornered.

"On who—" The words choked off, and I took a deep breath. "On whose authority are you asking questions now? Has not your master been masterless, since old Lord Hunsdon died?"

"Not at all. John Clement is now engaged by the new Lord

Chamberlain. William Brooke, Lord Cobham. Perhaps you know him?"

"We've not met." All I knew of William Brooke was his son's complaint against our portrayal of their noble ancestor. "Is . . . is this about Sir John Oldcastle?"

"Fat Jack?" he asked quickly. "What has he to do with it?" But Starling, who had pulled up a stool beside me, was shaking her head vigorously.

"Put the theater aside," she told me. "There are greater things afoot. Bartlemy is on the scent." I shot her a venomous glance: *Bartlemy,* now, was it? She had as little reason to like him as I did, yet somehow he had laid siege to her confidence and won it completely while I was away. "Go on," she urged him. "Tell Richard what you told me."

Just then, a serving man brought a roasted capon on a platter. Bartlemy straightened at once and drew his dagger, then remembered his manners enough to ask, "Have you et?" When we both nodded, he zealously tucked into the bird. During the next half hour, Starling and I watched in growing amazement as he dismembered his dinner and ate it entire, even down to cracking the larger bones and sucking the marrow. In between swallows and wiping his greasy mouth on his sleeve, he told a fascinating tale.

His master, John Clement, was looking into an incident that took place late in May, in which the Lord Chamberlain's son was robbed. Henry Brooke was on his way to London from his country estate, accompanied only by a manservant. Around sunset, he marked a traveler following him but was not alarmed because his follower appeared to be a gentleman, dressed in a fine black doublet trimmed in gold. Brooke suspected nothing amiss until the "gentleman" closed in, drew a pistol, and pleasantly demanded his money or his life. Brooke recalled his saying, "And since your life is worth more to you than to me, I would liefer have the money."

Those words sounded familiar. I was about to ask why, but then they rode into memory on the back of a lively tune: *Your money or your life, demanded he/And since your life's no use to me/I'd liefer the coin. . . .*

Bartlemy continued, still chewing: Henry Brooke's servant lunged forward, but the highwayman quickly knocked him in the head with the long barrel of his pistol. He drew a short sword next and parried Brooke's stab into a harmless thrust that wounded his clothes, not his person. An expert twist of the sword disarmed the victim, who was finally persuaded to part with his traveling money. The thief, again in most gentlemanly terms, asked for both the rings on his left hand—and got them, without argument this time. Then they parted company, leaving young Brooke to rouse his serving man and skulk to London, hoping that word of the humiliating encounter would never get about.

But soon after, the ballad of "The New Robin Hood" began circulating in the London streets—a tale of a gentleman bandit who robbed a foppish young nobleman called "Lord Puff" and shared his bounty with the poor. Henry Brooke had never paid much attention to street ballads, but when one of his friends bought a copy and showed it to him, he recognized the particulars. Within days it was all over court, and Brooke's enemies were making up additional, mocking verses. A furious Lord Chamberlain engaged John Clement to bring the culprits to justice.

Three weeks had passed since the robbery and the trail was cold, but in a painstaking search of the pawn shops along Houndsditch Lane, Bartlemy found one of the stolen rings. He traced it back to an old crone who picked rags on Gracechurch Street. All she could say was that a fine gentleman in black and gold had given her the ring near Aldersgate, and she had pawned it for a few sovereigns.

Our narrator paused to stuff all the meat from the capon's thigh into his mouth—I didn't think a mouth could hold that much and still leave room to chew, but he managed it. I was trying to remember when I had first heard the song. It was in May, after a performance of *Henry IV* at the Swan. I had walked with Robin and Master Condell up St. Andrew's Hill and saw an Egyptian girl with scarves in her hair, two musicians . . . "Who wrote the ballad?"

He swallowed, another amazing feat. "If we could discover that, our fortune's made. A new one began going the rounds early in July, just before the Queen left on her summer progress. It tells of another robbery at dusk, in Greenwich

Park. The victim this time is old 'Lord Stuff,' who has drawn aside to relieve himself in a corner of the garden. Just as he is lacing up his breeches, Lord Stuff feels a knifepoint in his ribs and a cheerful voice demanding his purse, along with the chain about his neck. The bandit is on foot this time, though still dressed in black and gold. And he makes off with the money. Tra-la."

Bartlemy paused to strip the meat off a capon leg, and I could not decide if he was prolonging anticipation or if he was truly as hungry as he seemed. Starling pressed her lips together and tapped her fingers on the table, finally bursting out with, "The new song was all over London—I never knew a ballad to get such play. They're still singing it. But wait until you hear: Lord Stuff was really—"

Bartlemy held up his hand and swallowed. "William Brooke. What's good for the son is good for the father, it seems."

"The Lord Chamberlain?" I gasped. "In Greenwich Park?"

"No; on the grounds at Whitehall Palace, where he had drawn discreetly apart. He has a well-known habit of looking upon the hedge, though the Queen forbids it."

"You mean, the elder Lord Cobham was robbed while—"

"Watering the roses; aye."

"Ha!" The laugh escaped from me before I could fight it down. It wasn't seemly to make light of a crime, and I sobered quickly under Bartlemy's frown. "Well, it *is* clever. Perhaps

155

whoever is carrying out these robberies means it as a jest. No one was hurt, and the money taken was probably no great sum—I mean, nothing such a wealthy family couldn't afford—"

"The money stolen was *theirs,* and I am working for them. Besides, Henry Brooke takes the loss of his rings hard. One of them belonged to his grandfather—a gold signet ring, set with rubies. Not the one I found, sadly. The robber may have kept it for himself, after giving the other to an old gossip who would spread the rumor of him. No doubt all the beggars and ragpickers are cheering on the new Robin Hood and hope to meet with him some day. But I wager he won't be so open-handed from now on."

I thought of mentioning that the beggars and ragpickers had little enough to cheer about, but it wouldn't have softened his heart, and something else occurred to me. "It sounds as though whoever wrote the ballads knows certain details that no one else but the bandit and the Cobhams would know."

"Very good." The way he said this sounded more like mockery than compliment. "But the tale diverges from truth in the second case. For one, William Brooke fought back—he drew his dagger and attempted to defend his goods, even though the thief was too quick for him. But my lord did manage to get a token." Bartlemy reached inside his shirt and took out a tiny wooden box. Tipping the contents out in his palm, he showed me a single black button.

"That's all?" The button was covered in black satin, with one edge discolored as though someone had tried to rub off a stain.

Bartlemy turned the button over to the shank side, and the stain looked now like something I should recognize—chalky and pinkish with a darker tinge around the edge. "Paint," he said. "Stage paint. This is what brought me to your door last month, to renew our acquaintance. You were off on tour, but Mistress Shaw was a help."

I looked to her, suspicious again. "What sort of 'help'?"

Starling could contain herself no longer. "This button, Richard—this very button—is from our wardrobe. I've mended the garment myself; it's a black quilted satin doublet trimmed with copper lace. 'Twas made for Richard Burbage, and a few of the others have worn it, but not many approach his size."

The garment was sounding familiar indeed: the same one Master Stewart reported missing just before we left on tour. "That's a long tale to get out of a button," I said carefully. "How can you be sure it's ours?"

"I showed it to Master Stewart, and he recognized his own work. Then he told me that the doublet had been missing since June!"

Stolen, I thought, as the strands of the tale came together. Stolen, to outfit a robbery. Too late I realized that Bartlemy had been very generous with his information, in a way he would not have been unless he expected an equal measure from me. "And, Richard—" Starling babbled on, "Do you remember the fine black damask that disappeared for a few days last spring? Remember I told you it had been cut, then mended?" I nodded, and she grabbed my arm. "It must have been used during the first robbery, when Henry Brooke was accosted on the road. The dates agree, and the cut on the side was where Brooke's sword went through!"

I stood up, seizing her hand. "One moment," I muttered to Bartlemy, then pulled Starling over to the unlit fireplace at the back of the room. "I can't believe this," I burst out. "I can't believe you gave up Company secrets to an agent of the Lord Chamberlain, who is no friend of ours—"

"What secrets?" she snapped back. "Richard Burbage made no secret that his black damask was missing—Bartlemy had turned up a lot, even before he talked to me—he would have discovered that, too."

"And that's another sore point: *Bartlemy*. You know what a rough cob he is. Look at him." I gestured to the table where he was contemplating us, at the same time gnawing a capon leg like a ravenous animal.

She didn't look, but her face set in a stubborn attitude. "There is more to him than meets the eye."

"Thank God—I would hate to go through life with nothing but a face like that."

"Stop being so mean, Richard. Your personal feelings matter not a whit. The honor of the Lord Chamberlain's Men is at stake—I mean, Lord Hunsdon's Men. The Company may be harboring a thief, unbeknownst to them. It's in your interest to help the thief catcher."

I stood for a moment, biting my thumbnail. Then I turned abruptly and marched back to the table, as Bartlemy looked up from the carcass he had demolished. "What are you after?" I demanded.

"Only answers to my questions. To wit: Has anyone in the Company, or any of the hired men, done or said aught to rouse suspicion? Do you know when this satin garment might have disappeared?" His tone sharpened a little. "Would anyone in your Company have a grudge against the Lord Chamberlain or his kin? Have you heard or seen a conflict—"

"Wait!" I felt that my back was being pushed to the wall. "You seem convinced that your prey is lurking somewhere in our Company. But I need better proof than a button to believe that one of my fellow players is the companion of highwaymen."

He sucked the remaining marrow from a leg bone and tossed the bone to a hound waiting nearby. Then he stretched his long arms above his head, belched, and reached for his cap. "Nothing simpler," said he.

After we escorted Starling to the corner of
Aldermanbury Street, where she could get home safely by
herself, Bartlemy and I set off southward at a brisk pace.
No words passed between us until we reached St. Paul's
landing, where Aldersgate Street meets the Thames. Since
the hour was past nine o'clock, half the watermen had tied
up their boats and gone home to supper, but the other half
had lit their lanterns and rowed on, trolling for fares. They
swarmed like fireflies in the weedy-smelling mist now
rising from the river. To Bartlemy's shout of "Westward,
ho!" two of them changed course and darted our way. We
stepped aboard the boat that reached us first.

"How far, sir?" inquired the waterman.

Bartlemy tossed him two pennies before replying,
"Whitefriars."

"Oho! As you please." The man pushed beyond the

reeds and steered his wherry to a place where the current was not so swift. "But when we draw nigh, I'll haul up and you gentlemen may leap ashore before I beat out to the open current." He chuckled at this, though I was not inclined to join him. Our destination was a haunt of cutthroats and thieves, its very name used to frighten children. "Be good," an exasperated mother or nurse might cry, "lest the devil come and bear thee off to Whitefriars!"

"You'll draw up to the landing and let us off like honest men," Bartlemy said, and the waterman laughed outright. Once past the rushes he stretched his oars and bent his back, bearing up against the current with long steady strokes as frogs along the bank raised a rackety chorus. We sat uneasily for a few moments, until Bartlemy asked me, "What's to become of Sir John Oldcastle, then?"

This was so unexpected I couldn't fathom his meaning at first. Once I did, the first thing that came to mind was, "Falstaff. We must call him Falstaff."

"Oldcastle!" the waterman exclaimed from the stern. "What a case! Will he get away with all his rogueries, you think?"

"We must call him Falstaff," Bartlemy informed him, in a solemn tone that seemed to mock me.

"Pffft! Falstaff, Oldcastle, makes no bones, he's a rare 'un. Claiming to be the slayer of Hotspur—did you ever hear the like?"

The waterman wheezed with laughter as he pulled on his oars.

"Most rare," Bartlemy said, in a voice that betrayed no opinion.

"Will he get away with it, think ye?"

"I'm not the one to ask," my companion said, gazing at me as though I could reveal the fat knight's fate. But so far as I knew, that was still locked inside Master Will's head.

"By the Lord," our boatman went on, "I almost hope he will. The tales he comes up with! Who'd believe he could twist his fat belly out of so many tight places . . ." He went on to recall his favorite bits of the play, and Bartlemy countered with his. I was amazed at how firm a hold Jack Oldcastle—Falstaff, rather—had taken on the public imagination. Coward, conniver, and cheat though he was, the waterman seemed to regard him as a hero—or at least juicy meat for conversation until he pulled up to Whitefriars stairs and tossed out a mooring line.

"Here ye be, gentlemen. Watch your purses, feet, and necks, and perhaps we shall meet again."

Once we were on the ground our boatman lost no time in casting off and pulling away. "Have you a dagger?" Bartlemy asked me. "Good—endeavor not to use it. Pull your cap down, meet no one's eyes and keep close—you'll be safe. Most like."

We were in the dreaded "suburbs," though at first glance it resembled nothing more than a down-at-heels section of London, with sagging shutters and tumbledown walls and a heavy smell of sour ale. The only light came from open doors and windows, and that little enough; they were like glowing patches on a sad, gray garment. Whitefriars once housed a monastery—hence the name—but all traces of religion had fled; the bursts of laughter and quarreling we heard sounded anything but pious. But except for the cat who flew out a window in front of us and hit the ground howling, I saw no violence. The place was quiet overall, but not with a comfortable quietness. The silence appeared to shift from one dark alley to the next, as though seeking its time to break out in lawlessness.

My companion had his route in mind: first along the wall marking Bridewell Prison, where he stopped to look into the windows of two alehouses. Then we cut across the old monastery grounds and paused at the window of another. When he shook his head and moved on, I protested, "I thought this was going to be simple."

"Simple, yes. Easy, perhaps not. I know one more place to look." He continued in a westerly direction, and to my relief the neighborhood improved a little. The Inns of Court lay not far away, which seemed convenient—with so many lawbreakers near to hand the law students had all the case studies they could ever want. After darting down too many narrow roads and alleys to count, we came to an alehouse with softly glowing windows and the merry notes of a fife and drum spilling into the street. By one torch mounted beside the door I barely made out the device carved on the sign: a crude bull with one bent horn.

After a glance in the window Bartlemy plucked my sleeve and whispered, "Here we are at last. Remember to keep your head down." I followed him into an alley, then through an open door that led directly into the kitchen. A drip-nosed, slack-jawed boy was turning a joint of mutton on the fireplace spit while a stout woman peeled onions at the table. The woman straightened and put her hands on her hips, but Bartlemy silenced all protest with a coin tossed her way. He also helped himself to a turnip just before passing into the tap-room.

A pall of greasy smoke stung my eyes and a hail of voices hammered my ears as we made our way around the wall. Bartlemy found a stool at one end of a table, dropped onto it, and disappeared. He possessed an uncanny gift for making himself inconspicuous, like a turtle disappearing into its own shell. I tried to do the same by not looking at anyone, or at least not anyone close by. A serving maid brought ale, splashing liberally at every step, and my tankard became a refuge to hide behind.

Shapes and sounds began to emerge. All around the room I could make out whiskered faces bent closely together and heard somewhere behind me the murmurs of a private meeting. Near the fireplace a buxom, frowsy-headed woman had begun a song with the fife player. The attention in the room flowed toward its center, where an imposing figure in a leather jerkin, sleeves pushed up on his brawny arms, sat at the head of the table shaking a dice cup. The dim and spotty light fell on his right hand, notable for the absence of two fingers. He made his toss and crowed in triumph. As he stood up to propose a health, the red face of Peregrine Penny leapt out of the shadows. "Behold the man fortune smiles upon!"

Fortune shone with differing brightness on the other players around the table—young men, all. One gloomily studied the dice, his face hidden under the brim of a flat cap. Another, dressed in the sober gown of a law student, made a throw and cursed when it went against him. The third bounced up to take his turn, saying, "Count not your grain until the last rat's killed, Captain." He also wore the sad colors of a student—except for his hat, a stylish, tall-crowned piece of work with a red plume. His accent marked him as a country squire's son. Perhaps his parents had sent him to the Inns of Court for polishing; if so, he hankered after polish of another kind. "Main!" he shouted after a favorable cast. "And now for the Nick—"

"Hold a moment, Master Coble." Captain Penny raised his hand. "The hour grows late. Would you care to hazard all on this next cast?"

The young man glanced around him. From the happy flush on his round, pockmarked face, I guessed he had come to the point where it seemed impossible to lose. "I might. I might—what of you, Knopwood?"

His fellow student waved a hand. "I've lost enough."

"You, then?" Master Coble offered his cup to the youth in the cap, who merely shook his head without raising it.

"It's between us lions." Captain Penny rose to his feet again. "To the victor belong the spoils."

All attention was now on the game. I have never played Hazard myself, but witnessed many rounds in the keeping room behind the stage, where hired players passed the time between scenes. Winning depends on rolling the right combination of numbers in a single or double cast. Master Coble's face gleamed with sweat as he shook the cup and made his toss. "Main!" cried the onlookers.

The young man scooped up the dice and rolled again. They struck the table with the sound of ice cracking.

"Three!" A bad cast—I knew by the falling tone of the voices.

The captain leaned forward to take the cup and rolled a seven. "Another Main," murmured a voice nearby. "Only a twelve will win it for him." The rattling in the cup filled the room like water as tension rose. Then Penny made his cast, and the dice clattered merrily on the table. "Twelve!"

The entire room let out its breath. The frowsy-haired singer swept over to give the victor a noisy kiss. A serving maid filled his tankard, even as the captain raised it, shouting, "May all honest dicemen prosper thus!" He drained the tankard to hearty cheers.

"—and live to dance at their own wedding, rather than the

166

end of a rope." Though I could not see who said this, I knew that voice—roughened by drink and smoke, but unmistakable. It almost knocked me off the stool.

"Pray contain yourself," Bartlemy mumbled through a mouthful of turnip. "You are not on stage."

Kit raised his head—and his cup—in tribute to the winner. He looked the same, yet not the same, and in an instant I recognized the difference: a light growth of black hair on his upper lip.

Penny was laughing at the hangman joke, his hands stretched out to rake in the winnings. But the next moment he was staring at the point of a dagger directly under his nose. Master Coble had lunged upon the table to point his weapon, though his voice was not quite steady. "You—Let me see those dice."

"Sir! What's your drift?"

"You play with false dice, that's my drift!"

A murmur rose from the tavern crowd, but the captain tempered it with a laugh. "Clean as a relic. See for yourself."

He handed the cup to his accuser, who sat up on the table to examine the contents with his companion the law student. While they were thus occupied, Penny scratched his upper arm serenely. "Watch his hand," Bartlemy murmured, startling me. "His right hand." I watched, as Kit stretched both arms above his head with a huge yawn, and his left hand came near Penny's right. Something may have passed between them, though it happened too quickly for me to be certain.

Master Coble looked up from his examination. "You switched them."

"I cry you mercy!" Penny held up his mutilated right hand. "Accuse me not of a dexterity that, alas, can hardly be mine. Search my battered body—you'll find no false dice on me."

Some of the bystanders protested angrily at this offense to an old soldier. The fellow in the legal gown tried to pull his companion off the table, but the latter seemed to be spoiling for a fight. "I know your kind!" he shouted at the captain. "All you 'old soldiers' should be locked up to keep you from preying on honest citizens."

Penny opened his mouth to protest, but the lad rushed on. "Yea, I said it, and I stand by it—if you would challenge me, I'll be in my rooms tomorrow between the hours of—"

"Put it up!" his companion hissed at him. "Haven't we been fools enough for one night?"

"What's your grief, Master Coble?" The captain's voice softened. "Have you wagered all your allowance for this term and fear your father's wrath? Here's fourpence back to see you through—"

"I'll none of your charity!" The young man knocked over a bench, and his round red face looked fit to burst. "It's my honor at stake. I'll not suffer—"

"*Un*stake it, then." Penny's voice took an edge, and for the moment he became a man one would not want to meet on a battlefield or a dueling green. Then his good humor returned as he signaled for his cup to be filled again. "Have another cup of sack, and let's hear no more talk of honor. What's it good for?" Raising his voice, he asked the room at large, "Will it satisfy a starving belly?"

"No!" came the answer, from a handful of no-accounts nearby.

"Will it fill an empty pocket?"

"No!" more of the onlookers chimed in.

"Will it keep a shrewish wife from your throat?"

"*No!*" By now the entire room had joined the chorus.

"Will it hold back the landlord from your door?"

"NO!"

"And—" Penny lifted his cup to Master Coble. "Will it keep a young firebrand from burning a hole in his breeches?"

"NO!!!"

"So you see, 'tis good for nothing useful, so I'll have none of it. Honor is a mere scutcheon—and so ends my catechism." He drained his cup on the last words, inviting all to join him, which they did with great applause and laughter. It was, of course, the ending of Sir John's speech. Penny was borrowing from the very character he stood as model for.

Master Coble, though not cheered, was cowed enough to back away from his challenge. His struggle to produce a witty reply twisted his mouth. "Go fry in your own grease."

"Aaaaaaah! Ooooooooh!" sang the tavern crowd, in mock

dismay. Knowing when he was beaten, the young man picked up his fine hat. His companion, Master Knopwood, counted what was left in his purse and gloomily settled his account with the singer, who appeared to be the hostess as well. Kit stood as they made their farewells and left with them.

The alehouse crowd broke up to their separate pursuits, including another game of Hazard at the center table. I turned to Bartlemy and asked, "Who is this man Penny?"

"A soldier, just as he claims."

"But he speaks so well—how came he by his education?"

"He was raised in a good house—a foster son, I think. But he fell out with his guardian and ran away long ago. Served in the Netherlands, then found himself turned loose on the country like so many others."

I could not help noticing that Penny was about the size of Richard Burbage and that he would look very much the gentleman in a black and gold doublet. "Do you think he's the new Robin Hood?"

"I think nothing before there is proof."

"Didn't his victims mark his nose? Or his missing fingers?"

"They marked gloves, and a mask. Every gentleman wears gloves, and many travelers wear masks."

I persisted. "But you have proof before your eyes that he's a coney catcher. Could you not arrest him for that and get a confession from him about the rest?"

He twirled the pewter mug between his long hands, as

though turning over in his mind how much to say. "A confession drawn off the rack would not satisfy me." He took a gulp of the ale. "Besides, we must cast a wider net."

"What do you mean?"

He did not answer. All this time, even while speaking to me, his eyes roved about the room so restlessly I almost believed they could turn over cushions and dart around corners. Now that the shock had lessened, I had to admit he had made good on his promise, proving to me that my fellow player was indeed a companion of thieves—an accomplice, even. A coney catcher himself, pulling in likely victims for a dice cheat. Kit could have served as the model for a sermon: "Behold the player's swift decline! From gowns to gambling to guzzling in alehouses and gulling young fools!" A chill touched my heart in that hot, stuffy room; Kit had irritated me, infuriated me, made me feel like a brainless lump of dough, but now he frightened me. If he had stolen costumes from the Company to dress "Robin Hood," he might be deep enough in intrigue to get himself hanged.

"Is it possible," I ventured, "that this scene is not as bad as it looks? That Kit lost his money as honestly as the other two and is even now slinking home with empty pockets?"

My companion pursed his lips, but didn't bother to reply. Next moment there came a stir at the door and Kit himself made his entrance.

There is no better way to put it: where before he had

clothed himself in insignificance, now he was every inch the player, gesturing to the third gallery—and, once again, making me feel like a brainless lump of dough as Bartlemy spared me a taunting glance.

"What ho, wanderer?" roared Penny in greeting. "Did you leave them in peace?"

"I did—and with a piece for myself." Kit reached into his doublet and pulled out a red plume, last seen on Master Coble's stylish hat. This he tucked into his own cap, to the applause and laughter of the tavern crowd. The hostess (who was not bad-looking, I noticed) wrapped her arms around him, and Penny clapped him on the back.

"Seen enough?" Bartlemy asked me.

"You shame me, boy." Penny wagged his good hand at Kit, pointing two fingers in a peculiar way that looked familiar. Then I recalled that it belonged to John Heminges, and Penny was now imitating Heminges's "lecture tone": "You're squandering your gifts on petty theft—have a care, or you'll find yourself on the road to virtue!"

"What's this?" Kit unwound himself from the hostess, after giving her the kiss she demanded. "Are you my father?"

"Perhaps—depends on where your mother was, seventeen years ago."

Amid whistles and guffaws, Kit set a stool upon the table and enthroned himself on it. "I warn you, good people!" His voice rang with such command the entire room fell into churchlike stillness. I had always envied how he could do that. "There is a devil haunts us in the likeness of an old fat man; a ton of man is our companion. . . ." He spoke in broad, measured tones, with wide gestures—another imitation of Master Heminges, but much better than the captain's. I drew in a quick breath, for this was an echo of the Boar's Head Tavern scene. Kit was quoting directly from the part where Hal pretends to be his own father, condemning the man the prince had chosen for a friend: "Wherein is he good, but to taste sack and drink it? Wherein neat but to carve a capon and eat it? Wherein cunning but in craft? Wherein crafty but in villainy?" As he piled on the accusations, Penny cringed like a guilty prisoner, to the delight of the audience. Suddenly, Kit rose from the stool and knelt at the end of the table, clasping his hands around the man's neck so their foreheads almost touched. "Wherein worthy, but in nothing?"

"Ah, lad." Penny seized Kit's arms and pulled him off the table, to loud applause. Once the two of them were steady on their feet, he threw an arm around Kit's shoulder and ruffled his hair. "To know all my faults and love me anyway. It's the sign of a great heart. We'll see the world, you and I—" Abruptly, he leaned forward and pounded the table. "But first, let's have a song!"

What struck me then was the expression on Kit's face. I could not recall seeing such unmixed happiness there before, not even after his great stage triumphs. It engrossed me so that I almost forgot Bartlemy, until he stood up. "I must go," he said shortly. When I rose also, he hissed, "No! You stay behind."

I made a grab for his sleeve. "You can't leave me here!"

I heard his sharp sigh as he pulled his arm free. "Then keep close." He was already slipping shadowlike around the wall. "And not a word—not a word, you hear?"

We went out through the main door, then darted across the dark street. Like my companion I flattened myself against a wall. From his utter silence I guessed he was listening, sifting the sounds: a church bell in the city tolling a death; a man and woman quarreling; an uneven step, like a man with a bad limp. After a moment Bartlemy rounded the corner and crept down an alley, with me close behind and just as silent—one learns to move all kinds of ways on a stage. At the next street we paused to listen again. Then Bartlemy took off at a sprint, his long legs covering ground with frightful speed.

The next moment there came a collision and a muffled cry. I ran to join him, thinking he might need help. Hardly— though I could not at first sort the shapes, it was clear Bartlemy had the upper hand. A moment's struggle put his victim in a pool of grayish light that fell from a window, and I could make out the sparse white hairs on his head.

"Have pity!" squeaked a thin voice. "I'm an old man, with scarcely a farthing to my name."

"I'm not after your purse, reverend sir." In spite of the

words, Bartlemy's voice sounded the opposite of respectful. "Where did you get the ring on your right hand?"

"What—say—you?"

"This ring." Bartlemy's knee was in the man's back as he held both arms secured. "The one I'm twisting off your finger."

"You'll have the finger and all! Believe me—'twas my father's, given for good service in— Arggggggh!"

The pathetic moan went through me like a spear. "Stop it!"

Hearing my voice, the old man turned his head in my direction. "Young master! Pity this poor gray head, in God's name—"

Bartlemy silenced him with a twist of the arm. "Stay out of this," he spat at me. The old man groaned, and in the dim light I saw his poor gray head loll in the mud.

Hardly thinking, I sprang forward and grabbed Bartlemy's arm. "No more—loose your grip! Can't you see—" He raised a hand to push me away, and in that instant his victim twisted free, rolled to his feet, and dashed off with the agility of a much younger man.

Next I knew, a sharp rock cracked against my shin and made me jump. "Milk-faced prig!" hissed my companion. "Lily-hearted lass!" He went on in this vein, tossing in some very insulting French phrases.

"I-I'm sorry. He seemed so—"

"*Felons* and *actors* share some of the same gifts. I would have had him, if not for your bone-headed—" More French, as he whipped the cap off his head and stamped on it.

I decided not to try his temper any further. And I'd had enough of his company, as well. Entrusting my safety to God, and my direction to instinct, I ran back toward the river as all the church bells of the city burst forth in a ragged chorus of midnight.

More Roguery

"*H*e has some rough edges," Starling conceded the next morning, when I told her of our adventure.

"Rough *edges*?" I was helping her spread new rushes on the floor, and their sweet dusty scent made me sneeze. "He could saw oak. And I can't fathom how he got you to even look at him, much less talk to him." She merely smiled. "That is your cue to speak."

"Oh, is it? Well, he was right simple and straightforward. On Tuesday three weeks past, before I left for the market, he arrived with a piece of raw meat and lured the dog out of the gate. While Roland was attending to the meat, Bartlemy tied a ribbon round his neck, and a message to the ribbon. When I came out, he sprang Roland after me. Of course the ribbon caught my eye first. The message read: 'A friend wishes to walk you to Bishopsgate Market.

If you would know who, turn around and let him speak first.' So of course I turned around and there he was, making a most elegant bow. In truth, I was so surprised I could not have spoken my own name."

"And you call that simple?" I said. "*Simple* would be appearing at the gate with a piece of raw meat for you."

This was meant as a jest—mostly—but she took it ill, turning her back and speaking in a small, tight voice. "Do you mean to say I'm no better than a dog?"

"No, of course not. But look you—the last time you saw him, he appeared just the opposite of a friend. Allow me to wonder how he won you over so easily."

"How do you know it was easy? You don't know what he said."

I held back an impatient sigh. "Right. Forgive me, I assumed too much. What did he say?"

After a moment she made a swipe at her nose and turned around. "Leave it at this: he convinced me that what's past is past and he means you no harm. He only wants to catch a thief."

"Well? Say on."

"That button led him first to the Admiral's Men, because of the Robin Hood play they put on last spring. He soon determined that their Robin Hood has nothing to do with the ballads, but some of the players told him about Kit's being dismissed. That was all the gossip this summer: according to rumor, Kit mysteriously lost his powers and tried to kill the Welsh Boy in a fit of madness. Some are even saying he succeeded, since Davy hasn't been seen. Bartlemy tried to find him but turned up Kit instead—in Captain Penny's company."

"Has he questioned them?"

"No; he's only watching now."

She and Bartlemy had had quite a little talk, it seemed. "Do you know if he's approached anyone else in the Company?"

"Only John Heminges, who refused to say much. He was Kit's guardian for five years, you know, and loved him like a son. But by the time you joined the Company, Kit was becoming difficult, and it's gone from bad to worse. Master Heminges feels betrayed, I think; his hurt goes so deep, he can't talk about it."

"So Bartlemy, sensitive hound that he is, backed away from Master Heminges and came to gnaw on me."

Angrily, she threw down a handful of rushes. "It's all of a piece with his work. It can't be easy, running down lawless men."

"Especially when he's not much better than they."

"Have some charity, Richard. That ring he saw could have been the other one stolen from Henry Brooke, else Bartlemy would not be so desperate to question the bearer."

"The alehouse was dark enough I could scarce see my own hand—am I to believe that he is so eagle-eyed he could glom on a finger from halfway across the room? Here's what I think:

he saw an old fellow wearing a ring, and thought it might be Brooke's, and waylaid him on the long chance that it was. And just a few moments before he was preaching against the use of torture. 'A confession drawn off the rack wouldn't satisfy me,' says he. As if *he* is the only one in this case who needs to be satisfied."

My voice was rising, and she held up a hand in warning. "He may have reasons for acting as he does."

"I care not. Whatever his reasons I want nothing more to do with him—that's flat." So saying, I scattered the last of my rushes.

"And what of Kit?" she asked.

"What of him?"

"He could bring shame on the Company." Her loyalty to the Company was as fierce as any player's, and she had never liked Kit.

"He *left* the Company, as you recall."

"He hasn't left London, and his name is still linked with ours."

I sneezed again; the rushes were irritating me, and I had slept hardly at all. Those two things made me sharper with her than I should have been. "Let Bartlemy bring him to justice, then. He doesn't need the help of a milk-faced prig like me." Before she could reply, I started for the stairs. "The fall season begins in two days, and after church tomorrow we'll be moving our things out of storage. That leaves me one idle day; pray tell the mistress I'm going to St. Paul's."

But this was not to be. I was dressed and on my way out the door when Master Condell called to me. "Richard! Doth my wife put you on some errand? Good—you may do one for me. Here are the receipts from our tour, all summed. Pray deliver them to Master Heminges—you'll find him at the Curtain."

There went the morning; with a bow I took the parcel he handed me and set off toward Shoreditch. At least it made a pleasant walk, with the sun climbing the sky, the hot season turning, and a fresh breeze blowing off the river. All this helped me sort my thoughts, which badly needed sorting after my quarrel with Star. The blame for that was mostly mine, and I resolved to buy her a book at St. Paul's by way of apology.

But deeper down lay my thoughts of Kit, in a hopeless tangle. Memories of him had thronged the night, in particular of our boxing match at the Curtain. Every time I drifted toward sleep, the bloody voice of the crowd jolted me awake, along with the recollection of how we had drilled into each other and seemed for an endless moment to become a single person. And then, half dreaming, I would see him in the upper tiring room, holding out the mirror. My white-powdered face reflected in it, and his emerging behind it, were like two planets crossing in their orbits.

He had always gone his own way. What could I do to stop him?

I reached the Curtain in a gloomy state of mind made worse by the sight of our old Theater, locked and barred on the other side of the road. Over the summer a wreath of brambles had grown up around its neglected walls until the building appeared to be caught in a stranglehold, like a castle under enchantment.

Inside the Curtain, Masters Burbage, Kempe, Heminges, and Shakespeare were gathered on the first gallery, huddled like conspirators. In the thick bars of light that fell from the narrow windows I saw eyebrows raised, heads nodding, fingers pointing. They seemed in a cheerful mood, making me wonder if they had come to an agreement with the landlord. A burst of laughter jumped out at me as I crossed the sawdust floor, then Kempe said, "But this must go no further. Keep it close, except for—" He broke off as Master Heminges nudged him, then turned to me. "What is it, boy?"

"Pardon, sirs. Master Condell sent me with the tour receipts."

"Well done, Richard." John Heminges, the Company treasurer, climbed over the gallery rail and took the packet from me. "I spoke with your master last night—so the tour went well, eh? He says you found your feet—and lost them once."

His blue eyes crinkled, inviting me to laugh along with him. I managed a smile. "Aye, sir. Thanks to Crab." He had some questions for me, which I answered as the other men broke up their meeting.

"By the bye," concluded Master Heminges, "pass along word that we will perform here at the Curtain for six weeks,

182

beginning Monday. Today is a bull-baiting—we will have to watch where we step."

He tucked the receipts under his arm and caught up with the Burbages, on their way out. The stage keeper of the Curtain had arrived, along with two of his boys, who began setting up partitions to form a bull pit. I turned to go, but a movement in the gallery caught my eye. Master Shakespeare had taken a seat and pulled out his table book. Since he was lingering, this seemed an opportunity to ask him a question that had gnawed for some time—and bit especially hard last night. I approached carefully, trying to read his mood.

To look at, he was like any other man of ambition: quietly but elegantly dressed, with a manner nicely calculated not to offend. But I had known him to snarl and snap, especially when under pressure to finish a play. Everyone left him alone when he tucked himself into an alcove behind the stage and set up his writing desk. At other times, like now, he appeared to be merely scribbling, setting down thoughts and lines as they came to him. "He leaks poetry," Robin said once.

To me it was more like spinning poetry, trailing lines like cobwebby strands that caught in the minds of other men. I learned his words because I was required to, often with little notion what they meant—but once learned they were not easily forgotten. They would come back to me on restless nights, or in jostling crowds, or apply themselves unexpectedly to situations I found myself in. Ever since last night, for instance, I kept hearing his words in Kit's voice: "There's a devil haunts us, in the likeness of an old fat man. . . ."

Master Will glanced up. "What is it, lad?"

I stopped. "If you please, sir. I would . . . I've had a thing in mind to ask, if you could spare the time."

He considered. Then, "Ben Jonson and his new play are to meet me here at any moment. Until he claims my time, it is yours."

"Thank you, sir." I stepped close enough to put my hands on the railing, like a petitioner before a judge. "There's a thing that troubles me about Sir John Oldcastle—Falstaff, I mean."

"Aye?" He made a little frown; it had irked him to change Oldcastle's name.

"What troubles me . . . is that everyone likes him so much. I mean, there is nothing in him that warrants liking, yet the stage seems duller when he's not on it, and that shouldn't be . . . should it? A man who lies and cheats like that should scarcely be tolerated, much less given the best lines of the play . . . and . . ."

A smile had lit on his face soon after I began my speech, and as I spoke on, it spread and quivered and finally broke out in a laugh. Embarrassed, I fell silent. "And that's your complaint?"

I wished some of his poetry would leak out on my clumsy tongue. "Well— Aye, sir."

"So your question is: Why do we love a rogue?"

"*I* don't love the rogue, sir—"

"Don't you?"

"Well . . ." Perhaps I did, a little. And perhaps that was the main thing that troubled me.

"Do you think Jack gets away with the king's ransom, and murder besides?"

"God is not mocked, sir. Thievery should not go unpunished."

"True." He thought for a moment. "You were raised in the country, were you not? So was I. Have you ever been close to a peacock?" Puzzled, I shook my head. "The great houses keep them for show. God never framed creatures so beautiful, but they bear it with ill grace—they're noisy, evil-tempered birds, and two cocks confined together will tear each other's lovely blue throats, ere long. The beauty and temper together are their nature. And there is in one part the capacity to destroy the other. Do you see the point?"

"No, sir."

He sighed. "Then wait for Part Two of the play."

"Wait . . . do you mean that Sir John's own nature will bring him down?"

"Ah. Now you are asking me to give too much away."

His smile encouraged me to go a little further. "But I know someone like him, sir." Master Will's expression of polite interest gave no hint he knew what I was talking about. "It's one thing to watch justice work in a play, but real life is . . . different."

He looked at me keenly for a moment, then shut his book. "Perhaps not so different. A good play is like life, except that it tells, swift and at a safe distance, what life can only tell over time and up close. And you cannot merely watch your life from a place of safety in the gallery; you must act in it, at your peril."

"But what if you don't know how to act? Or what your role is?"

His eyebrows rose. "Are you asking *me* that? I am a humble poet, not Holy Writ."

"Of course, sir. Forgive me, sir." I dropped my hands from the railing and backed away. "I shall look forward to Part Two."

"You and all the rest of London. I pray you will not be disappointed."

He had a reputation to maintain as the city's leading author, and it must have weighed heavily on him at times. I bowed a farewell as Ben Jonson bustled into the theater with a bulky manuscript under his arm. Master Jonson's plays had thus far been the property of the Admiral's Men, but we were to perform one of them in September. I had heard that our rivals were not pleased. "Ho, Will!" he cried. "I made the cuts—raw butchery, I call it!"

I took my leave, mostly unsatisfied, but more eager to learn the outcome of Part Two. For now, half the day remained for me to snatch some time for myself in St. Paul's churchyard.

As the day was fine, most of London seemed to be struck with the same notion, and I had to dodge shoulders and elbows while making my way down the rows of stalls. St. Paul's is home to almost all the booksellers and stationers of the city. The larger shops cluster around the cathedral walls, where a patron might find elegant bound copies of theology, poetry, history, and law. The stalls were friendlier to my purse, and livelier as well, with broadsides, ballads, and quartos rippling in the breeze and apprentices bawling their wares: "What do you lack, sirs? Here's a marvelous strange account of the late voyage to the New World, and the wild men there encountered!" "Here, friends! Here be the last words of the murdering fiend Black Hand before his hanging on Tyburn Hill!" "What do you lack, gentlemen? Here's news of the latest adventure of him they call Robin Hood—"

"What's that?" I stopped, as though I'd run against an invisible wall, and made a grab for the paper.

"Ah no, sir." The boy who had been crying the ballad stuck it behind his broad back. "I'll see your penny first."

"Little chiseler! Ballads are a halfpenny."

"Not when they are this fresh, and no other stationer has them."

I didn't believe this, but paid the penny anyhow and stepped aside to scan the sheet of paper he gave me.

It was illustrated with a woodcut showing a young girl beside a river, hands raised so stiffly she resembled a fork.

Two men in a wherry were rowing toward her, while another man stuck his head out of the water off their bow, grinning like a crocodile. The picture raised all sorts of questions, answered by the ballad: a tale of how Robin and his accomplices set up a vague, colorless knight called "Sir Biscuit." At "dusk of day" (Master Hood's favorite time for mischief) while on his way upriver, Sir Biscuit was diverted by a cry of distress from the bank. A pretty little child in costly dress was sobbing that her brother had fallen into the water.

> *"Ay me!" cried she, in woe and weal.*
> *"My brother slipped below the peel*
> *Of cruel Thames—*
> *Yonder he floats amongst the reeds;*
> *I fear he's dead. O help! Make speed!*
> *Thy vessel trimmed . . ."*

Sure enough, a body was floating facedown near a bed of reeds. But when Sir Biscuit's boatman rowed closer, the "corpse" rose up, grabbed the oarlocks, and turned over the wherry, spilling both knight and boatman into the river. Robin, in black and gold, sprang out from behind the tree and offered to throw a line to Sir Biscuit (who couldn't swim) at the price of his ruby cuff pins—and his purse.

So Robin, corpse, and decoy made off with the money, tra-la.

I returned to the stall where the boy was still crying the ballad and selling one copy after another. "Look you," I demanded. "Is this all true?"

"Of course it's true," he said indignantly. "We sell nothing untrue."

"Who is this 'Sir Biscuit,' then?"

"I dunno—some gentleman at court."

"When did it happen?"

"Dunno that either— Thank you, good sir." He took another penny for another ballad. "'Twas only printed up last night. My master kept us at the press until near dawn."

"Who wrote it? How did your master come by it?"

"Do I look like an oracle?" Turning his back on me, he raised his throaty voice again. "What do you lack, sirs! Here's news of the latest exploit of the new Robin Hood—!"

I read the lines over and over while making my way down the narrow aisle. If the ballad was a disguise for a real event, why had Bartlemy not mentioned it the night before? Might it have happened so recently even he had not learned of it? If so, these robberies seemed to be occurring at intervals of about one per month. And who had played the part of drowned corpse—Kit, or another accomplice? The quilted satin doublet taken from our wardrobe seemed to be still in use, but a costly gown for a little girl might be harder to come by, unless . . .

At this point, I pulled rein on my galloping thoughts. "Here." I thrust the ballad at the nearest passerby, a young 'prentice with his maid. "The latest deeds of Robin Hood." I shouldered my way through the crowd, angry with myself for wasting a penny on what I had decided was not my affair. With the little money I had left, all I could buy for Starling was a pair of ribbons.

Robin Bowle returned from Kent later that day, more than glad (he said) to be home. The holiday with his mother was marred by his stepfather, who (he said) could not abide him. His arrival made an incomplete set of three apprentices, and I devoutly hoped the Welsh Boy would not be the one to round our number to four. My feelings about him clashed too violently for comfort, even though I could hardly blame him for the fault of being himself. So I could not suppress a groan, Monday morning, when Gregory came back to the tiring room to tell me that the streaky-bearded uncle had brought Davy to the Curtain and left directly after, like a cuckoo depositing her young in another bird's nest.

A brief audition showed Davy's reading had improved and his delivery too—not greatly, but enough to keep his place for the present. On the previous Saturday evening, the chief players had met to set a schedule for September and shuffle apprentices to fill the gap left by Kit. They had lost lead boys before and managed to survive, but this loss might prove difficult to cover. Our first play, revived from the previous spring, featured a scheming queen whose part was clearly written with Kit in mind. As our most experienced boy player, Robin took it, but he lacked a certain snap and fire. He had grown almost two inches taller over the summer and gained more weight too, which he seemed unsure what to do with. His voice still rang pure and unbroken, but there was a threat in it. Some boys' voices changed without obvious cracks or drops—mine had, even before I came to the stage. But one never knew. Robin's might play him false when the time came. That fear, and his disappointing holiday, and missing Kit, all combined to set him off balance at the start of the season.

As for me, I found another reason to bless the summer tour: I walked back onto the stage of the Curtain with scarcely a ripple in my confidence, as though I had never been off. Gregory had gained in assurance, too, and the Company seemed to think that, for now at least, the three of us could make up for Kit until one emerged as the leader.

Meanwhile, Davy seemed less inclined to hang on me, except for one morning when he sought me out, sniffling and wide-eyed. He said that a tall, ugly, red-headed man had come to Thomas Pope's house and asked him some hard questions about Kit. "I know naught, but he kept asking and asking and went away mad. Will the Queen's Men come for me, Richard? Will they take me away?"

I assured him that this would not happen, taking a measure of satisfaction that Bartlemy had stubbed his toe on this particular stone. But then the stone fell on us.

In the middle of the second week we performed a comedy, followed by a Morris dance. The dance had just concluded and we players were capering off the stage with bells jingling, when a sharp cry from the second gallery stopped us in our tracks. After a heartbeat of silence a clamor arose from that quarter, informing us that a cutpurse had been caught there, like a weasel in a trap.

Will Kempe marched to the corner of the stage. Or perhaps I should say he pranced, since he was dressed as the hobby-horse rider, with the head and body of a stuffed horse around his middle. "Order in the house!" he called. "Order, I say!" But the shouts continued until Richard Burbage strode forward with his powerful voice.

"We'll not abide a thief. Pass him forward, good people!"

In a moment we saw the culprit being lowered from the second gallery to the first, and thence passed along over the heads of the groundlings. All participated willingly. No one likes a cutpurse, who is as apt to prey on a poor laborer as a rich gentleman—all he requires in his victim is a money-pouch hanging from a belt. The Company could not tolerate nips and pickpockets during their performances, lest word get out that they ran an unsafe theater. But the next moment they were stunned to silence when the thief was heaved upon the stage, and rolled over, and turned out to be the Welsh Boy.

Davy lay so still he might have been dead, except for the quick rise and fall of his thin chest. Master Kempe was the first to recover his wits. Betraying no hint that he knew the boy, he turned to the crowd and raised his hands, crying, "Safely delivered, God be praised! We will deal with him—may all evil-doers take heed! Justice awaits all who harbor such—"

In the midst of the sermon Davy came to himself. He blinked once, then jumped to his feet and screamed out a few words in his own language, directed at the Company. I shall never forget the sound: the soft burbling syllables were twisted into spiked metal by his screeching voice, and I needed no Welsh to know it was a curse.

Then, quick as a cat, he disappeared through the discovery space at the back of the stage. Gregory bolted after him, followed closely by me. Just as we reached the tiring room we caught sight of a curly head disappearing from the ledge of a narrow window. Since neither of us was small enough to take the same route, we circled around to the door. But by then he had vanished among the rows of dikes and irrigation channels that lay to the north.

A search by many dozen self-appointed scourges of justice failed to turn him up, which did not surprise me—why would such an accomplished thief not be an accomplished escape artist as well? "That settles it," Gregory remarked dryly, as we trudged back to the Curtain. "The boy has no future with this Company."

Davy had left behind the bag that held his personal belongings. When we returned, I took it off the hook and drew aside to spill the contents. I found a spoon and a needle, a fox's paw, and a broken arrow fletched with black feathers. There was also a vial of some powdered herb which, when I shook a little in my hand, made me sneeze for a good five minutes and itch for the rest of the day.

But one object stopped my breath for an instant. I recalled it clearly: a small black velvet pouch with a golden cord—the one given to Kit by someone who had "certain expectations" of him. My hands trembled as I opened it and shook out a silver brooch, of the kind that gentlemen use to fasten their cloaks. It was in the shape of a crescent moon within a circle, set with a single pearl.

Apparently the boy was not scrupulous about stealing from his fellow players, either.

The Prince Returns

$\mathcal{W}$here had Davy come from? the men of the Company wished to know. Who brought him in? By piling all their memories together, they recalled only that the boy was first presented at the Mermaid Tavern by his uncle, who asked that he be taken in trial. All who were present at the Mermaid remembered that the uncle lived outside London, but could not agree if he had said where, or even given his name. He never lingered long enough for chat. So the boy's appearance was as mysterious as his departure, though not so dramatic. Richard Burbage was all but gnawing stage timbers in his wrath at being cozened: "Suppose he's been robbing patrons all along, directly under our noses?"

"Sure we would have heard some complaint," Cuthbert said reasonably. "Though he must be a better cutpurse than a player, else he'd be hanged by now."

For myself, I felt a little sick, recalling the time Starling and I had taken him to the Rose, and he stood us for a boat ride afterward. The money for that had doubtless come from some unsuspecting theater patron. Now knowing Davy's true vocation, I could see his brief stage career in a new light: his steady watching while he sized our character with the instincts of an animal, his tricks of winning sympathy, his skill at pitting Kit and me against each other. The uncontrollable itching, the needle in the corset, and the tripping behind the stage—he had done those things to himself. And I had fallen in perfectly with his schemes. He'd played me like a flute.

But that was nothing to what he had done to Kit. Stealing the crescent brooch was only the final outrage; it might have been one reason why Kit had attacked him so furiously. At any rate, Davy was the proven thief; suppose *he* had taken the costumes?

Starling agreed with me that an injustice had been done, but was not ready to absolve Kit of blame. "We know he consorts with thieves—even helps pull in victims for them."

"True, but—" I sighed; it was such a muddle. "Oh well, we're rid of both now, so perhaps it doesn't matter. Except I don't know what to do with the brooch."

"I would just hold on to it and wait," she advised. "If it's worth anything to Kit, he'll claim it somehow."

The episode of the Welsh Boy left a sour smell in the air, but a sweeter wind blew the following week. Master Will announced that the Revels Office had approved Part Two of *Henry IV,* and we might proceed with casting. The Swan was already pledged to us for the second week in October, and filling it with this play would build up the treasury again. An air of expectation lightened our mood when we gathered on the stage of the Curtain after Saturday's performance. Casting sessions usually occurred at the Mermaid Tavern, but such was the fame surrounding Part Two that it was decided to keep its outcome private until the play opened. Master Cuthbert ordered up a joint of beef and two kegs of ale, and the Company lay about on cushions and stools like outlaws in the forest, eating with their fingers.

Master Will chose to begin the play with a curious device: a character called "Rumor" who appears, as the author put it, "painted with tongues." Rumor is spreading false reports about the battle of Shrewsbury, with the result that Hotspur's father first hears of it as a victory for the rebels. "But soon enough the truth reaches him," explained our reader, "and he must deal with disaster on two sides—the death of his son and the blow to his rebellion. He determines to fight on, even though—"

A stirring at the back of the stage interrupted him. Someone had joined us, a tallish presence in the shadows that moved forward until it stood at the edge of the lamplight. Beside me on the wardrobe trunk, Robin made a gasp and dropped the beef rib he was holding. We all recognized our visitor and yet he seemed changed enough to be a stranger, standing with a worn cap in his elegant hands and a growth of silky black hair on his upper lip.

"If you please, sirs," Kit began. "Pray forgive the interruption, but . . . I wish to be taken back."

Starling and I had much to talk about that night. "Is he up to mischief?" she asked.

"I wish I knew. He's accepted hired man's terms—housed and fed at his own expense, taking any role the Company assigns to him and subject to dismissal whenever he's no longer needed—all for seven shillings a week. It's a mighty fall, yet he took it humbly. And 'Kit' and 'humble' are two words I never thought to join."

"Even a king may be humbled," she said. "Look at Nebuchadnezzar of Babylon, eating leaves and grass. Suppose Kit has fallen out with Captain Penny?"

"Then he could have offered himself to any other company in London and they'd have taken him gladly, on better terms. But he comes back to us, only ten days after the Welsh Boy left. It's almost as if Kit is supposed to be a replacement."

"If that's so, they must have known each other all along."

"Aye, and if *that's* so, they may have been forced to work together. I would wager anything that Davy was the little girl who helped waylay Sir Biscuit in his boat, and Kit may have been the corpse."

She thought about this, then shook her head. "Whoever played that part had to be strong enough to turn over a wherry by himself. I don't think Kit could do it."

"Then he must be serving some other purpose. Davy overstepped himself by getting in trouble, so Kit had to come back." I struck the bench we were sitting on. "But *why*? Merely to steal costumes?"

"Perhaps someone still has 'expectations' of him. But what might the Company expect? Were they willing to take him back?"

"John Heminges absolutely opposed, Richard Burbage a little less. Most of the others seemed inclined to give him one more chance. The one who spoke most round for him was Master Will."

"He's always liked Kit. Spoiled him, I think."

"I wish they'd turned him down. I wish he'd go away."

"Well, it does no good to fret."

"Who says I'm fretting?"

"Your poor thumbnail. You've gnawed on it for the last ten minutes." I resolutely put both hands on the bench. After a pause, she said, "If you would know more, you know who to ask."

I gripped the bench. "I want *nothing* to do with Bartlemy. And after our scrape in Whitefriars, he'll want nothing to do with me."

"What you will. But it may fall out that you have no choice."

Kit showed himself on time Monday morning, accepted three small parts in that day's play, and performed them faultlessly, with little effort and no passion. He played a messenger, a groom, and a captain of the guard—drudge work, the sort of roles handed to the lowliest apprentice or the newest hired player. His mere presence in such roles felt uncanny to me, like performing with a ghost—the ghost of the best boy player of London.

The only fire I saw in him occurred in the tiring room, when Robin cornered him after the play. I paused, on my way to the stairs, as Robin was pulling out every trick of persuasion he knew to interest Kit in an adventure: "slipping out," as they used to do, to find a bear fight or a dice game. But Kit, as I well knew, had grown far beyond pranks. Though his back was to me, the very set of his shoulders signaled resistance, until he reached out and seized Robin by the shirt. I could not hear the few words he put directly in Robin's face, but I saw that face fall so hard it hurt. I continued on toward the stairs, my anger toward Kit boiling up again.

Evening rehearsals lasted only long enough to walk through the next day's play with speeches cut to a few lines. Hired men were not usually required, and Kit left directly after changing his clothes. Robin suffered through the rehearsal, and when it was time to walk home, his eyes were still reddish. We were halfway to Bishopsgate before I ventured to speak. "About Kit . . ."

"I know," he muttered fiercely. "He's changed. It seems I'm supposed to change as well, but I'm not ready. Change is working on me without my consent."

Kit was not his only grief; his own body was threatening to betray him. Rapid growth had tricked him out of the Juliet parts and might yet grow him right off the stage. He had seen it happen over the years with other apprentices, many times.

"You're doing well with the comic parts," I said, in an effort to cheer him. "They could support you for years."

"Aye—years of playing Juliet's nurse."

"That's no disgrace. Will Kempe and Richard Cowley have made a noble living of clowns."

Robin only snorted. "All well for you. Your voice has already changed, and you'll probably never be much taller than a woman."

If I were still living in Alford, a statement like that would have earned him a punch in the stomach. "I resent that. You might at least say a *tall* woman."

He didn't smile, and I turned serious. "You can't stop what you're changing into. If it happens to be a clown, then why not be the best clown London has ever seen? Embrace it."

"If it happens to be a clumsy lout, should I embrace that?" Suddenly he flung out both arms, bashing me in the chest. "Come, O croaking voice, hair on chest, feet like barges—I embrace thee!"

We had been speaking low, to keep our inmost thoughts

from Masters Heminges and Condell up ahead. At Robin's outburst they jerked their heads around in unison, with looks we could only meet with sheepish grins until they returned to their conversation.

"As for Kit," I murmured, "I would just—"

"As for Kit," Robin stated firmly, "from now on he can do all his changing by himself."

The next morning after rehearsal Master Shakespeare called me over to him. "Well?" he asked. "What think you of the fate of our lovable rogue in Part Two?"

I had hoped he would forget our conversation on this subject—or, failing that, would not stoop to ask me this particular question. "It pleases me well enough. I think."

"I hear an unspoken 'but' hanging over your judgment. Is the rogue not justly served?"

"Aye, but . . . at such a cost."

He sighed explosively. "Come now, boy—are you so innocent?" While I gaped, he went on, "Justice *always* comes at a cost."

"Aye, sir. But still, one should feel satisfied at the end, and not . . . sad."

"All change is sad, even if it is change for the better. That's because something must be left behind, and oftimes it is a thing you never expected to miss."

This formed such a neat commentary to Robin's troubles

that some days passed before I recognized its aptness for mine. The next two weeks felt a bit like my early days as an apprentice; there was that same sense of groping to find my way. Kit's new attitude was far more unnerving than his former one. The old Kit was surely something I had never expected to miss, but now I did. His cross-grained character had sharpened and stretched me and made me a better player. And perhaps I had done the same for him, to a lesser degree. Now I looked back with longing to the days when we struck sparks off each other on the stage.

Taking parts that he had once played came especially hard, with him standing by in some trifling role. In the middle of September the Company staged a return of *The Merchant of Venice* and assigned me the role of Portia: one of those keen, witty women Master Will liked to give the best lines to. Kit had created that part, and I kept trying to play it as he had, instead of finding the way myself.

And if that were not enough, I had to worry over what his presence meant to the Company. Already a month had passed since the last adventure of "Robin Hood"; it was time for another if they were keeping to the pattern. I couldn't convince myself that the gentleman bandit had retired, but neither could I determine what to do. "Perhaps," Starling said after one of our fruitless talks on the subject, "if you won't speak to Bartlemy, you should speak to Kit."

This made perfect sense, but ill use. There was a barrier

around him, a wall of glass that none could penetrate. I intended to return his brooch in its velvet pouch any number of times, but somehow never carried through. And I was not the only one to find him unapproachable: late one Saturday evening he brushed aside a friendly invitation from two of his fellow hired men to join them in an archery meet at Newington Butts.

"I'm no archer," he replied shortly, as he gathered his things and started for the door.

"Go to! We saw you there, one Sunday last month; did we not, James?"

"Aye, with your soldier friends . . ."

That was all the conversation I heard as they left the theater, but it was enough to start the wheels of speculation in my head.

Newington Butts? Sunday? Soldier friends?

Every Englishman is supposed to own a bow and a full complement of arrows and keep in practice enough to help defend our shores in case of invasion. Over ten years had passed since the last attempt at invasion, and archery practice has fallen off. Even so, Newington Butts remains a popular spot for a Sunday afternoon. It lies below Southwark—quite a little walk for a Londoner, but when I arrived, with Harry Condell's borrowed bow and quiver over my shoulder, the field before me was well populated with archers lined up before a long row of targets.

My purpose was to see if this might be a meeting place for "Robin Hood" and a merry man or two. It seemed a slim chance, based only on the broken arrow I had found among Davy's things and chance remarks from two hired players—Starling agreed on the slimness, but also agreed that it was worth a look. She planned to come along, until Ned Condell fell off the front gate and cracked his head on a flagstone and screamed he would die if she didn't stay to tend him. Starling was too soft-hearted where the boys were concerned, but I assured her I could carry out this mission alone.

A low stone wall separated the bowmen (and women) from bow-less citizens merely out for a stroll. I walked slowly along this boundary, surveying the other side as though seeking an acquaintance or a favorable spot. It was a perfect September day, scrubbed and shining, and I counted myself wise for venturing out—when suddenly before my eyes was reason to count myself lucky as well. On the opposite side of the wall, nocking bowstrings and comparing shots, stood Peregrine Penny and another man whose streaky beard I recognized when he turned to take a drink from a bottle. I could not have asked for better confirmation that Davy was in league with Penny, as here was his so-called uncle.

Forcing an air of unconcern, I took a seat on the wall, my back to them, and pretended to sharpen the point of one of my arrows. The air was filled with tiny zings, as each missile sped from its string and thumped the straw-packed targets. General cries of "Well shot!" and "A pox on wayward bows!" made the conversation behind me difficult to hear. But Penny's voice stood out enough for me to gather that they were wagering shots, and he was losing money. Finally he announced, "My throat caves in a parching thirst! Where's that bottle?"

They paused to take a drink, and their voices came a little more clearly. I sharpened a few more points and sharpened my ears as well for any useful words that might come my way. They came in patches, amongst the *whizzz* and *thonk* of arrows all around, but in a sudden gap I heard Penny say, "Patience, Tom! Leave him to me. I know his humor: air and fire mixed in such a balance he can be made to go off like a cannon, in any direction he's pointed."

I missed the first part of the reply, but then the man called Tom must have turned his head: ". . . have reason to fear cannons, if ever a man does." Something in his voice—the hard tone, the curious accent—made me think I had heard it before.

The captain laughed, a strong and manly laugh that made light of troubles. "I can do without a finger or two. But we must keep Tewkesbury in our sights." While he took another drink, his companion said something I could not hear, and the sputtering that followed sounded like a gulp of ale going down the wrong way. Penny's voice came after, thick with scorn. "'Evil eye,' say you? That's so much Welsh fog. Blow it back to wherever it was you picked up your light-fingered brat." A single blast from the field horn signaled a break in the shooting to allow for arrow gathering. "And speaking of him, where *is* the little goose turd?"

Penny's voice sounded good-humored, in spite of the insulting words, but Tom's struck my back like a fist. "You! Boy!"

He could only mean me. I turned my head so that not much of my face showed. "Sir?"

"A farthing to fetch our arrows from yon field. Be quick."

In the spark of time I had to decide, it seemed better to take the job than run away and risk being pursued. I swung my legs over the wall and came forward, my eyes cast down.

"The ones with the raven fletch, like this." Penny showed me one of his arrows, and I was not surprised that the black feathers on it matched the ones on the broken arrow in Davy's pouch. As I trotted down the field, the words I had heard buzzed in my brain. Kit had to be the one they compared to a cannon. "Air and fire mixed" summed him up neatly—or at least, it summed up the old Kit. Tom seemed to regard him with suspicion—perhaps even distrust. But what did Penny mean by "keeping Tewkesbury in our sights"? Tewkesbury, I recalled, while plucking raven-fletched arrows from their target, was a place—somewhere west of London, known for—

A recollection twanged in my head. Tewkesbury was famous for mustard. Might it also be the name of a hot-headed young gentleman, mockingly ordered back to his mustard pot after he leapt upon the stage of the Swan and called out a challenge to Henry Brooke? And someone else had called him by that scornful nickname—

I pulled in my breath sharply and glanced back at the pair calmly testing their bowstrings. Now I knew where I had heard Tom's voice: on the street outside Buckingham Tavern, where he had dueled with a haughty young man over the honor of the Earl of Essex. I did not remember his having a beard, but beards could be shaved. "The privilege was mine, Lord Mustard. . . ." "Tewkesbury in our sights . . ." Had I discovered, purely by chance, the name of Robin Hood's next victim?

Captain Penny was putting another string on his bow when I returned. "Many thanks, boy. Hand them to the corporal there"—with a nod toward his companion.

I did so, and the corporal looked at me closely for the first time. "Wait." He took my chin, tilting up my face to get a clear view of it.

My heart leapt wildly. To my knowledge he had seen me only once, when he brought the Welsh Boy to the Theater last spring. He would have had no particular reason to notice me then, and on the stage I was usually so painted that even steady play-goers seldom knew me off it. "What is thy name, sirrah?" His voice felt as hard as his hand.

"R-R-Richard, sir." The stammer was no sham, as I forced myself to look at him, searching for any sign of recognition in his eyes. They were black, as unflinching as marble, and told me nothing.

The captain twanged his bowstring. "Simple," he remarked—meaning me. "Let him go; I must win my shilling back before dark."

Tom let me go, but I found it hard to breathe while making my way back toward the city. His hard eyes seemed to bore into my back, and his cold voice wrapped me in an eerie chill. Not until I reached Southwark did I begin to feel safe—proof of my disordered brain, for the south bank of the river, with its brothels and dice dens, is no place for safety. By now it was late in the day and everyone seemed to be hurrying off to some forbidden occupation. I hurried too, making for the Bridge. To get there faster, I cut across some narrow lanes, where the overhanging storeys of crowded buildings blocked most of the light, even at midday. By now the setting sun had abandoned them to premature night.

The more I thought of Corporal Tom, the more gaps he filled—why, he might have been the "corpse" who turned over Sir Biscuit's boat in the third robbery. He looked strong enough to perform such a feat—

At that moment, a weight like a sack of rocks caught me from behind, spun me halfway around, and knocked me to the ground.

YELLOW SLEEVES

✤

A dirty hand clapped over my mouth, as small as a child's. A voice piped in my ear, "Don't speak a word, for both our lives."

I could have sobbed in relief and rage, for the voice belonged to the Welsh Boy—and so did the sharp little knees straddling my back. "Let me up!" I hissed. "Did they send you to follow me?"

"None sent me," he replied calmly. "I came on my own, after sighting you in yon field. What be you after?"

"Lift your elbow and I'll tell you." Once he did, I sat up slowly, feeling every dent the cobbles had made in my body. One hand had slid though a mass of slime. While wiping it off on the wall behind me, I tried to frame an answer. "I'm after . . . I wanted to know if Kit is still a friend of Captain Penny's."

"Why don't you ask him?"

"We're not on good terms—thanks to you, in part. I

know you're the one who harried him out of the Company."

"Aye."

His voice, as placid as a pond, made my temper rise. "Why? Was it because your 'uncle' didn't trust him and wanted you in his place?" When the boy didn't answer, I pressed on. "But you weren't so trustworthy either. You couldn't keep your little hands from nipping, and so—"

"Stop *talking.*" The words came out in a whine, followed by, "My talk is worth a power of yours, anyway."

Something in his voice put me on guard. "What do you mean?"

"You will want to keep me from telling who you are."

"And why?"

"Because," he said patiently, "you don't want them to know."

"*Why?*"

"They don't like spies."

Very slowly, I inched back against the wall. "Davy. Wasn't I always your friend?"

"Aye . . ."

"Then let me go quietly. I shall steal away and keep this a secret between you and me and all will be well."

"Except that I'll not have what I'm wanting."

"And what's that?"

A bitter, aggrieved tone crept into his voice. "I want my pin back—the silver one, with the man in the moon."

I spoke before thinking: "But it's not yours!" He remained

silent, and I heard the feebleness of that protest, when spoken to a thief. "Anyway . . . what makes you think I have it?"

"You have it," he said in a tone useless to deny.

"Look you, I have two shillings saved. That's probably more than the thing is worth. I'll give them to you this very night."

"Nay. It's the man in the moon, or naught." He spoke with the blind stubbornness of a little boy—which of course he was, in spite of his skill as a cutpurse and sneak.

"But you can't even wear it! Money is much better use to you. Think what you can buy—gingerbread, meat pies, shoes—"

"That, or I'll tell."

"And what will your telling bring about?"

"Dark Tom—my uncle—he's cold of heart."

"He's not really your uncle, is he?" The boy did not answer. I felt the silence in him: the superstitious dread of speaking overmuch of what he feared most. "How long have you known him?" Still no answer. Now that my eyes had adjusted to the darkness, I could barely make out an ugly bruise under one eye and guessed that Tom had made him pay for losing his place in the Company. "Davy. If you want to get away from him, I could help you. There are places where you'd never be found. Mistress Condell has relatives in the country—"

"No more talk! Get me the man in the moon."

"Well . . ." It felt like a betrayal of Kit, but I could see no way around it, short of smothering the boy. "All right."

"Stick out your hand," he commanded.

Honor among thieves, I thought sourly, and extended my hand. But instead of shaking it, he performed a very swift motion with his fingers, thrust a mass of string over my hand and released it. The unseen pattern disappeared, leaving a length of string around my wrist.

"There," he said. "You're bound. If you don't do what I say, one of your eyes will fall out."

I worked the string loose and threw it at him. "Don't come over me with your charms and spells."

He jumped up on his feet. "Heed what I say."

"Never fear. Where will I find you?"

"I'll find *you.*" He dashed away down the alley and disappeared like a puff of smoke.

"Stop fretting!" Starling almost shouted at me. "You needn't be so high-minded when your life is at stake. I wouldn't underestimate this Tom fellow."

"I'm not. But the brooch belongs to Kit."

"Then why have you not given it back to him?" I could think of no answer to this sensible question, so she supplied one. "Here's why—because prudence told you it might serve some purpose later on, and behold, it has: buying Davy's silence."

"Prudence doesn't speak to me so plain," I said miserably.

It was true what she said: if I had given the trinket back to Kit, Davy would still have expected me to steal it for him. How much easier to simply hand it over to the boy with Kit none the wiser—except for my conscience.

Fortunately, Starling abandoned that subject for another. She agreed with me that Tewkesbury might be the next intended victim of Robin Hood; the more we talked, the more likely it seemed. "But one thing doesn't fit," I said. "They spoke as though Kit has a certain connection with him that's important to their schemes. Yet they know Tewkesbury already—at least Tom does. I can't see how Kit figures in."

She made an impatient shrug. "What's more to the point, if we know who is like to be the prey of Robin Hood, is it not our duty to warn him? Or warn somebody?"

The "somebody" could only be Bartlemy, which was the first reason I objected. The second reason was my reluctance to do anything that would directly harm Kit. If he was bound for a fall, I did not want to be the one to give him a push, especially for the likes of "Lord Mustard." "A man so hot and haughty could probably benefit from a meeting with Robin Hood."

"What are you saying? That we leave the hot and haughty to their fate? The law must protect all men, whatever their disposition."

"Look who's being high-minded now," I muttered. But on this matter, right was clearly on her side. The upshot was that together we composed an anonymous note suggesting it would be wise for agents of the Lord Chamberlain to watch young Philip Tewkesbury in the event that he might be robbed. Starling promised to see it delivered in a way that concealed our involvement, and I promised to carry the silver brooch with me, against the time when Davy would demand it. I was not happy about any of this, but there seemed to be no choice.

All these burdens combined made me not worth much the next day. Gregory scored two hits on me in fencing practice, and Master Will found his patience tried when he took me aside for a speech lesson. They had given me the role of Rumor in Part Two, along with one scene as Lady Percy—not a heavy burden, except for the author's particular notions of how Rumor should sound. "I want a special quality of voice: airy and disembodied, like a flute. Begin at the first: 'Open your ears! For which of you will stop the vent of hearing when loud Rumor speaks?'"

My flutelike voice failed to please him. "That's more like a banshee, shrieking through the night. Rumor sounds pleasant to the ear—the words go down like honey, though they oft turn bitter as gall. Pray you, try again."

I tried again, and again, until my voice was coming out of my nose and it was almost time for rehearsal. "Well," he sighed. "We will practice more anon."

Since the fall season began, we had performed Part One of *Henry IV* twice, and today we were doing it again. The play was still pulling in happy crowds and helping to build anticipation for Part Two, now less than two weeks away. By now it needed little rehearsal except for brushing up the scenes in which Ned Shakespeare had taken Kit's former part. Ned showed little brilliance as a player, but he had a youthful enthusiasm that suited him well for Poins. Kit was nowhere in evidence while the first scene was being rehearsed. "Can't bear to see Ned carry off what he could barely pick up," Gregory murmured to me as we sat on one corner of the stage to watch.

I made no reply, but was struck once again with the mystery of Kit's failure in the part. It made no sense, especially knowing that he had real experience in planning robberies. "We may do it as secure as sleep," Ned gushed to his companions. "If you will go, I will stuff your purses full of crowns; if you will not, tarry at home and be hanged."

Thomas Pope, as Falstaff, thumped Ned on the back and turned to Augustine Phillips: "Hal, wilt thou make one?"

"Who, I rob?" replied the prince. "I, a thief? Not I, by my faith."

Not I. Not I . . . The words echoed in my head. Prince Hal had his limits; perhaps Kit did, also. Perhaps he was being pushed in directions he did not wish to go. I knew he had set up at least one crooked dice game—and cheerfully, too—but if he was unwilling to do more, could they force him?

"Hark," Gregory said in my ear. "A storm brews in the east."

I looked toward the northeast corner of the stage, where some of the chief players gathered. A servant in blue livery stood by, having delivered a letter which John Heminges was now reading. The contents had frozen him, or so it appeared; only his eyes moved, sweeping across the paper.

Richard Burbage plucked the letter from his friend's hand and perused the lines. On him they had the opposite effect; instead of freezing, he erupted in a blaze of profanity, followed by, "We won't—I care not how much gold is in it—We will not!"

This outburst was sufficient to break up rehearsal, and calming him took some time. Once he was quiet, the chief men huddled together for a short council in the first gallery, after which poor Cuthbert was sent out with messages. We muddled through a few more scenes and made ready for a performance with Rumor's fiery tongues spreading havoc among us the whole time. Just before two o'clock more blue-coated servants arrived, one with a wooden chest and another with a bound manuscript. Throughout the performance Master Shakespeare could be seen in his writer's closet off the main tiring room as he read through the manuscript, shaking his head and muttering curses.

"It's a play," Gregory told me, from what he had overheard.

"Commanded by someone at court," he added later, "just like that putrid *House of Maximus*."

As the performance was ending, he speculated, "I wonder if it's by the same author?"

Worse than that—it was the same play, with the title and some lines changed. The Company saw fit to tell us this much when we gathered in the tiring room: the performance had been requested by a prominent personage who was seeking this favor for the love and regard between himself and the Company. And paying handsomely for it, too. "It had better be a lot," Gregory whispered.

According to Master Burbage's outburst, no amount would be enough, but there must have been other considerations—perhaps the Company could not afford to offend any more gentlemen at court. As John Heminges began handing out the sides, Master Will gave us one curious instruction: "When you speak your part, pray leave out any references to brooks, or cobs, or hams, or old castles. Simply do not speak them. Is that plain?"

It was anything but plain. The performance was set for Monday—our first day at the Swan—and with so little time to prepare, all players would take their previous roles. I hoped that my part had been eliminated, but no such luck. Nor had Kit's. Under the circumstances, no one was surprised to see such an important part settled on a hired man; it was the response of the hired man that caused a stir.

"No, sir," Kit said firmly when his side was offered to him. "I will not take it."

John Heminges stood with the scroll in his hand, stunned. "What's that?"

"I will not take this part, if you please, sir."

"I am not offering it to you, Master Glover. I am laying it on you. You have no choice."

Kit's eyes flickered as though seeking a way out. "My answer is still no. Sir."

"Come with me." Master Heminges dumped the box of scrolls on Henry Condell, then drew Kit aside. Richard Burbage joined them presently, and I was reminded of the old days (not so far back) when they would band together to straighten out their most gifted, most difficult apprentice. Together they broke him. When the Company dispersed that evening, it was with the understanding that Kit would play Adrian. He would receive a bonus for it but, judging by his face, that was no consolation.

A quick scan of Silvia's part that night turned up a few references to brooks, and one to an "old castle." Speaking around them would not be difficult, as long as I stayed alert. But I began to understand the reason for Master Will's instruction: the entire play was an insult to the Brooke family. Whoever wrote it must have held an enormous grudge. We were already in bad odor with the Lord Chamberlain and his son for our portrayal of Oldcastle; if we performed this play as written, we might as well bathe in a sewer. Leave out all references to brooks, cobs, hams, and castles? With right good will!

Two days passed—dreadful days, while I expected the Welsh Boy to ambush me at any moment and the Company fretted their coming ordeal with *The House of Maximus*. The play was now titled *A Son's Revenge* but remained as putrid as ever. In fact that's what everyone called it now—the Putrid Play—as though calling it by its right name would bring us further ill fortune. Kit went through our one rehearsal like a sleepwalker, which made me feel all the worse.

Our rehearsal broke early on Saturday because Shakespeare, Heminges, Kempe, and both Burbages had arranged a meeting with Giles Allen—though none of them seemed to expect much good to come of it. I watched them go, wondering if this would be the day Davy jumped me. Shortly thereafter, Kit went by with his cloak rolled up and tucked under his arm.

I found myself staring at the cloak. Why was he carrying it, on a cold day? It looked too big a bundle for just itself—suppose there was something inside?

At that moment my mind flashed with a recollection of him, last spring, handing a rolled-up cloak to Corporal Tom after the fencing match with "Lord Mustard." Suddenly I knew—*I knew*, as surely as if I had seen through the wool—what must have been inside the cloak: a doublet of fine black damask, needed to outfit a robber. A few weeks later I had seen him leave the Curtain after John Heminges dismissed him from the Company. He'd carried a bundle under his arm then, too, and shortly afterward a black satin doublet was reported missing.

He did it, and he's doing it again! I thought. Willingly or not, he is smuggling costumes to his criminal friends, and how long might it be before the consequences come down on all our heads?

I scrambled upstairs to the tiring room to fetch my cloak, then dashed out of the Curtain and caught up with Kit on the Shoreditch Road. "I'm bound for the Bridge," I panted. "May I walk with you?"

"As you please," said he with something of his old regal manner. He spared me hardly a glance, though I stole many sideways looks at him. He still chewed his fingernails.

We walked for some time in silence, as a brisk wind sprang out of the west and made me pull my cloak tighter around my shoulders. He kept his tucked under his arm. "Aren't you cold?"

"What do you want?"

I wanted to knock him to the ground, sit on him, and shake out the contents of that bundle. But what I said was, "Nothing. I'm on my way to the Bridge, that's all."

He made a noise, between a laugh and a grunt.

After a moment, I tried another tack. "Where are you staying these days?"

"In hell," he replied, with a stagey drawing-out of vowels.

I suppressed an angry sigh; this seemed to strike an overly tragic pose. "Is that the only place that would take you in?"

We had reached Bishopsgate. Watchmen were lighting

torches over the portal, and by their sputtering light his features twisted in a bitter expression. "Yes."

The word reproached me—after all, I knew not what demons were driving him. "Kit . . . What's happened to you? If I could help—"

He turned away and stalked through the gate. I followed a moment later, berating myself for mangling the conversation. On the other side of the portal, always thick with strolling musicians and peddlers, I spotted him in front of a puppet motion: a little booth enclosed by curtains, within which the puppet master was trying desperately to hold a thin crowd with the antics of Punch and Judy. As I drew closer, Mr. Punch was attempting to sell their baby to a roving Egyptian. Then Judy appeared and the battle developed into a tug-of-war. The play was neither kind nor clever, yet for the moment Kit appeared to be entranced by it. However, as soon as he sensed my presence, he whirled around to face me. In the torchlight his pale face leapt like a flame, his eyes flinty sparks. For an instant I thought his remark about hell might be true, in spirit. If he didn't live there, it lived in him: burning, restless, caged.

"Help me?" he burst out. "*Help* me? That's what you want, after coming out of the provinces and pushing me out of my place in scarcely more than a year?"

I swallowed a mouthful of wind. "What— How so?"

"I see you've learned to act innocent, too. Or perhaps you

started with that and used it as your staging ground to conquer all."

"What are you talking about? The Welsh Boy's the one who pushed you out of the Company. I know now how he baited you—"

His hand flew up, so swiftly I flinched, but it was only to silence me. "Soft," he said. "That music . . ."

I recognized the thumping refrain of the Robin Hood ballad, sung in a pleasing baritone voice to the accompaniment of a single flute and drum. On the west side of the gate, a tiny stage had been formed by laying two planks across a pair of barrels. On it stood the singer, a young man with an aged face, and perched on the platform at his feet a child in a motley tunic and a parrot's mask, beating upon a hand drum.

In highway or city, near river or wood,
No mark stands too high for the new Robin Hood.

The audience drawn by the refrain grew in number as the singer embarked upon new verses:

In yellow sleeves to honor his maid, he
Rides far afield with the beauteous lady,
*   A bold deed in hand;*
Here Robin and Marian choose their ground,
A mantle of forest circling round . . .

The gathering crowd laughed and cheered, welcoming the appearance of Maid Marian. The mention of yellow sleeves indicated that "Robin" had changed his garb from black and gold. I glanced at Kit's folded cloak. Sleeves could be taken from one garment and laced to another and would be easy to smuggle. The ballad singer spun a tale of Marian posing as a lady whose son has been stolen away by kidnappers: "The scorpion whips of cruelty/Have stolen my child!" she cried. A vain, boastful knight called Sir Flatter rides to her rescue (once she has promised a reward) and takes her up on his saddle, whereupon Marian pulls a dagger and Robin charges out from the surrounding forest. The token they demand is Sir Flatter's watch, in its pearly case.

And then they made off with the money, tra-la . . .

Kit turned abruptly and shouldered his way through the crowd. I watched him with a sickening weight in my stomach: Could the ballad be predicting an event that had not even occurred? Did that cloak contain a pair of yellow sleeves? I hesitated, then decided to follow a little farther.

Kit turned west on Threadneedle Street, headed toward Cheapside. I kept him in view while hanging back as far as I dared. Dusk had fallen, held at bay here and there by lamps in doorways; shopkeepers were boarding up their stalls and street vendors cried their last cries for hot mutton pies or periwinkles alive-o.

A curly-headed child ran past me, dodging cart and horse as deftly as a rat. His clothes flashed like a rainbow in the gray light; it was the little parrot from the singer's platform, without his mask. He pelted on toward Kit—then swiftly snatched the rolled-up cloak and made off with it. All that remained of him was a childish laugh and a mocking salute: "Hail, Marian!" I recognized the voice in a heartbeat.

Kit bolted in pursuit of the Welsh Boy, and I closed in behind—with no second thoughts this time. Davy led us a grueling chase down many a twisting side lane, through a crowded courtyard, across busy streets. Our twisting route led us in the general direction of the river, but all of it soon blurred for me, as I tried to ignore the knifing pain in my side. A high stone wall scrolled out beside me; I spun around the corner and almost ran into Kit.

He was holding on to Davy's motley tunic. The boy wriggled like an eel, landed a hard kick on his capturer's shin, and got away, diving into a narrow opening in the wall. His hard soles clattered on stone steps, fading away as they sank out of hearing.

Next moment, I heard a high-pitched scream, abruptly cut off by a thumping sound, like a full bag of oats striking a hard floor again, and again, and again.

I shall hear it forever.

*W*e stood at the top of a long set of steps built into the slope that led down to the river. Walls narrowly enclosed both sides, and cold air gusted from it like the stony breath of a cave.

My voice trembled, not just from exhaustion. "D-d-don't go down there. S-suppose it's a trap?"

Kit's arm was in my grasp, a fact I did not realize until he peeled back my fingers. "I think not. And I need my cloak."

His calm voice steadied my jangled nerves. I went with him to find a torch and stayed with him as he lighted it from a householder's lantern. He never spurned my company—perhaps he was secretly glad for it, especially when we entered the dark passage and went down about thirty steps.

The steps ran along one side of a house, enclosed on the other side by a wall. The building had probably once belonged to a wealthy merchant or church official, but now it had fallen into neglect. On the way down, the torchlight flashed on two shallow recesses, each with a small door. The steps ended in a little courtyard paved with rough-cut flagstones heaved up by sprouting weeds. A sagging gate led to the riverbank, so near we heard the cries of ship pilots as they took soundings.

The Welsh Boy sprawled faceup on the stones where he had fallen, his neck oddly bent to one side. Kit swept the light over him, and even a glance was enough to confirm he was dead.

My first thought was that he would never threaten me again. Then a pang of guilt: how had this child become such a foe that his death meant my liberation?

"Waste no pity on him," Kit said, as though reading my thoughts. "He was more beast than boy." His cloak had been flung across a stone bench—in a way it could not have landed if it had merely fallen from the boy's hands. Someone had thrown it there. Kit tossed it over one shoulder, then bent to retrieve something from under the bench.

"Bring the light closer," I said, my throat so tight the words could scarcely pass. "I think—there's something around his . . ."

He came over and stuck the torch in a bracket on the wall. The light fell rudely upon the boy's startled face, with its scarred cheek and blue eyes beginning to dim. Around his neck, cinched tight, was a doubled string. Kneeling, Kit pulled the end of the string loose, revealing the knot that tied it into one large loop.

"Where did that come from?" I whispered. "Wasn't it the fall that killed him?"

"Aye. His neck is broken." Kit looped the end of the string through his fingers, and I remembered Davy weaving his endless figures, casting his malevolent spells.

"Kit—what deep plot is this?"

"Plot?" He spread his cloak on the ground and placed on it the object he had retrieved from under the bench: an ordinary shirt, not a stolen costume. He rolled shirt and cloak together, stood up, and tucked the bundle under his arm. "What plot?" The hinge on the little gate squealed as he opened it and stepped through. "I'll leave you the torch—pray don't follow me this time. You were never here. And I am nowhere."

Next instant, he was swallowed up in the river mist.

I turned to face the stairs, rising into darkness, and remembered the two recessed doorways I had seen on the way down—perfect places to wait, concealed, for a hapless victim. In my disordered state I could not help wondering if someone was now waiting there for me. Would Kit regard my death with the same uncanny calm he'd shown the Welsh Boy's?

One thing sure: I was not going up those steps.

After picking my way across the bank, I scurried up to Thames Street, where by good fortune a gentleman from France hired me to light his way to Cheapside. When I reached home, a penny richer, Starling met me, waving the ballad about Robin and Marian that she had bought at Bishopsgate. At that moment Master Condell was calling for Jacob to carry a message to the Heminges house, so I offered to carry it myself and asked her along for company.

"I know all about the ballad," I told her, as soon as we were outside the gate. "Something has happened. You must tell no one of this, especially . . . Well, you know."

"I am not in communion with anyone called You Know," she sniffed. "If you mean Master Finch, he only sought me out one time, and I've not heard from him since the night you—"

"Be that as it may. You have my drift. And here's my tale."

I told her of my walk with Kit, and of hearing the ballad, and of Davy snatching his cloak. When I came to finding the boy dead at the bottom of the steps, she halted abruptly and covered her mouth with both hands. "Oh, poor Davy! Why?"

"I'm not certain. He is—or was—a cunning little creature in his way, but not reliable. He talked too much and made foolish mistakes."

"But still, if they wanted to be rid of him, they could have chosen simpler ways to do it."

"I know. It seems as if he was placed at Bishopsgate to wait for Kit, then snatch his cloak and lead him that merry chase. But nobody told Davy how the scene was staged to end. Someone was waiting for him on the stairs. Dark Tom

I'd wager. A trip or a push is all it would take, with time to follow him down and make sure he was dead, and wrap that string around his neck . . . but I still don't know what that was for."

"A signal to Kit? 'Do what we want or this will happen to you'?"

"Perhaps. They do want something. When we got to the bottom of the steps, someone had searched his cloak."

She made a gasp and grabbed my arm. "Looking for a pair of yellow sleeves! Recall what the ballad says, about Robin wearing yellow sleeves to honor his maid."

"That was my suspicion, too. But there was nothing wrapped up in the cloak but a shirt."

"Tom or whoever it was may have already taken them. Though if they got what they wanted, why leave a warning for Kit?"

"Perhaps they want more. Think of it: Who else of their band could play Marian? Davy is too young, and Tom would never be convincing. But Kit would have to shave, and so far, he hasn't."

We walked a few steps in silence, then she said, "So someone still has 'expectations.' He's put himself in a pretty bind."

"The trouble is, I may have bound myself with him, after this night. If Tom got a good look at me, he would recognize me from the archery butts."

She stopped and made another gasp, and the next thing I

found myself bound in was her arms. As I was holding a lantern, this was a little awkward, but I didn't mind. Just then a pair of men came around the corner of Aldermanbury Street and headed our way. Starling let me go as we heard John Heminges's voice saying, ". . . all in all, though, it pleases me. Now our course is decided, and we may proceed with a clear conscience— Hold! Who's there?"

I named myself and handed over the message. "Very good, Richard; my thanks. Now go home and get a good night's rest. Tomorrow is another moving day."

His preoccupied manner, shared by Master Shakespeare beside him, told me nothing about their meeting with Giles Allen. Starling remained uncommonly silent during our walk home, but at the door she held back and whispered, "Will you report this? Davy's death?"

I sighed, knowing already that this question would keep me awake tonight. "I probably should, but . . . Kit told me not to. 'You were never here,' he said. What do you say?"

She paused a moment to consider, then touched my cheek, but her answer was not a model of clarity: "Look to your safety."

The following afternoon, as we packed our carts once again for a move to the Swan, Robin ventured to ask about the meeting with Giles Allen. Master Heminges hesitated, then unloaded his news along with a box of costume jewels. "No harm in telling you now. The landlord has made up his mind which side of yes-and-no he prefers. It's no."

Robin's face fell as he took the box. "Is there no more use in talking, then?"

"None at all. After you finish loading that cart, you and the other boys may take it on to Southwark." Master Heminges resumed his packing as Robin turned away, biting his lip in a manner picked up from Kit.

I relieved him of the box, saying, "Don't take it so hard. They've only given up on the landlord, not the stage."

"Why do you think so?"

"Are they sunk in despair? They have a plan in mind, or I'm an onion. Do I look like an onion?"

"No. Though you smell like one, betimes."

"The same to you. *Esperance,* as Hotspur would say."

"*Esperance,*" he repeated, looking a bit more cheerful.

"Hope" was a word equally meant for me, for I was still in a quandary over whether to report a murder. That evening, as we were arranging the last of our properties in the tiring room of the Swan, one of the hired men arrived in a high state: "Have you heard the news?" My heart stopped.

But the news had nothing to do with the Welsh Boy. It seemed that Ben Jonson, whose *Every Man in His Humor* had been one of our more successful plays that season, got himself embroiled with a player from the Admiral's Company. The two had met on a Finsbury field that very morning, and Jonson had killed his rival. Now he was being held for manslaughter and could be hanged.

"Another good playmaker cut off before his time," sighed Richard Cowley, in a feeble jest. "Pray *you* don't provoke any hot-headed players, Will." No one smiled; Master Jonson's fiery disposition had landed him in prison before, and he had emerged with no apparent scars. But this time he might emerge only to face the hangman. It made a sad beginning to our week at the Swan—and we still had the Putrid Play to perform on Monday.

That morning we arrived to find stage keepers setting gilded chairs in one of the "gentlemen's rooms" in the first gallery. This happened only when some prominent personage planned to attend. Every face wore an anxious look as we gathered for rehearsal at nine o'clock, especially the faces of those who had leading parts—Ned Shakespeare, and me, and . . . where was Kit?

I am nowhere.

Rehearsal began without him, as Richard Burbage muttered about heavy fines while his brother read Adrian's lines from the prompt book. By ten o'clock the chief players were considering a substitute play, and at half-past Master Will sent a message ("to Essex," Gregory whispered to me), expressing our deep regret that his request could not be honored, due to Adrian's unfortunate absence. At eleven we were all on stage, waiting for the chief men to decide which of our plays would be brushed up and outfitted within three hours. They sounded almost cheerful, for an air of relief had swept the entire Company. I even overheard Richard Burbage say, "God bless Kit Glover—whether he meant to or not, he's done us a good turn. If I see him again, I'll toss him a shilling—"

At that moment one of the stage keepers hurried up to inform him that we had a visitor. Directly after, my jaw dropped as a young gentleman in yellow silk strode to the very center of the stage and introduced himself as Philip Tewkesbury, Baron of Wellstone. . . . Lord Mustard!

He looked in fine health—not as if he had fallen prey to Robin Hood—perhaps the anonymous message sent by Starling and me had done him some good. But his presence here had nothing to do with that. He had heard of our dilemma from his good friend the Earl of Essex and was here to propose a solution. "We long to hear it, my lord," said Master Heminges, though his eyes suggested otherwise.

"Very well." Philip Tewkesbury peeled off his kidskin gloves and used them to fling gestures around the theater as though he owned it. "'Tis a matter very close to my heart that this play go forward. Therefore, if no player in the Company can be found to take Adrian's part, I propose . . . myself."

For a heartbeat or two, none of us caught his meaning. Then I heard a distinct groan behind me, and Augustine Phillips left the stage, perhaps to tear his hair in private.

Robin whispered, "How can he walk in and claim a role of that size? How does he know it?"

Gregory and I looked at each other as the reason became clear. "Because he wrote it," we said together.

Meanwhile, Lord Philip was insisting that he knew the play "as well as any man here." Master Will stepped forward and explained with the greatest tact that performing before an audience was much harder than it looked, and the Company would be sorely grieved if the gentleman met with some misfortune on their stage—

"Fear not for that." The young man pulled a strip of black silk from his sleeve. "I shall disguise myself. Adrian will be masked, and we shall add lines to say his face was disfigured by his enemies. That will enhance the play; increase his motive for revenge, you see?" He glanced about with obvious pleasure at this brilliant stroke, while the men of the Company stared at the mask as though it were a viper.

He got his way, though. The most determined arguments failed to discourage him, and a brief audition proved he could at least put out the lines. He sealed the decision at last by references to important friends who would be very disappointed if the play was not performed. "I'd like to tell him where he could send his important friends," Will Kempe muttered, but of course that would not do. Every player understood his obligation to help prevent Philip Tewkesbury, Baron of Wellstone, from making too great a fool of himself. A most difficult task in so putrid a play.

235

While the dresser laced up my gown, I dutifully read the corrected lines I had been given: something about Adrian's face being o'er raked with the scorpion whips of cruelty. Once I had it in memory, to be forgotten as soon as the play was done, I folded the paper, pushed it into the deep cuff of my sleeve, and climbed down to the lower tiring room. Tewkesbury nodded to me—his first concession that I existed—but continued his pacing.

This close, he looked no older than nineteen. Overconfidence may have propelled him thus far, but now he looked as if the reality of walking out onto the boards was sinking in. I was wondering what reason would drive him to expose himself this way, when a ragged cheer sounded in the half-filled house, indicating that the Prominent Personage had taken his seat in the gentlemen's room. Gregory scampered up to the musicians' gallery and came down directly to tell us who it was: "Essex." No one seemed surprised, but Lord Philip turned a bit green, as though the earl were not his "good friend" so much as his examiner. But no more time for nerves now; Ned Shakespeare made his entrance as Sylvester, and the play began.

To Tewkesbury's credit, he was not dreadful. With training and practice and the addition of another skill, like sword-swallowing, he might have commanded some attention. But new players are always surprised at how little weight their voice carries when surrounded by a crowd of strangers. To one accustomed to having his every word obeyed, it must have been a shock.

Besides, it soon became apparent that he and the Company were at cross-purposes. While we dutifully left out all the veiled references to the Brooke family, he resolutely left his in—and even repeated a few when quick-witted players spoke over him. In our courting scene the conflict became painful when he took my hand. "Alas!" said I. "I do fear the bloody streams of treachery will yet rise up and o'erwhelm our jocund hope—"

"What mean you?" he interrupted. "Bloody *brooks* of treachery?"

He squeezed my hand so hard my next line came out as a squeal: "Aye— Heaven defend us!"

Tewkesbury was almost panting with effort when we came off the stage. He flung aside my hand and approached Master Will to ask why some of the lines had been changed.

"Changed, my lord?" asked Shakespeare, all innocence.

Tewkesbury found himself in a delicate situation: what right had he to protest alterations in the play, if he was unwilling to admit his authorship? The Company, meanwhile, pretended to have no idea what he meant by "changed lines," thus creating all sorts of undercurrents (streams or brooks) behind the stage. But those were soon o'erwhelmed by the very obvious currents in the house.

By the second act four young gallants were sitting together

in the first gallery, across from Essex. They were obviously not his friends, nor Tewkesbury's, for by the third act they were causing enough disturbance to destroy any possible interest in the play. Every time I came on, there were fewer people in the galleries and more hazelnut shells and orange peels on the stage. Directly after Silvia's death scene, Essex departed, too.

After that, Master Burbage strongly suggested cutting large sections of the remaining text, and Tewkesbury agreed. He kept his head high, like Hotspur going to his doom with "Die all, die merrily" on his lips. Lord Philip at least had the sense to die quietly, wrapping himself in the poisoned cloak with the least possible fuss and cutting down his speech to:

"O happy garb, that ends my vile disgrace!

Ye fates—bear me up to a happier place!

O cloak most black, consume me into dust—

The pale smoke of honor to the gods I trust."

When he fell (with a thump), his tormenters in the first gallery rose and flapped their arms, as though helping to bear him up to that happy place. Behind the stage, the players groaned. While Edmund Shakespeare was making a speech over the fallen Adrian, his brother said to Master Burbage, "You deal with Lord Mustard; I will do what I can to calm yonder beast"—by which he meant the remaining audience. On his way to the stage Master Will bowed politely to the body of Philip Tewkesbury as it went by on a litter. Thus the gentleman did not hear Shakespeare's public apology for his play, because Richard Burbage was at the same moment apologizing to *him*—a noble effort that summoned all the diplomacy Burbage possessed. Tewkesbury left the Swan with a straight posture and flaming cheeks, while Master Burbage clutched the bag of coins paid to him as Judas might have held his thirty pieces of silver. "If Kit Glover ever shows himself hereabouts again," he said, "I'll cheerfully kill him."

That night I complained to Starling, "I wish you hadn't talked me into sending that message to John Clement. If ever a man deserved to be robbed, Tewkesbury does."

"Well, one good thing came of today's performance—it silenced Mistress Critic. She came early and stayed for the whole play, but after the first act I heard not a word from her."

"All the rest of our critics were loud enough."

"Put it behind you. Part Two will save your reputation."

She was very likely right. Boys were already posting playbills throughout London, and a full house, at double admission, would boost our fortunes again. When Thursday arrived, eager play-goers began lining up outside the Swan long before the first trumpet.

The Company had to borrow a boy from St. Paul's Chapel to play Falstaff's page. The part had been written for Davy, and to see young Lawrence Bates strutting around in a short cape reminded me painfully of a child lying at the bottom of a stone staircase with a broken neck. By now, five days had gone by without event, but I was increasingly on edge, and Lawrence's habit of humming monotonous tunes needled my conscience. Nor could I escape it, for the boy perched on the loft just over the place where Richard Burbage was painting me.

Burbage was an accomplished painter, and "Rumor, painted with tongues" gave him an opportunity to stretch his skills. I had pictured something like cow tongues hanging all over me—not a pretty sight, but Master Burbage thought tongues of fire: flame-tipped points, layered like feathers. The wardrobe master had made a pair of breeches covered with strips of red, yellow, and orange that would spin out when I whirled upon the stage. The effect was far more pleasing than I could have imagined, though art could not disguise the fact that I was stripped to the waist and perched on a stool next to a window, while a man in a smock applied paint to my chest in preparation for me to go out upon a stage and expose myself to three thousand pairs of eyes. This was one of those times when the player's life felt every bit as unnatural and devilish as my sister had said.

"By my faith," Master Burbage complained, "it takes twice the quantity of paint to cover thy goose bumps. Hold still."

I made an effort to hold still, as my breath streamed out upon the cold October breeze and Master Bates overhead hummed his song without end. Then Gregory appeared, in scarlet taffeta. He was playing a whore named Doll Tearsheet, but at the moment his face under the paint was so pale that he resembled a real doll. "Please, sir," he said breathlessly, "Master Heminges would speak with you."

Burbage frowned. "Can it not wait? I'm almost done."

"No, sir. We have a visitor—a constable, sir."

"What *now*?" The painter threw down his brush, leaving a bright red spatter on the floor. When he was gone, Gregory leaned forward and whispered to me. "He's looking for Kit Glover."

"Who is?"

"The constable. He wanted to ask me about that time last June, when Kit tried to kill the Welsh Boy. He asked me every detail."

If I was cold before, my veins now turned to ice. "Why?"

"Because Davy is dead! Murdered, most like! They found his body at the bottom of some stairs. They think Kit did it. But he can't be found."

Burbage and Heminges sent the constable packing with their assurance that none of us had any notion of Kit's whereabouts, but all the players were shaken. Bad enough that Ben Jonson should now be in prison for manslaughter, but this was cold-blooded murder, with a former colleague as chief suspect. Robin was so undone he had to be fortified with doses of cider and *Esperance* before he could even think about Mistress Quickly.

But I was worse. I alone knew that the suspect was not guilty.

"This is a blow to all of us," Master Condell told me

kindly (and much more truly than he knew). "But set it aside as best you can. It falls to your charge to begin what is perhaps the greatest opening we have ever had. Pray put your speech forward with every particle of energy that's in you, and . . . Richard, *what* is behind those great staring eyes of yours? Is your part less than perfect?" I managed to indicate that there was no fear for my part. "Very good—but there's no harm in going over it again, eh?"

Some of the other actors were looking at me curiously. "You *will* be able to speak, will you not?" Augustine Phillips asked. I nodded and took out the paper that contained my lines, hiding behind it as I gathered my wits. There was no longer a choice of standing apart from Kit's trouble. Kit's trouble had broken loose like a team of horses pelting madly downhill— with me tangled in the traces. I was the only one who could speak for him, and I must speak quickly. Immediately. Rumor's first words rolled out before my eyes: "Open your ears . . ."

In those words, I saw a chance. A slim chance, but it was all I had to hope for. God grant that the ears I must open would be present in the house today.

The third trumpet blew, and Master Will's hands rested lightly on my painted shoulders. "Not yet—let them wait a little longer. Anticipation, you know. Breathe deep. Again. Remember the voice—high and disembodied. One moment. One moment. Now—"

"Open your ears! For which of you will stop
the vent of hearing when loud Rumor speaks?"

The greatest compliment to a player is not applause;
it is silence. From the moment I spun out upon the stage,
"tongues" flying, the house fell into my hands, hushed
and spellbound. Partly because I had been entrusted with
opening one of the most eagerly awaited plays of the
Company's history—a well-trained dog might have led
this audience by the hand. But the burning in my heart
fired Rumor with uncommon energy, as I whirled "from
the Orient to the drooping west" and swept both hands to
the west door of the theater.

"Upon my tongues continual slanders ride,

The which in every language I pronounce,

Filling the beaks of sparrow and *finch* with false

reports . . ."

The line Shakespeare wrote was "Stuffing the ears of men with false reports." My change altered the rhythm, and Master Will would not be pleased. For the rest of the speech I made my hands talk, sketching "present danger" in the air as I flew across the stage in a fluttering of tongues.

"*Now* (pointing west) the posts come tiring on,
And not a man of them brings other news
Than they have learned of me. *Now* from Rumor's tongues
They bring smooth comforts false, worse than true
wrongs."

The audience held perfectly still as I whirled off, then erupted in applause. "Well spoke, Richard," remarked John Heminges in passing. Master Shakespeare was adjusting his nightcap before his entrance as the ailing Earl of Northumberland; he lifted a finger and an eyebrow to indicate we must have a serious talk later. "Later" suited me—at the moment I would have been hard pressed to explain my rewriting the text. I only hoped it had done its work.

In a few moments, still wet from a hasty scrubbing, I slipped out the west door of the tiring room. The autumn breeze gilded my cheek like cold silver. Shivering in my cloak, I looked about but saw only a few beggars waiting patiently for the play to be done so they could work the theater crowd. A Yeoman Guard, in his red and yellow livery and steel helmet, paced slowly in my direction while peeling an orange. I glanced toward the river, where watermen had docked their boats on the Paris Stairs. My chest was tightening with despair when Bartholomew Finch spoke behind me. "Well, what is it?"

I spun around to face the Yeoman, who had removed his helmet and was fanning himself with it, blowing the lock of red hair that had escaped from his leather hood.

"Thank God you came!" I gasped in relief.

"Small wonder, that. You were as broad as Cheapside. From the way you pointed I expected a whole flock of sparrows and finches to join me in my exodus."

I was thanking God that he'd come to the theater that day; a dozen reasons might have kept him from it, though he was as eager as anyone to learn what Falstaff was up to. "Why are you dressed so?"

"I've been enlisted to guard the Lord Chamberlain's son."

"Henry Brooke is here?"

"Aye," he said patiently, "else I could not be guarding him here. I've been excused to relieve myself, but if you don't get on with it, he'll suspect I've fallen in."

"It's about Kit Glover. Do you know he's accused of murder?"

"Aye," he said, most carefully.

"Do you know who brought the accusation?"

He chewed and swallowed about a quarter of the orange. "I did not come out to answer questions. Suppose you tell *me* somewhat."

"All right." I took a breath, knowing that what I was about

to say would make me his ally. "You must call off the constable somehow. Kit didn't do it. I know because I was with him when it happened."

His only betrayal of surprise was that the waving helmet came to a halt and his eyes shifted, as though to make sure we were alone. "Speak fast and low."

In few words, I told him of my walk to Cheapside with Kit, of Davy's appearance, of the chase he led, and how we found him at the bottom of the stairs.

Bartlemy nodded. "A vagrant found the body two days later. Witnesses swore they saw a boy in motley being chased by a tall pale fellow they recognized from the stage—just one fellow, so far as I've heard, not two."

"There was a constable here earlier, asking questions about Kit's attack on the boy last spring. Is it possible he's being set up?"

"'Set up'?" he repeated, with a sly inflection. "By whom?"

"Well . . . It's a long tale."

"It always is." He popped the last of the orange into his mouth and spoke around it. "I will talk my way free and meet you directly after the play. Where can we be private?"

My mind raced over possible places to meet. "I know— under the stage. No one will be there for this performance. If you come around to the back right corner, you may slip under it without being seen. But I can't stay long."

"Ten minutes, no more," said he, replacing his helmet. "And be prepared to tell me all."

With that, he turned and strolled back toward the public entrance. Though his last words fell with an ominous ring, he left me in a more settled state, now that I had done something. True, it might turn out to be something I would regret, but at least half the weight was off my shoulders, and I could think about my part as Lady Percy. As I slipped back into the tiring room, Thomas Pope hitched up his stuffed belly and marched upon the stage with little Lawrence Bates in tow. The roar that greeted Sir John Falstaff's first appearance felt as solid as a clap on the back.

I knew the outcome, but as usual with a new play, the first performance was like seeing it for the first time. And see it I could; my main contribution was already over, and Lady Percy appeared only once. At the end I would help swell the cheering crowds of London, but between times lay a rare stretch of leisure for me to sit at the back of the musicians' gallery and watch the play.

Part Two begins much like the first. Though crippled by Hotspur's death, the rebellion is not yet put down. The king still frets over his son's wild ways, in spite of Hal's courage and loyalty on Shrewsbury Field. Falstaff has received a reward for "slaying" Hotspur and swaggers about London with his new clothes and his little page, chiseling money out of anyone foolish enough to lend to him.

He soon runs afoul of the Chief Justice of London, who wants to question him about the robbery on Gad's Hill. To make matters worse, Mistress Quickly has brought suit against him for money he owes. True to form, Sir John not only squirms out of the suit, but also cozens another ten pounds out of the lady. The justice likewise finds himself no match for Falstaff in a battle of wits, and so leaves the knight's correction to God. But he adds a judgment of his own: "Thou art a great fool." (Boos and hisses followed the worthy gentleman off the stage.)

Prince Hal, meanwhile, is restless and troubled. The old reputation sheds harder than he thought, and the old ways still appeal to him. He resigns himself to the hope that events will prove him true: "Let the end try the man." But when Poins suggests another trick to play on Falstaff, the prince goes along with it willingly enough.

He and Poins disguise themselves as ale servers to eavesdrop on a flirtation between Falstaff and Doll Tearsheet, a lady of very common goods. (Gregory played much of this scene on Thomas Pope's lap and complained of having to pretend to kiss him behind a fan: "It wouldn't be so bad if he didn't eat boiled eels for breakfast.") An old soldier named Pistol appears, whose heroic poses and bombastic speeches sound like a broad, comic echo of the late Hotspur—and since Will Sly was given this part, the comparison may have been intended.

But by now it was evident that Part Two had taken a

different tone than the first. It lacked a hero: Hotspur was slain, King Henry dying, Falstaff moaning to Doll, "I am old, I am old."

"Rouse yourself then, you ton of flesh!" came a cry from the groundlings. As if in reply, Sir John was soon up to his old tricks.

Commissioned to raise a company of soldiers, he travels through the countryside drafting able-bodied farmhands—who promptly pay him off so they won't have to serve. Those who can't pay are the lame, the halt, and the unemployed; scarecrows so thin "they present no mark to the enemy." While making his rounds, Sir John stops at the home of a friend from his school days, a country justice named Shallow. True to his name, this gentleman is a doddering old fool who thinks no deeper than his ale glass and whose favorite subject of conversation is his wild youth: "What days we have seen!"

"We have heard the chimes at midnight, Master Shallow," Falstaff agrees—secretly plotting to milk this useful friend for every penny.

Meanwhile, King Henry feels death creeping upon him and fears for the kingdom once it falls into Hal's frivolous hands. While meeting with his advisors, the king falls into a swoon and must be carried to bed. Hal arrives to find his father in such a deep sleep that he appears to be dead. The prince carefully lifts the crown from a nearby pillow and sets it on his own head. . . .

And for the first time I understood what both parts of this play were about: not loyalty to the crown, or glory in battle, or outwitting the law—it is about how a prince becomes a king, or how a boy becomes a man. And the hero of *Henry IV* is not King Henry IV or the lovable rogue Falstaff or the gallant, reckless Hotspur: it is Hal.

The king revives, but only long enough to make peace with his son and pronounce his blessing. Wild Prince Hal is now King Henry V.

But what sort of king? Everyone, from his brothers to his disgraceful companions, expect that the royal court will now be turned into the Boar's Head Tavern, with Mistress Quickly pouring sack at council meetings and Falstaff merrily hanging the Chief Justice. When word of the old king's death speeds to Justice Shallow's country house, Sir John believes his fortune is made. Hurrying back to London, he arrives just after the coronation at Westminster, in time to greet the new king's procession.

By this time I was out of the gallery and on the stage as a member of the cheering crowd. Augustine Phillips, resplendent in a coronation robe, marched solemnly down one side of the stage and across the front, followed closely by Richard Burbage as the Chief Justice. Phillips was one of the tallest players in the Company, but he seemed a very tower in this scene, as though stretching to reach the height of his crown. The two trumpets in the gallery blew a mighty fanfare worthy of ten, as the groundlings cheered and tossed their caps in the air, becoming players as well as audience. Slowly King Henry V turned at the corner of the stage, then paced up the opposite side, where Falstaff was shouting, "God save thy grace, King Hal; my royal Hal!" and Pistol chimed in, "The heavens thee guard and keep, most royal imp of fame!"

Though told to be silent, Sir John cried all the more: "My king! My Jove! I speak to thee, my heart—"

"I know thee *not*, old man." The king's cold, hard voice fell like an ax, chopping off their friendship. The house fell silent as he went on to compare his past life—the wild escapades, the witty word wars, the carefree drunken nights—all to a dream. Now he was awake. His former companions could expect a decent allowance from him, but they must not come within ten miles of his royal person—"on pain of death."

Trumpets blaring, the king then paced off the stage as Falstaff remained—speechless for once, and the groundlings stricken with him. My own sympathies were confused. Surely King Henry V, if he meant to rule justly, could not be advised by the Boar's Head crowd; in cutting them off, he had done only as he must. But did he have to do it so cruelly, exposing his friend to public ridicule? Then again, it was the friend who had exposed himself, blinded by his own vanity. For all his cleverness, his wit, his endless invention in borrowing money, Falstaff was as great a fool as the Chief Justice had said.

Though they may have understood this, the audience did

not like it. When officers arrived to bear Sir John and his companions to Fleet Prison—in payment at last for the Gad's Hill robbery—boos and catcalls followed them off the stage.

"And that," remarked Will Shakespeare ironically, "is my cue." He walked onto the empty stage with a parchment in hand, then made three bows: one to his left, where the wealthiest patrons sat, one to the top gallery on the right, and the lowest and most sweeping to the house as a whole, taking in all classes as the noise gradually died.

He began his epilogue with an apology for Monday's "displeasing play": no doubt a peace offering to Henry Brooke. Then he went on to pray their patience for Part Two—almost as if he expected some displeasure over Falstaff's comedown. He promised to write another play about Henry V and restore everyone's good humor with the further antics of Sir John (not in any way related to John Oldcastle, "who died a martyr"). His little speech won the fickle crowd; their shouts and cheers rang in my head as I made my way to the trap door at the back of the tiring room. With no one about, I let myself through it and dropped to the packed earth below.

The players' dance had begun; rhythmic steps thumped the boards overhead as I slouched toward the near corner of the stage. Bartlemy had placed himself just outside the only patch of light; I had to look hard to see him, cross-legged on the sawdust with his back against a trestle, his Yeoman's tunic and helmet laid aside.

He spoke first. "A sorry end."

It took me a moment to understand he was talking about the play. "But that's how it must end. How else could Hal become a great king?"

"He's a great hypocrite. 'Reply to me not with a fool-born jest,' says he to Falstaff. Those fool-born jests were his very meat in the old days."

"A king must live up to his calling."

"I've heard of plenty who don't. And these 'nobles,' so called, I know them firsthand. At least Fat Jack and his crew go about their thieving honestly, but gentlemen of the court mew and fawn over Her Majesty and snipe at each other like pug dogs behind her back— But enough of that." He wiped his sleeve across his nose.

I gestured to the Yeoman's tunic. "Why is Henry Brooke going about with a guard now? Does he fear another robbery?"

His long face stretched even longer with annoyance. "Never mind what he fears. I'm wasted in this office. Tell me this: do you know aught about an unsigned message regarding a certain gentleman at court named Tewkesbury?" This took me by surprise, and my face gave me away. He slammed his fist on the ground. "I *knew* it. I was working out a likely doctrine of the crimes when your warning arrived. And my master insisted that we pay heed to it, even though it shot holes in *my* theme, and Henry Brooke suggested that since we could not even agree on our path, I might better serve him as a guard until we did—"

"Hold a moment!" I knew his temper and thought it best to stop him before he worked it up. "The message wasn't a whim. There was good reason to send it." And Starling talked me into it, I might have added, except that it did not seem honorable to blame a girl.

He inclined his head in a sarcastic bow. "Very well. Your reason?"

I told him of my visit to Newington Butts, and the conversation I had overheard there. After hearing me out, Bartlemy asked only one question: "Are you certain those were Penny's words exactly? 'We must keep Tewkesbury in our sights'?"

"That's my work—remembering words. Do you know this man Tom?"

He nodded. "Tom Watts, a Welshman. Served with Penny in the Netherlands."

"Well, mark this." I leaned forward, confident that I was about to shake his "likely doctrine," whatever it was. "Tom may have a score to settle. I saw him last May fighting a rapier match outside the Buckingham Tavern. He had insulted a gentleman, who called him out. The gentleman was Philip Tewkesbury."

His jaw did not drop; he did not even blink. He merely took in what I said, turned it over in his mind, and came out with, "Did you ever consider that scene might have been staged?"

"Ah . . ." This took me aback, though now that he mentioned it, I could see it made sense. After all, if Kit had used

254

that opportunity to pass a borrowed costume to Tom, he must have known the man was going to be there at that time. "But," said I, thinking aloud, "even if it was staged, that doesn't prove Tewkesbury was party to it. Unless—" I had just remembered yet another "staged" incident from the past.

"Unless what?"

"Last spring, Kit got into a bit of trouble. He was arrested for breaking the peace, along with Captain Penny. But there was someone else involved in that scrape. His name never came up, but we reckoned he must be wealthy because he paid Kit's bail."

This finally captured Bartlemy's imagination. He sat up straighter, eyes bright. "The magistrate's record doesn't show that, nor mention a third offender. It merely says that Glover was released on bail—I assumed it was put up by the Company."

"What—you looked into it already?"

"That's *my* work."

"But if Tewkesbury is a part of this scheme, then . . . then perhaps he is the author of the Robin Hood ballads!"

He nodded, unsurprised. "If I could prove that, I'd be a made man."

"Then who was the victim of the Robin and Marian episode?"

He thoughtfully picked at one of the pimples on his chin before deciding to share what he knew. "Listen close. Last

Sunday—the day *after* the song appeared—Sir Walter Raleigh and two of his men rode out toward Devon to visit his home estate. At dusk, about ten miles west of London, he came across a tall gentleman on a bridge, crying for help to get his horse out of a bog. The gentleman was dressed in a black satin doublet with yellow sleeves—and no Marian in sight. Raleigh sent one of his men down to see to the horse and soon after heard a scream. The tall fellow then pulled a pistol and made the usual demand for money or life, along with Sir Walter's watch. While pretending to hand over the watch, Raleigh went for his sword instead, and he and his other servant both attacked the robber. Would have had him, too, except that an accomplice appeared and helped beat off Raleigh and his man long enough for them to leap over the bridge and make their escape, on a pair of horses that—needless to say—were stuck in no bog.

"Sir Walter found his other servant badly wounded under the bridge—he almost bled to death while the fight was going on, but is on the mend now. The rogues got away, but Sir Walter believes he paid one with a gash in the arm. And though it was too dark to get a good look at the face, he matched the man's size and manner to the description given by his brother-in-law, Lord Throckmorton—otherwise known as Sir Biscuit of the boat."

I tried to sort this out. "So, was the Marian story a sham?"

"I think it more likely they had to change their plan because Marian failed to show."

256

"You mean Kit."

"Aye. He's vanished. Which, if he *is* being set up by his so-called friends, would be a sensible thing to do."

"Why would they do that to him?"

"Advantage. To have something on him; to make him do their will."

"But he didn't."

"No? How do you explain the yellow sleeves?" That was a sticky question; most likely they were rolled up in the cloak after all, and Tom had made off with them. Bartlemy went on to say, "Glover is vital to our case. If you have any notion, any glimmering, where he might be, you are obliged to tell."

There was a hardness in his voice and eye that got my back up. "I don't. I asked him where he was staying, and he brushed me off. Perhaps he has fled the city."

"Not likely."

"How do you know?"

Bartlemy paused. "His mother has been doing his laundry."

"She *talked* to you?" He seemed to have a gift for winning female confidence, though for my life I couldn't see how.

"Aye, though all she will admit is that he leaves it for her, in a place she would not tell. We're watching her now, of course."

That explained the shirt Kit was carrying. Such a plain, homely concern emphasized how far he had fallen—so far that his poor mother had to be watched for trying to look after him.

"You'd spend your time better looking for those stolen jewels."

He pulled a sardonic smile. "The jewels have been returned, after a fashion. The Lord Chamberlain's gold chain was found in his privy, and Throckmorton's cuff pin was tied to the collar of his hunting dog. But the other Cobham ring is still missing."

"That makes all this sound like . . . a prank."

"Except that one boy is dead and one man gravely wounded."

The theater had mostly emptied; boards overhead creaked as stage boys swept up and put away the furniture. Soon the Company would be assembling for evening rehearsal. "I must go."

My companion stirred. "So must I. Well, now—you've told me somewhat, and I've told you likewise; was that so bad? If you discover anything else, you must get word to me at once. Send a message through Mistress Shaw that you will meet me between . . . say, seven and eight of the evening, or six and seven of a morning, in the south transept of St. Paul's. She will know where to bring it." My displeasure must have showed, for he asked, "What is it?"

"Why must you involve her?"

"Because she has more freedom to move than you—unless you want this Starling to be kept in a cage?"

"I want no harm to come to her."

"She is not the one in danger. You may be, if you're not

careful. And Kit Glover is, sure." He crouched on his heels and pulled the yellow and red tunic over his head. "It would mean a deal to me to know where he is."

We parted ways, Bartlemy ducking out from under the stage and I backing through the trestles. Under the hatch door I paused, listening to make sure my way was clear before opening it. And as I crouched there, it suddenly came to me where Kit must be staying.

After all, he had told me himself.

ehind stage, the men of the Company were congratulating each other on their success. Richard Burbage declared a holiday: the play would hold good for the morrow, and Saturday as well, and at least eight more performances by Christmas. So after the costumes and properties were put away, all would adjourn to the Mermaid Tavern for dinner on the Company's account.

If nothing else, this made a very neat opportunity for a private expedition. Starling would assume I was stuffing myself at the tavern; the Company men and boys, if they missed me, would assume I had gone home. The gloomy pall cast over them by the constable's visit was now dispelled; in the cheerful mayhem I slipped out before anyone could tuck me under his arm and haul me off to the Mermaid.

Since most of the boats were taken with theater patrons,

I walked up Bankside to the Bridge. By the time I reached it, the hour was creeping upon five o'clock and a watery sun pierced itself upon St. Lawrence steeple. The milliners and fine-goods merchants on the bridge were packing away their costly wares and closing their shops. One of them, his traveling cloak still draped over one shoulder, was grandly giving his opinion of Part Two to his clerks and apprentices. ". . . taken altogether, I conclude it will be fitting for you to see, because at the end—"

He was drowned out by a chorus of, "Nay, Master Percival—don't tell us how it ends!" and others begging, "Pray, how does it end, Master Percival?"

I followed Gracechurch Street through the east side of the city and passed under the wide portal of Bishopsgate. A low mist hung over Moorfields, heightening the autumn chill. I tightened my cloak about me and stepped up my pace in order to squeeze more light out of the day. The field was near-deserted; only a flock of geese crossed my path, and an angry young goose-girl soon after, screeching abuse at them. Before long, two familiar, many-sided structures loomed over the horizon: the Curtain and Burbage's Theater, one polished and spruce in the honey-colored light, the other rank and overgrown. Leaving the road I cut across the field toward the Theater.

Agents of the landlord kept the way clear that led to the public door. But I was looking for a less evident path, and after circling behind the building, I found it—more thread than path, marked only by a crease in the tall grass. It led to a cellar opening built out from the theater wall, covered by a hatch about two feet square.

One would need sharp eyes to see it, or else be very familiar with the Theater. I had almost forgotten it myself, since it opened to a passageway that players never used—a route for workmen to carry timbers in or garbage out. A heavy padlock on the hatch gave me pause, until I noticed that the bar had been filed. I removed it, and swung the door aside on a well-greased hinge that made little noise. I stooped through the opening and lowered myself to a narrow corridor that ran under the tiring room, leading directly to "hell."

"Halloo!" I called, receiving no answer but my own heartbeat, which sounded loud enough to summon the Yeoman Guards. Little clawed feet scurried overhead: rats making free with our tiring rooms. As soon as my eyes were accustomed to the darkness, I crept forward along the passageway until it opened to a wilderness of trestles—the timbers that held up the stage, black against the fading light that fell from the open roof. Beyond them I could see the floor, still covered with mildewed rushes, and the lower edge of the balustrade that separated groundlings from the first gallery—all draped in ghostly silence like a corpse under a shroud. But near to hand lay signs of life.

A decent little habitation had been created under the stage, with a thin straw mattress laid on a wood pallet to keep it off the damp, a tattered quilt nailed to the trestles to hold back the drafts. There was even a hearth of bricks laid together, with the ashes of a fire on it, placed directly under the trap in the stage to let out the smoke. A pile of wood was carelessly stacked nearby. For a home in hell, it wasn't bad.

My plan was to offer Kit's brooch back to him and use it as leverage to open some sort of conversation—if he would talk to me, I might gain some idea what to do. While wondering how long to wait, I noticed the corner of a paper sticking out from under the bed. I lifted the mattress to reveal a collection of quartos—cheap copies of plays or poems that could be bought for a halfpenny at the stationers' shops on St. Paul's. Some of the plays were by Shakespeare: *Romeo and Juliet, Richard III.* A glimmer caught my eye from under the papers. Pushing them aside, I uncovered a thin gold chain and pulled it free. Looped on the chain was a gold signet ring set with a cluster of rubies, their splendor dulled in the gray light.

The other Cobham ring is still missing, Bartlemy had said.

I quickly dropped it, and the mattress. But a single sheet of paper shot out under the force, and I scrambled to recover it. Though my heart was still racing, I marked the lines of verse on the paper and edged toward the light at the rim of the stage, to make it out. It was the Robin and Marian ballad, handwritten, with a note scribbled across the top. Squinting, I read: "The upstart Malory may have supplanted you on stage, but you have a chance to prove yourself a man on another ground—"

"Ill met by moonlight," chimed a familiar voice. If I had jumped any higher, my head would have cracked the stage boards.

Trembling, I folded the paper and pushed it between the buttons of my doublet before turning around. The voice had come from the back of the theater, but all I could see when I looked that way was a reddish glow, bobbing toward me. Country folk speak of fairy fire in the forests at night, ducking and weaving as the spirits hold their revels. I felt my flesh prickle. "My faith! You make no more noise than a ghost!"

"A useful skill to know, when one's quarters are apt to be invaded." The light separated itself into bars and I saw it was only a common coal carrier. Gradually a face took shape behind it—eyes first, gleaming like caged coals.

"Kit—what are you doing here?"

He set the carrier upon his "hearth," then arranged a nest of kindling on the bricks and used a bent gardener's trowel to spoon the live coals on top. As a ribbon of smoke spiraled up he let down the trap overhead. "Should I not be the one to ask you that?"

"I . . . I happened to think of what you said, the other day, about living in 'hell,' and it just popped into my head. That this might be what you meant. I came because I have something that belongs to you."

Trying to compose myself, I fumbled among the effects in my purse and took out the black velvet pouch. I handed it to him, watching his face.

His eyes narrowed a fraction, but he gave no other sign as he took the pouch, opened it, and tilted out the silver crescent just enough to confirm what it was. Then he slipped it back, pulled the drawstring, and tossed it on the bricks as if it were of no more value than a potato. Not a touch, not a flicker of the agitation it provoked in him last June. And not a word of thanks to me, either. But then, he had something of much greater value under his mattress.

I swallowed, my throat suddenly dry. "What are you living on?"

"Bad ale, mostly." He leaned over to an open-topped keg and uncorked a bottle, taking a long swallow from it. "But I neglect my duty as a host. Will you have some?"

"I meant, how are you supporting yourself?"

"I know what you meant." His kindling had come to a blaze, so he set down the bottle and went about building a fire on top of it. The firewood was a mix of green twigs, rotted timbers, and bits of scaffolding that put out more smoke than heat while he fanned it with a tin plate. In the white belch of flame his cheekbones stood out like buttresses, his eyes red-rimmed and sunken. But there was an elegance of gesture in his hands, even while flicking a rat turd into the fire.

"You're being sought," I told him. "You're accused of murdering the Welsh Boy."

"I know." He laid the tin plate aside and took another swallow from the bottle.

"How? Where did you hear it?"

"On the street, of course. The flaming tongues of Rumor."

"But they're looking for you! How can you go about on the street without being caught?"

"Ah." He stroked his upper lip. "I've been *watched* all my life. But now I have become the *watcher*."

An odd tone in his voice made me sit up straighter. Something was not right with him; was it hunger, or drink, or had he slowly gone mad indeed? "And what does that mean?"

"Look at me: what do you see?"

"Well . . . a ruin."

"True! A wreck of my previous self. Who would know me now?"

"The constable would."

"I doubt that. He's looking for the chief boy player of London. Who has been supplanted."

This theme again. "*Not* by me. It was Davy who—"

"Davy is nothing. Robin's day is over and Gregory's ambition surpasses his ability. But you turned out to be the player." His pale eyes glittered. "I must compliment the way you played the country lad and tripped and stammered through your trial term and put us all off guard. You tricked me, sure."

"That's fool's talk. How came you to dream this fantasy that I was out to—" I stopped, remembering the taunting message I had just read about the "upstart Malory."

"I'm not saying you did it out of malice or design. It was

instinct, more like. You were a weasel and a toad on instinct. It comes easy to you."

I have been told this before—that one thing or another is easy for me—and swear I do not know where it comes from. "*None* of it was easy, then or now. I wasn't born to the stage, like you—"

"Born to the stage." The words clanged in his voice like cold metal. "You know what I was born to. The blood of generations of tradesmen runs in these veins."

"There's no taint in the blood of honest tradesmen—"

He stood up suddenly, stuck his head through the trap and hoisted himself to the stage. "Come up here," he commanded. Not knowing what to expect, I followed him more slowly. We sat on opposite ends of the trap, legs dangling into "hell," with the fire from below casting a diabolical light on Kit's gaunt features.

"Now *listen*," he said fiercely. "I'm going to tell you a story, and then you can tell me how honest is the stock I come from.

"I was the only child of my parents to survive, and I fancied they would die for me. I loved my father; we used to sing together as we sorted turnips or stacked cabbages. Singing was my joy then. But one day an agent from St. Paul's happened to hear us. . . ."

"Robin told me," I prompted, when his voice trailed off. "An agent from St. Paul's heard you, and thought you not only sounded like an angel but looked like one too, and secured you for the Chapel choir that very day. Robin speaks as though you were transported to the heavenlies, and you only seven."

"Six. I was only *six*. And the place I was transported had no heaven in it, except for the music in the Chapel. Imagine yourself at a tender age, being ripped away from everything you have ever known, carried off, and set down among strangers. Boys, no less—if you shut a crowd of boys together with not enough government, what you get is a herd of beasts. They set on me in the quarters that first night and hung me out the casement window by my feet. They do that to all the new boys, and rare is the child who doesn't piss all over himself, or worse. Later, a big chunk of an alto named Gabriel Vance carved his initials into my rump, to show I was not my own anymore.

"Three times I ran away, and every time my father brought me back. My mother begged to keep me home one more year, but he held firm. Because he's such an honest tradesman, you see: he had made a bargain. I was bought and paid for. I saw the money change hands."

I recalled Kit's father watching him in performance, standing afar off as though too humble to approach. Or too guilty. "Surely he didn't do it for the money. He must have thought it was best for you. Think of it: if you were in his place, and an agent from the Chapel told you that your only child is like a bright shining star in the firmament with a brilliant future, what would you say?"

He frowned, as though the question had not occurred to

268

him. "I would say . . . I would say, the boy is too young. Give him time. For God's sake, give him time. But time is the thing I never had.

"For once thrown into a viper's nest like the boys' hall in St. Paul's Chapel, you either fight your way to the top, or you sink under the heap. When I knew there would be no return, I set myself to go up, and fast. The road is clear marked: you work toward becoming the choirmaster's favorite, so he will give you solus parts, then you work to gain the attention of the voice instructor for the Chapel players and you work to catch the attention of men who matter. Along the way you hang a few little boys out of windows and carve your initials into a few rumps, so they'll know not to trifle with you. And once you've worked your way to the top of a children's company, you must begin plotting a way into a men's company, because by now you have gained the wit to know you won't be a boy forever."

He began speaking faster. "I got that, too—the best place in the best company. Shouts from the crowd, and commendations from the Queen. Messages from women who wanted to meet me—women of all stations, all ages, with flattering lips. They'll set upon you, too."

I felt my eyes widening, unsure whether I wished to follow this track. "Kit . . ."

"In short, I gained everything I could want from being the best boy player of London. Except, perhaps, a boyhood."

I was thinking it would have been better for him if he had

not been so talented, so good at his profession. Better if he had stumbled at the beginning and gained his feet slowly, rather than shooting out like an arrow from the bow. And much better if he had started older, as I had, with some sense already of who he was. But he had been playing parts from the age of eight, putting on roles and taking them off with frantic speed. Which one was Kit? Or was he all, or none?

I spoke slowly, feeling my way. "Whatever happened to you in the past is beyond changing. It's there . . . to learn from."

"True. I've learned that I'm done with the stage."

"But that would be throwing away all your talent, all you've achieved!"

"And what's that?"

"A reputation; a name. Christopher Glover, if I mistake not."

His gaze was fixed on the fire below. Now he looked up, and his eyes mirrored the light with a peculiar gleam. "You speak as if I would deny my name."

"What?" The words sounded familiar.

"But I am Prince of Wales and think not, Percy, to share in glory any more." Now I remembered: these were Hal's first words to Hotspur when they meet on Shrewsbury Field. "Two stars keep not their motion in one sphere. Nor shall one England brook a double reign."

I marveled at how well he knew the lines. My own recall was much less certain, but the opportunity to play Hotspur was too good to miss. "Nor shall it, Harry—for the hour is come, to . . . to . . . to end the one of us, and . . . Something about he wishes Hal had a name as bright as his so the glory of slaying him would be greater—"

"Never mind that." Kit leapt down into the trap, then tossed up two straight sticks, each the length of a sword. Scrambling out of the pit, he cried, "All the budding honors on thy crest I'll crop to make a garland for my head!"

I barely had time to catch the stick he threw at me. "Wait! I didn't come to fight you! And I don't remember what comes next."

"'I'll no longer brook thy vanities!'" Kit rushed at me, and I had to defend myself.

The sticks were mostly green, with some bend to them; otherwise they would have snapped in that first exchange. Gradually my alarm faded as I realized he wasn't trying to kill me—we were merely playing parts. Or perhaps not "merely"— there was a fever in him to play this particular part. As for me, I made up my mind to give back as good as I got before Hotspur fell. To my surprise, for the first several minutes we were evenly matched—either I had greatly improved, or he was out of practice. I warded all his strokes and got in a few of my own. "Well struck!" he panted once, then went on to shout out Falstaff's line, with gleeful abandon: "Well said, Hal! To it, Hal! Nay, you shall find no boys' play here!" Reddish light brimmed from the trap, casting a ghoulish glow as we circled around it.

It *was* no boys' play, even though we fought with sticks. He gave it his best, and so did I. In time, though, my treacherous right foot bent at the ankle and put me off balance, whereupon he slipped past my guard and poked me in the chest. Judging this a good time to fall, I stumbled back on one knee, crying, "Harry! . . . Um, Harry . . ."

"'They have robbed me of my youth,'" he prompted, very solemn.

"Right." Clutching my chest, I rolled to the floor. All I could remember of Hotspur's dying speech was the last line: "The cold hand of death lies on my tongue. No, Percy, thou art dust, and food for—"

Will Sly could die with a rattle in his throat that moved the coldest heart, but I simply choked on the last word and let my outstretched hand fall.

"—for worms, brave Percy," Kit said, and went on to speak Hal's eulogy over his fallen foe. "Fare thee well, great heart:

Ill-weaved ambition, how much art thou shrunk.

When that this body did contain a spirit

A kingdom for it was too small a bound.

But now two paces of the vilest earth

Is room enough . . .

Adieu, and take thy praise to heaven . . ."

I wondered why he had stopped, for he was speaking well—better, perhaps, than Augustine Phillips in the same part. "As for me . . ." Kit tossed the stick aside and spread his arms wide. "Happy garb, that ends my vile disgrace: Ye fates, bear me up to an honorable place!"

He crashed to the floor with his head near to mine and burst out laughing. I laughed too, partly from exhaustion, aware that we had never shared such a moment. Nor would we be doing it now, except that he was a little drunk and I more than a little confounded. Even after the laughter subsided, I felt him shake and pound the floor, from mirth or rage.

"You should have taken Hal's part," he said after a while. "I could do worse than die like Hotspur."

"Why don't you live like Hal? Cast aside your worthless companions and assume your rightful place."

"I cry you mercy." His voice thinned with sarcasm. "What if I am in my rightful place at this moment? Isn't my reputation wrecked on the shores of Hebrides, as Master Heminges would have it?"

A wintry wind breathed over us, drying the sweat on me as my flesh clenched up in a shiver. "You're only seventeen. And Hal overcame his reputation."

"At too high a cost," he shot back.

"*Too* high? Giving up the Boar's Head Tavern, to gain a crown?"

"Look you—" He propped himself on one elbow. "Hal is a figure in a play, made up to please the public. Besides, he's a hypocrite: not too proud to gad about with common folk but when the time comes, he'll scrub them off like lice." Kit lowered himself to the floor again. "My folly was to mistake copper crowns for gold. To think that acting noble makes one noble."

I gazed up at the stars, gathered close in the clear cold sky. The round opening of the Theater ceiling framed them like a picture: a little off-center swung Charlemagne's Wagon, circling the North Star. The constellation bent at an angle, reflecting Kit and me on the stage boards, our heads together like two stars in one sphere. "Few can wear crowns," I said slowly, "but anyone can wear honor."

"What is 'honor'? Can it set a leg, or an arm, or take away the grief of a wound? No; 'tis just a word."

Learned men claim the stars are indifferent to us. But gazing up at them, I fancied their vast hearts burning with a passion for honor. "Perhaps," I said slowly, "it's no more than a determination to be true to the best that God has put in you. Whatever the cost." Perhaps, in the confusion of parts he had played, Kit could no longer determine the best.

"I may have been wrong about your calling. You belong in a pulpit, not a stage."

I sighed. "Better than in a prison, like Falstaff."

"Spoken like a self-righteous prig. Falstaff makes no pretense, and in his company Hal can drop all his pretenses, too. It's a blessed relief."

"But suppose he means Hal no good? Suppose he has designs?"

"He is not a 'designer.' And his love is true."

"It may be . . . so long as it suits him." By now I knew we were speaking of Kit and Penny, not Hal and Falstaff. "Have you never had a friend turn against you?"

"I have never had a friend," he replied simply.

The statement was bare truth, naked and shivering: in the track he laid out for himself to climb to the top of every heap, there was neither room nor time for friendship. But if he counted Penny as such, he was deceived. "Kit," I said urgently, "I must speak plain—"

"You must go," he said, rising from the floor.

"You know who killed the Welsh Boy, don't you?"

He was walking toward the trap, a black shadow against the red glow. "I'll light your way out."

"It was Dark Tom! And he and Penny are partners—they set you up to be charged with murder!" He dropped below the stage and I followed. "Are you deaf? I speak naught but the truth!"

His only response was to pick up the coal carrier and lead me out through the passage, ignoring all protest. When we came to the outside hatch, he pushed it open and crouched to one side so I could pass. Our eyes met, in the sickly light of the coals. "Turn yourself in," I entreated. "I'll testify for you—you'll be cleared."

He jerked his head toward the opening. I climbed through it with an angry snort, then turned around. "The net is closing.

We know who wrote the Putrid Play and likely more than that. He's not so clever as he thinks."

Kit stood up and lifted the hatch to close it. "Perhaps you're not so clever as *you* think." Then he stepped down, and the door banged shut over his head.

A Fine Italian Hand

$\mathcal{I}$ went directly to the Mermaid Tavern, to avoid any hard thought. This was a mistake, for the next morning my head felt so stuffed that even simple thoughts could barely get through it. Most of the Company were in the same state, but by noon our brains had cleared enough to present a brilliant Part Two to a full house. For me the only snag occurred when I was getting laced up for Lady Percy and my gown ripped down the side.

Muttering about cheap thread, the dresser scanned the wardrobe racks and pulled out a rose-colored silk. "This 'un seems whole. Skin off that garment and I'll see what I can mend before Master Stewart gets a look." He exchanged gowns with me and helped me pull on the rose silk. Stifling a yawn, I adjusted my sleeve and felt a crackle in the cuff.

A piece of paper was hidden there. Pulling it out, I recognized the revised lines for Silvia that I had stuffed there on Monday, when we performed the Putrid Play. I nearly tossed it, but the writing looked familiar.

Once the dresser had grumbled his way down the stairs with the torn gown, I fumbled through my street clothes and found Kit's handwritten ballad. My eyes went at once to the line where Marian cries, "The scorpion whips of cruelty have stolen my child!" On the other paper, Silvia described Adrian's face as "o'er-raked with the scorpion whips of cruelty." Though the latter was written in haste, the slanted Italian style and peculiar flourishes appeared also on the ballad. The same hand, and the same bad poet, had written both.

When I met Bartlemy in St. Paul's the next morning, the first thing I said was, "If I could prove that Philip Tewkesbury wrote the ballads, would you let up on Kit?"

His eyes kindled, but his voice held steady as he replied, "Perhaps. What have you got?"

I showed him the papers and told briefly where they came from, and the look on his face was my reward. His customary expression is foxy and knowing, but as I talked, his mouth softened and his eyes sparkled like a child's when presented with some new toy. At the end, he so forgot himself as to take my head between his hands and kiss me resoundingly on the forehead.

"Leave off!" I cried, outraged. "I'm not your pet."

"Better than that," he said, smiling. "You are my fortune."

We stood in the south transept of the old cathedral, much like any two Londoners coming to an agreement. Since our Queen began her reign forty years ago, St. Paul's has been turned into a meeting place for every sort of business except religious—employers find help, smugglers find acceptors, lovers find each other. And Bartlemy had found priceless information, though not quite all that I had to give. I told him of Kit's hiding place, but not of Kit, nor of the ring I found in his possession. "By itself," Bartlemy said, "the fact that the same words appear in the play and the ballad proves nothing. Authors steal words from each other all the time. But the fact that both come from the same hand—oh, this is good."

"Is it good enough to leave Kit alone?"

"Pray, sit down." A row of benches furnished that part of the building, left over from its days as a house of worship. Bartlemy motioned me to a spot on the nearest bench and seated himself about two feet away, facing in the opposite direction. His head was down as he studied the lines of the ballad again. Anyone looking our way might remember me; never him. Just loud enough he murmured, "There's a great rivalry going on in court between my Lords Burghley and Essex. Raleigh, too—if he were choosing sides, he would choose Burghley, but he prefers to go his own way. The Brookes are of the Burghley faction."

"I know this," I said. "Everybody does."

"Hear me out: Essex attracts the young bloods at court, Tewkesbury among 'em. They all long for fame and glory, and they're right put out that Her Majesty has not been obliging enough to start any wars for that purpose. But there's a rebellion on the boil in Ireland, and Essex is begging her to send him there. If she does, he will take his favorites along with him as officers." He paused again, then said, "Young Tewkesbury is mad to go. What better way to prove his worth than by lining up the enemies of his hero, one by one, and humiliating them through these robberies—in a way that everyone suspects but none can prove?"

I turned this over in my mind. "Is this the theory you were working on? That these crimes were mainly a ploy to attract the attention of Essex and advance the fortunes of—"

"Of one young fool of high birth and not enough money. Tewkesbury fit that description best, to my mind. We suspected someone at court all along, because whoever was planning the robberies had an intimate knowledge of where each target was likely to be at a given time. But my master has been reluctant to pull any gentleman aside, at least without evidence. And we've found precious little of that. Until now." He looked at me so fondly I feared he might kiss me again.

"So you can arrest Tewkesbury and bring the business to an end."

"Not yet."

"But you have proof!"

"A question: you found this copy of the ballad on Thursday night. Why did you wait until Friday night to get word to me?"

"Because— It's no light matter, to inform on a fellow player."

"Could it also be because you met and talked with the player?"

Lord, he was sharp. I looked away, but could not lie.

"Even though you knew," Bartlemy persisted, "that you were giving him a chance to pack up and find another hiding place." After a moment, I nodded. "Why are you protecting him?"

The only answer was that Kit had somehow entrusted himself to me, for reasons I did not understand and certainly could not explain. "I'm not. I mean—I begged him to give himself up, but that's a decision he must make."

"To comply with the law? Is that a 'decision,' or a duty?"

"Isn't it plain he's not a criminal?" My voice broke on the last word.

"He is plainly an accomplice."

"But he didn't pose as Marian for them, even though they brought great pressure to bear. Isn't that worth something?"

"Then why doesn't he turn himself in? If his hands are so clean, why does he fear the law?"

"Well *perhaps,*" said I, with a sarcastic curl on that word, "he knows that the law will come down harder on him than it will on the gentle Philip Tewkesbury. I handed you the proof you need to charge the real culprit. But wait—Essex may be offended. Isn't that what most concerns you and your master?"

To judge by his face, I had hit a sore spot. "What concerns me and my master does *not* concern you. But you should understand that we're not done. Steel yourself, I pray—you may have to bear a little more of my loathsome company." He flung his knitted scarf around his neck, rose, and marched away so stiffly I might have thought I had hurt his feelings—if he had any feelings to hurt.

Starling, once she had heard all, believed I should surrender my knowledge of the ring I had found under Kit's mattress: "Holding stolen property is a *crime.*" Indeed, I said, the clearest proof of Kit's guilt yet. And exactly why I could not report it: because Kit was not a criminal. "Then what do you call one who commits crimes?" she demanded. This point was hard to counter directly, so we circled the theme more than once, our conversation ending when she threw up her hands in disgust. "This is wrong!"

"Perhaps—but pray keep it to yourself," I charged her.

"Don't fear me for that—but it's for your sake, not his. What do you intend to do?"

"What *can* I do? Only wait. If Kit has a change of heart, he knows where I am."

She sniffed. "Little hope for that, I think."

Late the following week a clammy wind blew out of the northwest, dragging a series of heavy rains in its wake. On the next Monday, after a downpour had interrupted our performance, we set about some housekeeping chores. Master Stewart put us apprentices to work at a long table in the back of the tiring room, sorting costumes: some for the ragpicker, some to the keeping room for mending, and others to be brushed up in preparation for our appearance at court.

That very day an engraved document had arrived from Whitehall, embossed with the seal of the Lord Chamberlain, formally and officially inviting Lord Hunsdon's Men to perform for Her Majesty during the two weeks after Christmas. So either the Lord Chamberlain had decided to forgive us for Sir John Oldcastle and the Putrid Play, or Her Majesty had simply overruled him. Good news, either way, but Robin was in one of his fretting moods. "I fear we won't have a stage when we come back from Whitehall. Our agreement with the Curtain is only good to the end of the year."

"Then it may be time for threats," said Gregory. "Tell the Queen to build us a new theater, else Falstaff dies in the next play."

Robin ignored this. "One of the hired men told me that Giles Allen means to tear down the Theater and sell the lumber, come spring. Can he do that?"

"If that were true," said I, "Richard Burbage would be

breathing fire. But he seems almost cheerful these days. I'm sure he has somewhat in mind."

"Aye," Robin agreed. "Retirement."

"Look, lads!" Gregory called. I looked, and a little cry escaped me. He had slipped on a pair of beaded yellow sleeves and struck a pose, singing, "In yellow sleeves to honor his maid, he rides far afield with the beauteous lady—"

"Where did you find those?" I asked, a shade too quickly.

"Why, here at the bottom of the court pile."

From the other end of the table, Master Stewart frowned. "I've been searching for 'em of late. They don't belong there, nor on thy twiggy arms. Put 'em on the pile to be steamed and stuffed."

Gregory obeyed, musing aloud. "Yellow sleeves, black and gold . . . By the bye, did that black satin doublet we lost last summer ever turn up?"

"Nay," muttered Master Stewart. "With all this shuffling between stages, one of the dolts at the Swan may have packed it away in their own wardrobe." Master Stewart was the most wonder-less man I have ever known. If a night-tripping fairy had visited him while he slept and left a perfect teardrop pearl hanging from his nose, he would have said, "Fancy that—my snot has calcified."

But if he was blind to coincidence, Gregory was not. "Strange, how things disappear from our wardrobe and show up in the ballads."

I made a vague reply, all the while calculating feverishly. If those were the very sleeves last worn by Robin Hood—and I had no doubt they were—then who had returned them? If it was Kit, then how had they come into his hands, unless by the last man to wear them, Peregrine Penny himself? I happened to glance out the window, and what I saw made my heart turn over.

Five men led by Richard Burbage were slogging through the rain toward the old Theater. Shakespeare made one, and Heminges another, but the other two were strangers. My first thought was that they were court officials, looking for Kit.

"Pray excuse me for a moment, Master Stewart?" He nodded without looking up from his work, and I dashed out, followed by Gregory's quizzical eyes.

Master Burbage had somehow obtained a key; when I arrived, the side door stood open and all five men were gathered upon the stage, below the overhanging "heavens" that gave them a little protection from the rain. I paused at the door to listen. Richard Burbage's voice carried famously well, and since he did most of the talking, I soon learned that the building, not Kit, was his subject. He was pointing out the structure of the roof timbers and the three galleries stacked one upon the other.

With their attention diverted, I ducked quickly under the stage. Their conversation covered my movement as I crept deeper into "hell."

Of course I did not expect to find anyone there, but even the wooden pallet had disappeared. A scattering of bricks and some gouges in the ground marked the former habitation— that was all. Had I flushed Kit out of his den, only to chase him back to Penny and Tom? The reappearance of the yellow sleeves made me wonder.

A rat brushed my foot, and I stifled a yelp. The men had climbed to the musicians' gallery for a better view; I heard Richard Burbage say, "Mind your step—the railing is loose. As I told you, Master Street, time is of the essence. With all your crew, how long might it take you to finish?"

An unfamiliar voice replied, "For the first, a mere matter of days. For the second, I must make a closer examination of the building before I give an account. . . ."

They retreated into the tiring room, leaving me an opportunity for escape. While scurrying under the boards, it occurred to me that Master Street might be a carpenter, and the Company wished him to build a new theater elsewhere. A simple and obvious solution to their problem, except that I knew from John Heminges it would take more money than they had. Far more pressing, to my mind, was where Kit might be. I paused at the door, staring at the rain with a gloomy apprehension that my effort to "help" him had only sunk him deeper in trouble.

Night came on early these days, and within an hour we were headed home, Robin and I following Masters Condell and

Heminges according to custom. Just inside Bishopsgate we paused for the men to bargain with a hot-pastry vendor. A few hardy musicians strolled about in the drizzle, and I listened as always for the Robin Hood tune. But over a month had passed since the ambush of "Sir Flatter"; it seemed the gentleman bandit had retired, or else he was nursing his wounds in some remote cave. Robin and I wandered over to watch the puppet motion on the south end of the gate.

The tone of the performance had changed. Instead of Punch and Judy tossing the baby, the puppets were acting a tale of thwarted love, wherein an elegant gentlewoman in purple silk rejected a young poet. A musician with a recorder piped the sad strains of an old ballad called "The Cold Lady," while the puppet master managed to make the squeaky voices of his actors provoke sympathy. Perhaps it was just the thing for a gloomy November day, for it held the crowd spellbound, and a kitchen maid nearby wept into her apron. Too sad for me, however—I was pulling Robin away to rejoin our master when a small boy ran out of nowhere and knocked into me. Recalling Davy, I felt for my purse, just before he slipped a piece of paper into my hand. "By your leave, sir," he gasped by way of apology, and ran on.

Turning aside, I unfolded the paper to a square smaller than my palm. The message inside was very brief, written in the overly careful hand of one who does not write much, or only recently learned how: "7 ante. BF"

In the south transept of St. Paul's at seven o'clock the next morning, on the same bench as before, Bartlemy said, "I finally got in to search the court records at Fleet Prison. The person who paid Glover's bail was not Philip Tewkesbury."

"It wasn't? Who else could it be?"

"Lady Tewkesbury, Baroness of Wellstone. Lord Philip's mother. After very much searching, I found not only the record, but also the message she wrote to the magistrate. The hand is the same as that of the papers you gave me."

In the long silence that followed, I marveled at how a single new fact can make all manner of odd pieces and recollections fall into place, and you wonder why the sense of it never occurred to you before.

I recalled the day a token was delivered, and the effect it had had, and the mockery in that more recent message that compared Kit to me, and his voice saying, "Women—all stations, all ages, with their flattering lips . . ." And what was the last thing he had said to me, when I claimed to know the author of the play? "Perhaps you're not so clever as you think."

"I see."

"Do you? Do you see clear enough to remember anything else? Such as when or how he may have met the lady?"

I shook my head. "It may have been during our last court season, almost a year ago. He changed after that, in some

288

ways. He used to roam abroad at night with Robin, but last spring he drew more into himself. If he went out, he went alone. Someone sent him a silver brooch last June—on the very day he was dismissed, in fact."

"Describe it," he demanded. After I did, he shook his head in exasperation. "This is the sort of thing you might have told me last summer."

"But it was common for ladies to send him tokens—and we didn't even know it was a lady. What sort of person is she?"

"A widow, twice over. About thirty-five, I should say, but looks younger. Philip is her only child. She came to London about a year ago to advance his fortunes at court, then returned to her home in Herefordshire for the summer. Now she is back in London but not so evident as before. She has made a bit of a reputation for herself."

"As a beauty? Or a poet?"

He shrugged. "She's fair enough, though too thin for my taste. Lord Philip resembles her. *He* is supposed to be the poet. She is known mainly as one who pushes too hard for what she wants."

"And what is that?"

"Three things." Bartlemy was picking at his chin, irritably. The joy I had given him with the handwritten ballad two weeks ago seemed to be all used up. "The most important would be the advancement of her son. The second thing might be revenge, for the family has fallen on hard times—six years ago they lost a deal of property in a lawsuit brought against them by none other than William Brooke. So they are sour on both Brookes and everyone associated with them. Her third wish, I reckon, would be to see her plays performed by the finest theater company in London.

"So look how it might have happened. When the finest theater company in London performs at court, she draws out the chief boy player for . . . conversation." Noticing the look on my face, he added, "I mean no more than that. She may have flattered and led him on, but she'd not compromise her position for him. I think she introduced him to her son, and they become friends, after a fashion. Perhaps Lord Philip met Penny and told his mother about him, and a bold plan began to take shape—the sort of stagey plan a playmaker would devise. By it the lady could get her revenge by humiliating her enemies and at the same time endear her son to one of the most powerful men at court, namely Essex."

"And wreck Kit's life in the meantime," I concluded. "Well? Is her work accomplished?"

"I fear not. Philip has slipped in the great man's esteem."

"Why? Oh—because of the Putrid Play?"

"The what?" When I explained that title, he nodded. "Very like, from what I hear. But the young man must redeem himself quickly. Essex has just received permission from the Queen to put down the rebellion in Ireland. He's making a list of friends to go with him, and at last count, Tewkesbury's not included."

"So—"

"There may be another robbery in hand—or a thing more sinister."

"Then why are you waiting? You've found your plotters and have your proof—arrest them."

"It's . . . not so simple as that." Bartlemy was rolling and unrolling the edge of his cloak between his thumb and forefinger. His irritation had become something else: a distinct unease, of a sort that I had never seen in him. "The perpetrators— Penny and Watts and Glover—have made themselves scarce, and we can't just arrest the Baron and Baroness of Wellstone."

"Oh. You'd throw Kit to the wolves, but we must forbear to touch the gentlefolk. He's no *perpetrator*—he's merely caught in the middle. Penny and Tom are wily enough to find cover and Lord Philip and his mother will go free. Kit bears the brunt, though he is the least guilty. What makes you better than those hypocrites you detest at court? You're just like them, advancing yourself by any means at hand—"

He grabbed a handful of my cloak and gave a hard shake to cut off my tirade. I was a little surprised at my own outburst, but this resentment of gentlemen, who could command bad plays and use our stage for personal duels, had been long building in me.

"Listen close to what I have to tell you," Bartlemy said in a voice that was absolutely cold. "It's not to justify myself, but to soothe your delicate feelings. The truth is, my master finds himself in a predicament. The Lord Chamberlain, who employed him, is gravely ill. Chances are, he will die. Did you know that?" I shook my head, too stunned to speak. "That means that someone else will be the next Lord Chamberlain, and chances are it will be someone of the Essex faction. My master wishes to see which way the wind will blow before causing an upset at court. This does not mean that anyone will escape. But if it can be done at all, he wants to catch the common criminals first, in the act of whatever scheme my lady cooks up, and use them to implicate their betters. Do you follow my meaning?"

I nodded, though sullenly. He went on, "This approach does not please me, but my master is my master. We will watch Lord Philip's movements, and wait a little, and make what use we can of Kit Glover."

"Why can't you leave him alone? What do you hold against him?"

"To the first question, I cannot. He's guilty of aiding and abetting highwaymen. To the second . . . I hold nothing against him. I've watched him for years; he is one of the few who have shown me what virtue and tenderness and nobility can be. True, that was all on stage, but seeing it there has helped me to recognize it in life."

Starling had told me there was more to him than met the eye, but virtue, tenderness, and nobility were not what I would have expected to find under that hard surface—or even the desire for them. "I need not tell you he is in peril," Bartlemy concluded. "His best hope is with us. If he surrenders himself, he can expect every mercy. If not, only God can save him. For depend on it, something will happen, and it will be soon."

Days passed, then weeks. November drizzled
into December, as icicles lengthened from the eaves and
shoes sank ankle-deep in the muddy streets, and the
spicy smell of mulled wine wafted from every tavern
door. Bartlemy's warning lost its edge as days slipped by
and nothing happened.

The Company drew up a list of plays that we could
perform at the Curtain with our eyes closed and bent
their energies toward preparing for the court season.
That was all the talk—no word about Giles Allen or the
sad fate of our old Theater, or the man Richard Burbage
had called "Master Street." The Company was keeping its
own secrets, as I was keeping mine, though surely they
had not so much to hide as I did.

Performances became irregular, subject to rain or
snow. On canceled days we often found ourselves at the
Curtain anyway, or in an unused hall at Blackfriars,

practicing the plays set for Whitehall. Both parts of *Henry IV* were included, at the Queen's request. Ben Jonson's new play made another (even though the author, having narrowly escaped the hangman, was now serving a prison term for manslaughter). A tragedy and a comedy rounded the bill, all rehearsed until we knew them like our own names.

Then, when I had almost made up my mind he was gone for good, "Robin Hood" reappeared.

Starling first heard the ballad sung among the fish vendors on Thames Street and immediately hurried to St. Paul's churchyard to buy a copy. A whiff of dried fish still clung to it as I scanned the lines that afternoon. I read it twice, then said, "This is pure fantasy."

"No, I'm certain it tells of a real event. It's like a riddle—you don't understand it until you see the catch."

"We know the catch. We know who is writing these, and we have a good notion why. But this is too bold for the purpose." The ballad told how Robin and his men kidnapped the Sheriff of Nottingham, nobly entertained him in their forest glen, and finally ransomed him for a bottle of nut-brown ale—"For we fear that is all you are worth, tra-la."

Ha-ha, laughed the Londoners, always eager to see some silken snob land splat in the mud. But it was one thing to rob a gentleman of his money and jewels and escape under cover of darkness, and quite another to steal the gentleman himself. Even if the Tewkesburys were foolish enough to try, Penny and

Watts would not gamble a hangman's noose for a bottle of ale.

"The streets are abuzz," Starling went on. "Everyone is delighted to see Robin Hood back. There's a strong vote for the Lord Mayor serving as Sheriff of Nottingham, though another opinion says it must be someone at court. I heard at least one argument: Mistress Browne the fishwife says it's a ruse to distract us from the real crime, and her husband claims there are no crimes at all—the whole ballad series is a trick played on gullible citizens. When I left, she was threatening him with a swordfish."

"Do you have an opinion?"

"Not yet." She tugged the paper out of my grasp. "But the answer is hidden in the text, depend on it. I'll have another look."

She did not take long to find it—once spotted, the "catch" stood out like a rusty nail. Supper was over, and the little children had been blessed and sent to bed when Starling joined me on the window seat at one end of the great room. I felt the excitement in her and knew she had made a discovery. "Look at this," she said, thrusting the ballad at me. "The third stanza, second line. What do you see in it?"

I read aloud, "'But under Rob's guardance he late entered York.' I see a line awkwardly phrased."

"Very true: either written too hastily, or too carefully. Look at the first letters only."

I lined up the letters in my head: B-u-r-g-h-l-e-y. "Lord Burghley? But that can't be."

Her green eyes were sparkling with excitement. "Why not?"

"He's the Queen's Secretary, her right hand."

"And everyone knows he's the chief rival of Essex."

"Well." I waved a hand impatiently. "This takes rivalry too far. They may as well kidnap the Queen herself."

"But suppose kidnapping is not what they have in mind? Suppose they only mean to . . . steal his dog. That would be insult without grave risk."

I scanned the lines again. "There's no reference to a dog here. No, wait—if you rearrange some of the letters of 'Nottingham' you get . . . 'hog.' They mean to kidnap his hog? Oh, cruel plot! Foul stain! Dastardly—"

She snatched the paper back. "Tomorrow is Sunday. I think we should take a walk after church."

Early the next morning she sent off a message. Later that day, as we took our apparently aimless stroll in the public gardens surrounding Drapers' Hall, not far from St. Paul's, Bartlemy joined us as quietly as a wraith. If I had to meet him, I had rather it be without Starling, but she claimed the right to share her own discovery. If that was all she wanted, Bartlemy's response must have disappointed her.

"Aye," he said, after hearing her out. "We saw the Secretary's name in that line, right off."

I did not look at her face, but allowed myself a secret smile. She had placed herself between us and likely fancied the picture of a fair maid taking in the gardens with her two squires—no matter that the wind blew raw and cold, the gardens had withered, and not many Londoners were out. "Has anything happened yet?" she asked.

"Nothing has happened, though the Secretary has been warned and there's a guard about him."

"Starling," I remarked, "thinks they may kidnap Burghley's dog to make their point."

"Does she?" Bartlemy's voice lightened with interest. "We never thought of that. He has a dog—a little pug that belonged to his wife. She died not long ago, so the dog means more to him than common. That's good. We'll follow it."

I felt a pain in my ankle—a little sideways kick from Starling. "But," I persisted, "you'll agree that there can be no intention of kidnapping the Secretary himself?"

"Nay, of course not. Too great a risk for an uncertain gain."

I delivered my own little kick, as she asked, "What about Tewkesbury's actions? Are you watching him?"

Bartlemy shrugged. He seemed distracted, as though his thoughts were elsewhere. "Lord Philip has been a model of faultless behavior."

"Any signs of Robin Hood and his Merry Men?" I asked.

"Only the ballad, which hints that wounded arms are healed, fears are quelled, and all stand ready for we know not what." Abruptly he reached inside his cloak. "I have a thing to show you."

He took out a folded handkerchief and unwrapped it. There on his palm lay a silver crescent moon within a circle, ornamented with a single pearl. "Recognize it?"

I nodded, speechless. The thing was like a bad penny, always coming back. "Where did you—"

"Pawned. Probably for food or firewood. He must be in dire straights—he's even stopped leaving shirts for his mother to wash." Bartlemy tapped the brooch. "If money from this is feeding him, it won't last much longer. He wouldn't have got more than two shillings for it."

I longed to ask if the Cobham ring had likewise appeared in a pawn shop, but could not risk bringing up that subject. I felt Starling's eyes on me, demanding: Tell him about the ring. *Tell him.* But I could not.

Bartlemy wrapped up the brooch and tucked it away again. "Remember: If you have any notion that would help us find him, it would be in his interest to tell." I shook my head, quite honestly, and we parted company soon after with very little wisdom gained.

On Thursday I was sent home early from the Curtain to inform Mistress Condell that her husband had invited some of the players home for supper. Passing through Bishopsgate, I noticed a small crowd around the puppet motion. The "Ballad of the Cold Lady" had drawn an audience even in the chill and the thickening dark. As I came closer, the climax was playing out, the young poet sinking before the lady who had cruelly broken his heart. His dying speech was rather eloquent, for a puppet. He died with a rose extended toward her, in a pathetic gesture that should have stricken the proudest heart. The cold beauty picked up this last token (or rather the puppet master did—I could see his fingers behind the black curtain, pinching the stem), and shrilled, "Good riddance to poetical milksops! Who'll be next?"

This made a curious end to a tragic story, but the audience seemed to expect it. Amid titters and chuckles they glanced about. The last thing I expected was for the paper rose to come sailing from the puppet stage and strike me on the shoulder. Bewildered, I picked it up. A couple of boys nearby howled with laughter and pushed me forward until I was only three feet from the lady, her painted wooden face turned coyly aside. "So," said she, in a voice that managed to be intimate and comic at the same time. "Do you wish to woo me?"

"Well, no—"

"Nay, lad!" shouted several voices in the audience. "Play the game—it's excellent sport!"

What game? thought I. But since I was holding the rose, there seemed to be no harm in giving it back. Her little hand, guided by a thin black stick, nimbly caught hold of the stem as the audience sighed with pleasure. "Will you meet me, Hotspur?"

This brought a new round of laughter, for I am short and blush easily—hardly cast in the warrior mold. Why would the lady choose that particular term to mock me with? A curtain of black gauze hid the puppet master; I could not see him, but he could see me.

I have become the watcher, Kit told me, the last time we met. And the last time we met, I had played Hotspur's part. "Ah—ah—" I swallowed, and managed to say, "I'll meet you." Catcalls and whistles scattered through the crowd. "When?"

"At midnight, on Holy Innocents' Day," she replied. That would be 28 December—two days before our court season began.

"He'll not be innocent for long!" a stout carrier guffawed.

"She likes you, lad," a woman remarked, nodding at me. "Most of the young ones are cut down to size by now."

As the noise died down, I asked, "Where will I find you?"

"In hell!" she screamed, and disappeared in a peal of devilish laughter.

This abrupt ending disappointed the audience. "Hah! I've seen her far cleverer." Apparently the Cold Lady was famous for putting down "suitors" with bawdy jokes that tickled everyone except the victim. But I, needless to say, was not disappointed—merely aghast.

No doubt of it: some business was afoot on 28 December at the old Theater. The business might well be the latest—if not last—adventure of Robin Hood, and I had received a special invitation to attend. Whether this was an honor or a trap, I knew not. Kit could not have expected to find me in his audience that very day. The invitation must have been an impulsive gesture. Was he in trouble and seeking my help at last? Or was he insane and seeking revenge?

One thing sure: I would not hesitate to inform Bartlemy. The next morning I was pacing the south transept in St. Paul's while my breath made little wads of cloud on the cold air. A couple of unemployed laborers approached to ask hopefully whether I was hiring, but Bartlemy failed to show—for the first time ever, now that I truly needed him. After half an hour I could wait no more, but hurried on to the Curtain, in a torment over what to do. Master Condell had begun to give me doubtful looks when I requested time for "private business"; strictly speaking, an apprentice was not supposed to have private business, much less the pressing, life-or-death sort that I had blundered into.

That afternoon, midway through a cold, sparsely attended performance of *Every Man in His Humor*, church bells all over London began ringing. We did not know the reason until the play ended, and the owner of the Curtain arrived to inform us that William Brooke, the Lord Chamberlain, had died. Though murmurs of "God rest his soul" scattered through the Company, I sensed a lightening among them, a hope that Brooke's successor might be more friendly to us and we could once more wear the proud title of Lord Chamberlain's Men.

For me, the news carried an entirely opposite meaning, confirmed when Starling waited at St. Paul's the next morning and Bartlemy again failed to appear. "He must be kept away on business," she declared. "I'm sure he would come in a minute otherwise."

"What if his master no longer *has* any business?" I pointed out. "You know who John Clement was working for. If his employer has died, what happens to the employment?"

"I'll go back to St. Paul's tomorrow," she promised. "He'll be there. He must be there, otherwise you'll be thinking of going to the Theater by yourself that night. You're not thinking that, are you?"

I did not answer; she knew me too well.

The Christmas season was rushing upon us and all business would soon be suspended for the great festival. Shops closed, law courts disbanded, and even the watch laid off their watching to some degree, though the season of peace and good will was not always peaceful. After the holy observance of Christmas Day came the twelve days of Epiphany, with increasing disorder in the wrong parts of London. At the Inns of Court the scholars held riotous celebrations on Twelfth Night, presided over by a "Lord of Misrule," during which they insulted their professors, drank the wine cellars dry, and broke the furniture. All of which seems a curious way for law students to behave, but consistent after all with the wild school days described by Justice Shallow in Part Two. The common folk were only too glad to follow their example, and Lords of Misrule reigned in the streets even before Twelfth

Night. Anyone who meant mischief could do it easily under cover of merriment.

Two days after Christmas, Master Condell, Robin, and I arrived home from a rehearsal in Blackfriars to find the household in an uproar. It appeared that a pack of ruffians had lured Roland, that happy, trusting hound, out of the gate—and strangled him.

The family and servants were at dinner when it happened, so none had actually seen or heard the culprits. They assumed that such a cruel, aimless prank could only be the work of cruel, aimless boys taking advantage of the holiday carelessness to work their mischief. I knew better once I saw the dog laid out beside the garden, stiff as a pike, with a doubled string around its neck.

"It must have been Tom," Starling said grimly. "We know his work. And it appears he knows you. He must have spied you with Kit when Davy was killed. Richard! Do you suppose he's been watching you all this time?"

We sat at one end of the table in the great room. Over by the fireplace, Master Condell attempted to cheer his grieving children with tales of Sir John Falstaff. Since Fat Jack made the perfect example of a Lord of Misrule, I would have chosen a more comfortable subject for mirth—especially with Captain Penny and his associates laying so heavily on my mind.

"I don't know." I thought it was more likely that Tom had taken cover with Captain Penny, but supposition was worth very little in the face of a threat like this. "Still . . ."

"You are *not* going to tell me you intend to be at the old Theater at midnight tomorrow. Are you?"

"I don't know."

"How can you even think of it? This well-named Dark Tom *knows who you are.* If he caught you meddling in this, he'd kill you as sure and quick as he did Roland."

"I know."

"And whose side is Kit on, after all? How could he tell you that something is afoot at the Theater unless someone told him—like his lady love, or Captain Penny?"

"I don't know."

"Now you have that look on your face that tells me you're going to do as you please, no matter what I say."

"I know."

"You *don't* know!" she burst out. "You can't see yourself."

Her voice cracked so sharp that others in the room stared at us. "Starling's mad at Rich-ard," chanted young Ned, in a singsong voice.

"*That's* not news," sniffed Thomas. "Come, father, tell us what answer Fat Jack made to the Chief Justice this time."

I turned around on the bench, my back to the room, and Starling turned also. After a moment, I said, "I must do this. He asked me to, and he's never asked anything of me."

"But suppose he means you harm?"

"I can't believe that. Rivals can be as close as friends.

We're not much alike, but we've shared the same space, the same sounds and smells, the same ambitions, even spoken the same lines. Our paths have met, and crossed, and . . ." And he's never had a friend, I thought—but did not say.

After a moment, she said, "That's not very clear."

"I know."

"Well—" A gusty sigh. "What do you propose to do?"

I stopped short of saying, I don't know, though it would have been mostly true. "We leave for Whitehall in three days. The Company will run our legs off all day tomorrow. After bedtime Robin should drop off like a stone, and I will be able to slip out to the Theater. After that . . ." I shrugged. "Tomorrow, you must try once more to reach Bartlemy. Tell him where I'm going, and when, and he may judge what to do about it."

She was silent for some time, which made me wonder if she was concocting a plan of her own. "You promise this is only a spying mission?"

"Of course! I know that place like my own hand. I can hide and not be seen."

"Very well. But if you get yourself killed, I will never forgive you."

As I predicted, the entire Company worked frantically all the next day from dawn to dusk, finishing up rehearsals and packing costumes and properties to be taken to Whitehall. Also as predicted, Robin could barely keep his eyes open during supper, and soon after prayers he dragged himself up to bed. The Condell boys followed directly, then I, yawning elaborately and ignoring all the anxious looks Starling sent my way. Even though we had had very little chance to talk, I knew that she had made several attempts to reach Bartlemy, all unanswered.

Once in my room I dressed for warmth, wrapping an extra length of wool around my legs before pulling on my nether-stocks and shrugging on a knitted waistcoat under my shirt. Then I lay down, shivering under the coverlet as a watchman passed below, crying, "Nine o'clock! Look to your lock, your fire, and your light; and so, good night."

I closed my eyes, expecting a long wait until eleven.

"**E**leven o'clock! Look to your lock . . ."

My eyes flew open, and for a moment I stared upward as the ceiling beam over my head took a shadow shape. The remnants of a dream scattered like a flock of ravens. We were at the old Theater, Kit and I, in the upstairs tiring room, getting ready to go on the stage. But it seemed we were the only players, and the house was filling with angry beasts. I felt as I often did when my lines were not perfect, or I wasn't confident of the play: as if a mouse in my stomach were clawing to get out. Kit appeared as cool as ever, but his fingertips were bleeding and I knew he felt exactly as I did. He stroked a line of blood on his cheek for color, and then handed the glass to me. I took it with apprehension, dreading what image might appear. But when I held the glass up to my face, I saw—nothing.

". . . and so, good night!" The watchman's call faded

as he moved on toward Lothbury Street. Slowly I sat up, took a deep breath to still my unquiet heart, eased out of the bed, and cracked open the casement window.

All the main gates of the city are barred at night, but smaller ones remain unlocked to allow for messages and urgent business. Moorgate was one of these and only a short walk from my master's house. It was seldom used because it opened to Moorfields, a dank and swampy stretch of ground. On this night, with not even a watchman standing by, I walked right through. Then my difficulties began.

I had hoped that the path across Moorfields would be frozen hard enough to walk on, but only the hollows held firm. A crust of rime covered the ridges, and when I stepped on them, I sank into miry mud. Stepping over them was risky too, as I could easily misjudge my footing in the stingy light of the half moon. Twice I slid into unseen hollows and soaked my legs, and once I tripped and fell to my knees. When the looming outlines of the old Theater finally rose into view, I felt my bones quaking hard enough almost to pull apart.

The midnight chimes had not yet struck, and no one appeared to be lurking outside. Reaching the high ground of spiky grass, I made my way to the hatch at the back of the building, then paused to feel around it. The padlock had been removed. This might mean that "hell" was occupied; I put an ear to the wood and listened for voice or movement. Hearing none, I slowly lifted the hatch on its oiled hinges and slid into utter darkness, letting it down behind me.

My teeth were chattering so loud I could hear nothing else for some time. My wool cloak made a pod, and I a quivering row of peas drawn together for warmth against the cold cellar wall. Many moments passed before the chattering lessened and another noise crept into my ears: a steady crunch on the other side of the wall, as though some unimaginable creature were chomping through the partition to get at me.

A cold night and a perilous mission can make sinister even the homeliest details—I soon realized it was only a horse munching up grass stems. The noise came from the east side of the building, opposite the road, where an animal could be picketed out of sight. Another sound came clearer to my ears: a regular treading of boards, first in one direction, then another. Someone was pacing the stage, back and forth. It wasn't Kit—I knew his walk—but as I listened, other small sounds began to creep out: a chink of spurs, a creak of leather, a sharp, impatient sigh.

And then I heard hoofbeats clattering on the Shoreditch Road, and the whinny of the grazing horse as it lifted its head to greet the newcomers.

A meeting was at hand; I must get out of the way as quickly as possible. There was another hatch nearby, an access from the tiring rooms for players due to make an ascent from hell or the grave. I crouched along the narrow passage-

310

way, pushing up with my hands, panic rising until I felt the boards give way over my head. The hinge squealed—I froze until the occupant of the stage shouted down into "hell" and covered the noise. "Ho! Late as always!"

I pulled myself through the narrow trap into the tiring room as the new arrivals entered. "Not so loud, my lord," Captain Penny wheezed in reply. His voice, even at half its normal volume, carried easily through the hatch I had just opened. While Penny and at least one companion made their way toward the stage, I cut across the tiring room, headed for the stairway to the upper level. I aimed to get to the musicians' gallery, from which I would be able to hear anything that took place on stage and perhaps even see a bit of it, all at small risk of being seen. While climbing the steep and narrow stairway, I spread my feet wide to tread only on the outside edges. My gain was a near-soundless ascent and I crept out upon the gallery feeling like a master of stealth—Bartlemy could hardly have done it better. The gallery extended a little over the stage and the railing was supported by balustrades. In daylight anyone looking up would see me between them, but at this hour, if I kept still, I should attract no more notice than a post.

Below me Philip Tewkesbury was saying, "This meeting place does well for security, Captain. But it lacks for warmth somewhat."

Penny heaved himself through the opening of the trap and onto the stage, panting with the effort. "A hazard of the profession, my lord. Those who live on the windy side of the law are apt to feel a chill, betimes."

"Are we all met? Tom, is that you?"

"Aye, sir." The flat, hard voice sent a shiver down my spine.

"The last I saw you, Tom, you bested me in a fencing match. I've been practicing since—in time, perhaps we can go another round."

"At your pleasure, my lord."

"After we've accomplished our present business, of course. Captain—is there still no word from Kit?"

"None, sir. Should there be?"

"I like not his being at large, knowing what he does."

"We've done what we can to silence him, sir, short of cutting his throat. If that is what you wish—"

"No! No—I've said no bloodshed, all along. I would just rest easier knowing his whereabouts."

I was wondering about that myself. I had expected a meeting, but if Kit was here, he had become one of the stage posts, still and silent. And if he was not here, then why was I?

"Have you asked your mother, my lord?" Penny suggested, most polite.

I heard a gasp and a whisper of steel as the young man went for his sword. Then he slid it back in the scabbard, with a snap. "I have told you," said he, in the cold, superior voice of one to the manor born, "not to mention my mother. I will not tell you again."

After a murmured apology and a brief pause, he spoke again, in a petulant tone. "She was only showing kindness to him. He took it for more than it was."

"Indeed, my lord."

"Her life has two aims, Captain: to restore our fortunes and to advance me. Nothing else matters to her. Nothing, I promise you."

This was an almost perfect confirmation of what Bartlemy had guessed and irritated me beyond good reason. I shifted, but the boards made an alarming squeak that froze me back to woodenness.

"Very well, my lord." Penny's voice sounded as bland as paste.

"And now to our purpose," Tewkesbury resumed. "All is going as we hoped. My man Jamie has become a friend of Burghley's chambermaid. She informs him that her master will stop at home tomorrow night, before going on to Whitehall. Tomorrow night it must be, then. Jamie will see to it that the gate of Burghley House is unlocked. He will meet you at the southwest corner of the garden and tell you the way to the master's bedchamber. From there you must go by your own wit, and I'm sure it will not fail you. Now, listen carefully. When you get to his room, according to the chambermaid—"

"Pardon, my lord." A creaking followed, as though Penny were getting up off the floor. "Allow me a word."

"What is it? Pray be quick."

"Quick it is—there's no need to proceed further in your plan."

"How's that? I've not even told you what you're to do yet."

"Nay; we've determined that for ourselves."

"What are you talking about? What do you—I pray you, let go my arm, you clod!"

Scuffling noises followed—what on earth? I inched closer to the railing and peered between the posts. But all I could make out was a dark shape lurching about the stage like a wounded crow, making stifled cries. Under cover of the noise I inched out a little farther for a better look, pressing my face against the balustrades.

Then I felt the gallery give way, and the next dark shape to land upon the stage was myself.

This was by no means the first time I had fallen from such a height. Falling is a practical skill of players, who must on occasion drop from a siege tower or the mast of a storm-tossed vessel. My training came into use about halfway down, and I made the landing with less injury than an amateur would. Still, it hurt. The pain, not to mention the sheer surprise, robbed me of all sense for a moment. I couldn't gather quite what had happened until a hand seized mine and hauled me up, and I felt the two empty fingers of the leather glove.

"What's this?" Penny boomed. "A messenger from heaven? State your business, angel."

Easy for him to say—I could not have stated my own

name. Tewkesbury's voice sounded only a little more workable than mine, as he sputtered out, "Run, fellow! Get help—" A blow to the guts—or that's what it sounded like—wrung his voice to a squeal of agony.

The next minute, firm steps were coming my way, a rough hand grabbed me by the hair and a hard voice asked, "Who's this, then?"

I could feel his breath, and his cold eyes. When I failed to answer, he pulled me over to a patch of moonlight and jerked my head back. Penny wandered over more leisurely and studied the exhibit I made. Over my pounding heart I heard the uneven peal of far-away chimes, silvered by the cold air: all the church bells of London, striking midnight.

"Malory, is it?" said Penny. "Or should I call you loud Rumor?"

"A fig for plays and players!" Tom hissed angrily. "He's the boy from the archery butts, and the one I later saw—"

"I'll grant your memory for faces, Tom, but why does his keep popping up? You said you would scare him off."

Tom gave my head a shake. "Speak—what are you here for?"

"Did Kit send you hither?" Penny's voice sounded the same as always: hearty, good-humored, meaning no offense. "You are by way of a special friend of his, are you not?"

"N-n-no, sir."

"Well then, you're in a pretty predicament—falling

friendless into a nest of thieves. I advise you to find your tongue, quick, or my comrade will just as quickly cut it out."

"Captain!" Lord Philip had finally regained his voice, after a number of gags and false starts. His black form against the meager light showed he had been tied to one of the stage posts. "What's this about?"

"Simple, my lord. We plain men favor simplicity. Instead of any complex mischief on Lord Burghley, we intend to make off with you."

A brief, shocked pause, and then a wild flailing and thrashing, as though to pull out the post and bring the painted heavens down on our heads. "You will never get away with that!"

"And why not? Your lordship has been very careful not to be seen in the company of such riffraff as I—at least since that misadventure last spring that put me in Fleet Prison. If your mother is so eager to advance your fortunes as you claim, she'll gladly put up, let us say, five hundred pounds for your safe return."

"Five hundred—! My mother could not raise that much in a year!"

"Then she may apply to the Earl of Essex or any other of your powerful friends."

"This was all to be a prank, Captain! I let you keep the money you took— We made a bargain, on soldiers' honor!"

"Lower your voice, my lord, or Tom will raise it for you." This threat silenced Tewkesbury altogether, and Penny went on, "A soldier's honor is only good among soldiers, and you are not one. But now we must deal quickly with this eavesdropper. Or is he a drop-eavser?"

I had been thinking, during these crowded moments, but found little to bargain with. "I'll carry your ransom note! Just—just tell me where you want it taken."

"A handsome offer," said Penny, with a touch of softness that might have been regret. "But we cannot allow even a Rumor to escape."

A dreadful silence fell, for I understood what he meant; my life was forfeit.

"Will you add murder to your crimes, Captain?" Tewkesbury had recovered some of his habit of command, or else he was feigning it nobly.

For answer, Tom pulled me by my hair to the back of the stage. I kicked and flailed for all I was worth, but his grip never faltered. As for my making any dent on him, I might as well have been kicking a rock. The next I knew, my back was against his chest, his arm around my throat, squeezing. His smell of sweat and leather crowded into my nose, and over my tortured gasps I heard the desperate color of Lord Philip's voice, commanding, "Let him go! Captain, for God's sake— he's just a boy!"

Just a boy—like Davy—a boy—let me let me let me go— My very thoughts were turning black, unable to complete themselves as I groped for air, sound, sense, life. I struggled with every ounce of strength in me—every muscle I could move strained against this bond. But he was as unyielding as iron, immovable except for that one arm, pressing tighter and tighter—squeezing out . . .

My life! A sound, high and persistent as a fly's drone, bore into my head.

Abruptly, the pressure on my throat let up, and colors flooded my mind in such a riot that I could take in nothing, except for one note from on high—a clear, shivery tone. A voice, though it was like no human voice I had ever heard. Delicately, it began to take shape: "My life! Give me back my life!"

"What's that?—" "Who's there?—" "Spirits preserve us!" I heard words but could not tell where they came from, who spoke them.

"Now dead, now fled . . . my soul is in the sky. My golden thread severed, forever—by thee, Tom Watts, by thee!"

The voice, already high, climbed even higher as though ascending a heavenly staircase. And though I would have thought nothing could frighten him, I felt the quick throb of Tom's heart and heard the quaver in his voice as he called, "Spirit? Spirit—what's your will?"

"Unhand the boy!" This came out in a shriek, with a reedy tremble that made the hair stand on end. To my astonishment, I was unhanded—practically ejected, as though suddenly too hot to hold. I landed on hands and knees, but jumped up and bolted to the edge of the stage—where Penny cut me off. For a large man past his prime, he moved with uncommon speed. "Idiot!" he hissed at Tom. "What's this that's made a quivering girl of you?"

"Didn't you hear?" Tom half whispered. "'Twas Davy's wraith!" Even in my desperate straits I was amazed to see him so undone.

"That's your Welsh blood babbling." Penny subdued me with a cruel twist of my arms that made me cry out. "'Tis no more than a trick, and I wager I know who's behind—"

A noise cut him off, a very ordinary, earthbound noise this time. It was the sound of a chain being rattled on the west door, and men's voices outside. Bartlemy! I thought, with a surge of heart. But the captain clapped a sweaty handkerchief over my mouth before I could cry out and tied it so tightly my jaw ached. "Quick, or all our plans come to naught! Seize Lord Philip, and follow me."

Tom was soldier enough to obey. The next few moments were confused, as the captain forced me down through the trap and pulled me along the passageway under the stage. I heard the scuffle and drag of Tewkesbury—now gagged as well as bound—as Tom bundled him along after us. All together we tumbled through the hatch, then circled around the building to where the three horses were passing the time as contentedly as old gossips.

Tewkesbury had to be subdued with another punch before Tom could hoist him up to his horse. Captain Penny vaulted into his saddle and pulled me up in front of him like a sack of onions. I kept thinking that our struggles would at any moment alert the men on the other side of the Theater, but they were making so much noise it must have covered ours.

Penny turned his horse toward the city. As we made a wide circle toward the road, I glanced back desperately. Stupid fools!—did they not know the criminals were escaping? Wouldn't the Queen's Men be wise enough to find these horses and secure them before blustering in at the front door, rattling chains loud enough to wake the dead? I longed to hear a firm voice ringing out, "Halt! In Her Majesty's name!" But as our horses picked their way over Finsbury Field, headed toward the road, no such cry sounded. I caught one glimpse of torches by the Theater door, lighting perhaps a dozen men who waited as calmly as play-goers to be allowed inside. If they saw or heard three horses circling around them, no one raised a cry. Perhaps, I thought with a shock, they were not the Queen's Men at all. But then, who were they?

"Now," said Penny, when we struck the firmer ground of the Shoreditch Road, "we go flat-out."

I felt his thighs clench as he spurred to a trot, then a canter. The clatter of hooves echoed behind me as the other two fell in behind. But we had not gone one hundred yards when shouts of alarm sounded up ahead. Next moment I felt a terrible jerk that pitched me forward, as Penny's horse staggered sideways. The creature fell with agonizing slowness, like the slow pitch of a sea vessel capsizing under a wave. I struck the ground and skidded over the gravel with one knee under his massive neck, but as the horse thrashed and surged, I scrambled free.

Gaining my feet, I heard at last those most welcome words: "Halt, in Her Majesty's name!" To my ears, Bartlemy's coarse-grained voice sounded sweeter than an angel's.

LET THE END TRY THE MAN

I heard a cry from behind me as Tom's horse bolted. Confused voices shouted, "After him!" and a few men set off in pursuit, on foot. Meanwhile guards closed on Captain Penny as he worked himself out from under his fallen horse and got to his feet, groaning under a badly twisted knee. The horse had galloped full-tilt into a rope stretched across the road, and now thrashed about in a futile attempt to get up. Tewkesbury meanwhile was untied and ungagged, and he immediately launched upon a stream of accusations against his captors. He had barely warmed to the subject when a scream burned the cold air. It came from the direction Tom had taken.

The captain of the guard rapped out an order for two of his men to lend their aid, and as they set off across the field, moonlight dashed off their polished helmets. I felt a tug on my sleeve as Bartlemy pulled me aside and loosened the handkerchief over my mouth, murmuring, "Good Mistress Shaw found me at Westminster. Stand here; don't speak unless you're called."

I could barely speak at all, owing to a badly bruised throat. Like a piece of furniture I stood where I was put. My body felt like an empty bottle, gradually filling with the Richard Malory who had been left behind at the Theater, in the iron grip of death. Soon my teeth were chattering again.

Steady hoofbeats sounded on the road as a new personage arrived: an imposing fellow, even after dismounting. He had brought a torchbearer with him, and by its light I recognized the stern, handsome features of Bartlemy's master, John Clement.

"So," he remarked to his henchman. "Fair caught at last."

"Aye, sir. We have witnesses."

One of them, I thought with a start, would be me. The other would have to be Tewkesbury, who was already testifying as fast as he could that two ruffians had ambushed him and were in the act of spiriting him away to hold for ransom when, God be praised, the stalwart guardians of justice had arrived and—

Master Clement tactfully interrupted him and with a few simple questions established the fact that Lord Philip had more to hide than to tell. "If you would, sir," he concluded in an oily tone, "we must detain you for a short time in order to plumb the depths of this affair. Please you, go with these worthy men and I will be with you presently."

"Go where?" As the "worthy men" in Yeomen's livery approached him, Tewkesbury's voice rose. "I demand to be told!"

"Please go quietly, sir." Master Clement turned to Bartlemy as Tewkesbury was escorted—not too quietly—down the road. "Right good work. I commend you—and the lamented Lord Chamberlain's son will too, once his rage cools. He was put out when you didn't report for guard service. I'll mend it."

"My thanks to you, sir—" A squelchy tramping was heard as two or three of the guards returned from their expedition over the mud.

"By your leave, Master Clement," panted one. "The man is dead. He was bad thrown when his horse fell, and it appears his neck is broken."

Well, Davy, thought I—you are avenged. Then I remembered the voice in the Theater rafters. Surely it wasn't . . .

"That's one bird down," Clement remarked. "Another flown, and as for you, Captain Penny—"

"Hark, sir!" called a voice among the guards. "Someone approaches."

Everyone turned—even I, now wrapped like a bundle in a cloak someone had thrown over me. A straight form, brushed by moonlight, was coming toward us on the road. From far behind him a light burned in one of the windows of the Theater. A finger of curiosity stirred in my addled brain: what was going on back there?

"State your name!" called Master Clement.

The figure on the road hesitated. Then: "Christopher Glover, so please you, sir."

"Kit!" That was Penny's voice, quiet but eager, as he strained against his bonds. Kit! I thought, more quietly yet. He must have been in the Theater all along.

"Approach," John Clement said. The cloaked figure came nearer and stood. "What is your business?"

Another pause, then Kit said, "To turn myself in, sir."

"On what charge?"

"Abetting armed robbery."

"Ah, lad!" Peregrine Penny surged forward, dragging a guard with him, and managed to come within a pace before the chain and the force of two men stopped him. "It's well done. Honor among thieves, they say—we'll face our doom together, eh?"

"Honor among thieves," Kit repeated. The company fell absolutely silent at the ringing, steely timbre of his voice. "Is that what you think it is?"

"Why, lad—what else? We were bound to France together, you and I. Now we'll to prison."

"Aye, to France. A new start, a new name. Or many starts and many names, while we doff the world aside and let it pass. But the world does not stand aside so easily." His voice took on a wondering tone. "You would have killed that boy, back there." With a start, I recognized he meant me.

"We do what is necessary," Penny replied, a stern soldier now.

"That we do." Kit raised his hands and pulled at a chain around his neck. As he walked around his mentor, I caught my breath, guessing his intent. "Here," he said to Bartlemy, holding out his hand. "Lord Cobham's ring."

"Kit!" Penny cried out. "What have you done? You've thrown away our fortune—"

Kit turned back to him and the light flickered on his face, which to my astonishment was wet with tears. His lips parted: "I-I-I . . ."

Often he had mocked my stammering speech in just this way, but now he was the one to have his words back up on him. He took a breath and started again.

"I'll see you hang, old man."

The words, so cold and unyielding, did not sound cold the way he said them. Indeed, they could have wrung the hardest heart. He may as well have said, *I know thee not, old man,* for Captain Penny looked as stricken as Jack Falstaff, and as speechless.

"Take him away." Bartlemy shouldered through the press of men and horses. When he reached Captain Penny, he struck the nearest guard on the shoulder with his fist. "Take him away!"

"Kit!" Penny cried as the Yeoman led him off, not without a struggle. "Speak for me—thy father in all but name!"

But Kit had turned aside, wrapping his cloak tighter around him. "Why did you come back?" Bartlemy asked him sharply. "You could have run in the other direction, and us none the wiser."

Kit turned his head without looking directly at the speaker—his way, as I had so often had occasion to notice, with people he considered beneath him. But he answered. "Because . . . I have a name . . . that I wish to keep." Then his pale eyes flashed, as he glanced around the gathering. "Is Richard here?"

I literally jumped—not merely at the sound of my own name, but the fact that, in the year and more that I had known him, I could not remember ever hearing him speak it. "I'm here." My voice came out at a croak as I squeezed between a pair of burly guards. Bartlemy stepped aside, and for a moment Kit and I faced each other as we had so often before, on or off the stage, in spite or scorn.

"From this time on," he said, "I want no argument when I say you will take over the stage."

"Th-the railing broke," I stammered out.

"A likely excuse. I meant to plant you there as a witness, not as a strangled corpse."

I nodded. By stalling Tom he had saved my life. "How . . . did you do that voice?"

His lips twitched, but the light was too dim to show it for a smile. He reached under his cloak and took out a small object, a reed of some kind. When he tucked it into his mouth, I knew it for a "swazzle," an instrument used by puppet masters to produce a high, shrill voice. But never used to better effect than that night. "Easily," he said, in an eerie tone that made me shiver. No wonder Tom had been unnerved by it.

I heard John Clement cough, somewhere behind us. "I fear we must arrest you, young Glover."

As his men came forward, I rasped out, "I'll come to you—tomorrow—I'll do anything—"

He took the swazzle out of his mouth. "You've done enough." His tone was surprisingly warm, as though to say I had done him more good than harm. Before the guards took hold of him, I stuck out my hand.

He looked at it. Then I felt his grasp, a quick pressure of cold fingers that released almost immediately as he was taken away.

In the space where he had been, the old Theater stood revealed. Every window now flickered like a firefly, as though sparkling with some fairy enchantment in a midwinter night's dream. "Kit!"

He stopped and turned his head, as the guards on either side paused with him.

"Those lights—at the Theater . . ."

He lifted his head toward the place where he had earned his greatest fame. "A new birth." When he moved forward again, it appeared that he was leading the guards, and not the other way around.

"It was *glorious*," Gregory assured me, two days later.

"Beyond belief," Robin chimed in.

"You should have been there," they said together.

We were in one of the royal barges—the white and silver swan, swooping upriver toward Whitehall Palace on the beat of twenty oars. The day glittered with a bracing cold that frosted reeds along the bank and marked every spoken word with a little gust of steam. Laughter cracked like gunshot in the sparkling air. The atmosphere aboard the barge was so expansive it made me feel that the Company had been in a box for the last several months, and the lid had just sprung open.

"Sorry to miss it," said I. It was still an effort to speak.

In truth, I was not all that sorry. When Bartlemy saw me safely home after our wild night, I collapsed into bed with no intention of getting up again. But at dawn Master Condell burst into our room in a state of high excitement. He almost never climbed to the attic, yet here he was, respected church-warden, family man, and gentleman player, bubbling over like a schoolboy. "Robin! Richard! Are you up to an adventure?"

I was up to a bad cold, hovering on a fever, and my throat had closed up entire. The master judged I'd better serve the Company by staying home. That was why I spent most of the day wrapped up by the fire with a poultice on my neck, while the rest of the Company tramped out to Finsbury Field and helped Peter Street the carpenter take apart the old Theater.

Gregory and Robin did not wholly regret my absence; otherwise, they would have had no one to tell. "The landlord discovered what was afoot and rode himself into a sweat to get there," Gregory was saying. "But he was too late—Master Street's men went up around midnight the night before. They had already taken apart the stage and stacked the trestles. They were dismantling the galleries by the time old Giles got there! He was almost jumping up and down, he was so furious."

"He'd have loved to throw a punch at Richard Burbage," laughed Robin. "You could see it working in him, except that Burbage could have smashed him with one fist."

"And his mother would've moved in for the kill," Gregory added.

"True—old Mistress Burbage was there, Richard, in her cap and apron, giving the landlord a piece of her mind—"

"With the rough side of her tongue."

"She picked up a broom, and he covered his head. Later, when the city watch arrived—he sent for them, though there wasn't a thing they could do about it—I heard him complain that the lady had threatened him with a pike!"

"Wait," I interrupted hoarsely. This story was moving too fast for me, although I understood the gist of it. Peter Street and his crew had chosen to break into the Theater, like a band of blundering angels, at the very moment Penny held me in his grasp. For which I was extremely grateful to them, and to God, but— "Was this legal? Can the landlord still bring suit against us?"

"We already told you that," Robin complained. "Your brains must be running out of your nose. Here, take my handkerchief—and *use* it."

Gregory explained slowly, as though to a half-wit. "According to the terms of the original agreement, the Burbages have the right to take down and carry away any of the materials of the building at any time, up to one and twenty years after signing the lease."

My head was not up to calculating. "I forgot—when does the one and twenty years expire?"

"Last April," said Robin.

"Oh."

"But never fear," Gregory hastened to say. "The deed's done. The old Theater is a stack of boards and beams and Peter Street is even now carting them down to his warehouse on the river."

"And as soon as the weather breaks," Robin continued, "he'll barge them to the spot of land in Southwark that the Company men leased a month ago. It's not far from the Rose— fancy being within spitting distance of the Admiral's Men!"

"How long is this lease?" I asked.

"Thirty-one years! We'll all be old men by that time."

Gregory sniggered. "As old and tottering as Richard Burbage is now."

"Well, you'll agree—our troubles are ended for a while yet."

"Our landlord troubles, at least."

"And Master Street thinks he may have the new theater built by this coming spring. Fancy it! Our own stage again—"

"With a bright new coat of paint—"

"A new name, a new start—"

A new birth. I listened to them, and smiled on cue, and tried to catch their high spirits. Here was a change even Robin could rejoice in—a most satisfying conclusion. Yet I felt about it the same way I had felt about the end of Part Two: sad. I was already missing Kit.

His fate was not general knowledge yet. Of the Company, I alone knew that Kit had been indicted that very morning on charges of accessory to theft and was now in Fleet Prison awaiting his trial. Bartlemy had sent word of the hearing, and since I could not risk being absent when the Company departed for Whitehall, Starling contrived to go. She returned home while Master Condell was laying down instructions for the servants and pulled me up to the stair landing to tell me what had happened.

She and Bartlemy had sat behind the bar in the magistrate's chamber while a clerk read the charges against the defendant. The murder charge had been dismissed, but what remained was enough to hang him, if he were prosecuted to the fullest extent of the law—a recommendation read by the clerk with no change in voice or expression.

Kit pleaded benefit of clergy, a privilege more often claimed by those accused of murder or manslaughter. Ben Jonson had done the same last month, which was why he was serving time in Newgate Prison rather than moldering in a criminal's grave. Kit was allowed to choose his text and turned to the Gospel of John: "Verily, verily, I say unto thee, except a man be born anew, he cannot enter the kingdom of God. . . ."

"He read it so well even the clerk was wiping tears away," Starling said. "I think the magistrate was persuaded to deal gently with him. Kit seemed to be speaking those words from his heart. I hope so: his poor mother sobbed the whole time, while his father sat there looking more stricken and guilty than the prisoner. But at the end, when they were leading him away, Master Glover stood up and walked to the bar and held out both his hands. Kit hesitated, but he took them. So perhaps he's making amends."

"What of the Tewkesburys?" I asked her. "Any mention of them?"

Her smile popped out, as though it had been waiting for this very question. "Not by name. But wait until you hear. The charges against Kit allowed that a certain person or persons unnamed had set the scheme in motion. There was an elderly servant in blue livery present, and the justice seemed to regard him as a proxy for the unnamed. I've seen him, Richard. He was the one who used to accompany Mistress Critic to the theater—the one whose ear she used to bend with her opinions.

Lady Tewkesbury has been attending our plays all along!"

I could not share her pleasure in the discovery. "'Persons unnamed.' What sort of penalty gets dealt out to phantoms?"

"Oh, they'll pay, though perhaps not in a court of law. Bartlemy says Lord Philip has thrown himself on the mercy of Essex. He'll be banned from court, sure, and they'll have to sell off more property to pay their debts. The House of Maximus is fallen indeed."

"And what's to become of Captain Penny?"

"He will hang, belike. So Bartlemy says. But he thinks Kit will serve no more than two years in Newgate."

Two years. It wasn't so bad, in a way. Ben Jonson was said to be writing another play in his prison cell; if Jonson could resume his career, then so perhaps could a young man formerly known as the best boy player of London. Still, my face must have reflected my dismay, for Starling suddenly wrapped her arms around me and squeezed tight, a comfort I had not recognized I needed. "You helped him, after all," she said.

I returned the squeeze. "He helped me."

"Sometimes it amounts to the same thing."

"What cheer, Richard?" Gregory slapped me on the back. "The landlord is beat and old Cobham's resting in peace and we're on our way to see the Queen! I've not heard you laugh all day."

"He's too busy sniffling," Robin said. "He's blown a whole bucket of slime into my handkerchief."

"Sorry," I mumbled. "D'you want it back?"

"Nay! Keep it, with my regards. The Queen will shower us with handkerchiefs. Money too, let's hope."

"Hotspur will fetch the handkerchiefs," Gregory predicted, "and Falstaff the money."

"What about Hal?" I asked.

"Hal?" Gregory frowned. "I never liked him—a conniver and a cold heart."

Somewhat more than that, I thought. "He's to become a great king."

Gregory shrugged. "So the histories say." He turned his attention to the riverbank, as Robin pointed out landmarks. It was Gregory's first time to play at Whitehall, and anticipation consumed his thoughts.

But I was already thinking of our return. Once back in London, I meant to visit Newgate, where I would tell Kit that acting noble can indeed make one noble and perhaps even inspire nobility in others. That honor is more than a word or a prize to be plucked from the pale-faced moon. That he had found the best in himself and been true to it, in spite of the cost—and *that* made his reputation, as far as I was concerned.

"Here we are!" cried Robin, as Whitehall gardens swept into view. "God guide the issue, as Master Heminges says."

Gregory laughed. "Die all, die merrily, as Hotspur says."

Robin turned to me. "What does Richard say?"

I could no longer resist their joy and goodwill. The grip of sorrow loosened, its cold memory trailing behind in the waters of the Thames. I raised a fist, croaking, *"Esperance!"*

They glanced at each other, then raised their hands likewise, clasping mine. *"Esperance!"*

⌒ HISTORICAL NOTE ⌒

The major events affecting Shakespeare's Company that I have presented in this story are all true: the change in the Company's name, their landlord problems, Henry Brooke's complaint against the portrayal of Sir John Oldcastle, and the midnight dismantling of the Burbages' Theater.

The new theater to come would be called the Globe. Giles Allen, who was not one to live and let live, sued the Company for "stealing" his building, and the case dragged on in court for years. Meanwhile, John Heminges, Augustine Phillips, Will Kempe, Thomas Pope, William Shakespeare, and the Burbage brothers set up a management arrangement that was unusual for its time: they divided the business into ten shares, with five of the players taking one share each and the Burbages taking five. The sharers took all responsibility for expenses, profits, and ownership of the building. Peter Street completed the Globe in the spring of 1599, at a cost of about 400 pounds—much less than the price tag would have been if he had used all new lumber. One of the first plays performed at the Globe was *Henry V,* continuing the adventures of "Royal Hal," but without Falstaff. Sir John dies offstage early in the play, and it's implied that he lost heart after Hal cut him off so abruptly. But the public, or perhaps the Queen herself, could not let Falstaff go that quietly, so Shakespeare wrote him into a comedy called *The Merry Wives of Windsor.*

Court rivalry in Elizabeth's time was every bit as vicious as presented here. The elderly Queen was not expected to live more than a few years, and ambitious men and women were maneuvering to win fame and fortune while they could. Younger nobles flocked to the Earl of Essex, who was handsome and dashing and something of a military hero. The Queen showered favors on him, but relied more on her Secretary of State, Lord Burghley. Cliques tended to form around these two men. Intrigue at court affected the theater companies of London, who depended on their noble patrons both for status and for protection from the city's mayor and aldermen (who generally didn't approve of the theater). For Shakespeare's Company to lose the title of Lord Chamberlain's Men was a drop in prestige for them, but their fortunes improved when William Brooke died and the Queen appointed their patron, Lord Hunsdon, as the new Lord Chamberlain.

Philip Tewkesbury is fictional, and so is the "Putrid Play," but the Epilogue of *Henry IV*, Part Two contains this reference: "Be it known to you, as it is very well, I was lately here in the end of a displeasing play, to pray your patience for it and to promise you a better [one]." No one has been able to identify this displeasing play, so I invented one of my own.

While most of the events are true, I've nudged a few dates together to tell this particular story. We know (thanks to the legal proceedings initiated by Giles Allen) that the Theater was dismantled in the dark of night in late December of 1598. However, William Brooke held the office of Lord Chamberlain from 1596 until his death in 1597, so the Company's brief stint as the Lord Hunsdon's Men would have happened earlier than represented here. It is most likely that the first performances of the Henry IV plays took place a year or two earlier as well. But the plays' themes of honor and reputation fit so well with the story I wanted to tell, and the parallels to the renaming of Shakespeare's Company and the dismantling of their Theater were so interesting, that I couldn't resist bringing them all together. I like to think that Shakespeare, who frequently did the same sort of thing himself, wouldn't mind.

J. B. Cheaney first fell under the Bard's spell when she and her sister wrote an adaptation of *Julius Caesar* and performed it in their backyard. Many years later, her interests in literature and theater have come together again. Cheaney's *The Playmaker*, also set amid the players of Shakespeare's company, was named one of the ten best first novels for young adults of 2000 by *Booklist*.

Ms. Cheaney and her husband live in the Ozarks of Missouri.